Valley Creek Station

Carl B. McDonald
&
Herschel McDonald

ISBN 978-1-64191-721-6 (paperback)
ISBN 978-1-64191-722-3 (digital)

Christian Faith Publishing, Inc.
832 Park Avenue
Meadville, PA 16335
www.christianfaithpublishing.com

Printed in the United States of America

CHAPTER 1

Homecoming

IT WAS A COLD AND rainy evening in September of 1860. Mark had brought in the wood for the night and was preparing supper, when he heard Uncle Edd coming up the trail. He always knew it was Uncle Edd long before he came into sight because Ada the mule would always bray and be answered by a nicker from 01' Cricket.

Even though Mark did not understand him, he was always thrilled to see his Uncle come home. It was not unusual for him to be left alone for three or four days and sometimes longer. Hanging around the cabin by himself could sure get lonely for a fifteen-year-old boy.

Mark hurriedly mixed the cornbread, greased the Dutch oven and poured in the contents. He set the oven on the live coals, put some coals on top, and then stirred the stew.

He was glad he had just made a fresh pot of stew because Uncle Edd had usually been drinking and could eat like a horse. A full stomach made him more agreeable and soon ready for bed.

01' Cricket came around the bend in that familiar, long running-walk that could cover lots of territory in a day. Mark had a great admiration for that jet-black coat with one white foot, but Cricket was strictly a one-man horse, Uncle Edd's.

His thoughts turned to 01' Ada. The mule was with him all the time and even gave a laughing noise of thanks when he began to draw her a drink of water from the well.

"Uncle, I'm glad you're home," shouted Mark.

"It's good to see you, boy," said Uncle Edd in a voice that Mark knew wasn't right.

He didn't speak, because he had learned a long time ago to not ask questions. He knew that if there were something he needed to know, he would be told, sooner or later.

He embraced his uncle with a sense of security, as Edd stepped to the ground. He couldn't smell "licker," so he knew something serious was at hand.

"Boy, while I unsaddle 01' Cricket, you go by the smoke house, and bring in that stone colored jug. I need to talk to you," Uncle Edd said firmly.

Mark hurried by the smoke house, brought in the jug, and took the cornbread off the fire. He set the table and was ready to dip the stew, when Uncle Edd interrupted him.

"Don't give me any, yet. I'm not ready to eat just now."

Mark set out a glass for his uncle, and put butter, molasses, and a pitcher of fresh buttermilk on the table. He cut a piece of bread and dipped a plate of the stew. He knew, in time, Uncle Edd would eat, so he ate silently and waited.

After three drinks of raw whiskey and four or five trips across the room, Uncle Edd sat and gazed into the fire. He remained deep in thought, while Mark finished eating.

"Pull yore chair over here by the hearth, boy. I'm ready," blurted Uncle Edd.

Mark pulled his rawhide bottom chair around the corner of the table and sat down in the chimney corner.

"In the first place, we're leaving here," Uncle Edd said roughly. "Got into it with a man, the other side of St. Jo, over whiskey money, and had to kill 'im. He pushed me into it, but there's several in the gang. They'll be looking for me."

As Edd reached for another drink, Mark asked calmly, "Uncle, when will we go and where are we going?"

Uncle Edd downed the rest of his drink and continued, "Son, we're goin' to a place in Texas. I've hired on with the Butterfield stage line that goes from here to California. They need a way-station

4

keeper and I dealt for it. It's roughly about four hundred miles this side of El Paso and about five hundred miles west of Fort Smith. Now, Son, I'm sorry things are like this, but it's too hot around here for me. Besides, it just ain't right, me leavin' you like I do. I need to be with you, boy."

Mark was shaken by the sudden news, but he tried desperately not to show it. He stood up and placed his hand on Uncle Edd's big, brawny shoulder, and said meekly, "Uncle Edd, you're all I've got in this world. What you say is the way it'll be.

Edd pushed up the end of the burned logs and said slowly, "Boy, I don't want you to feel like I owe you a damned thing, but I love you. I can't stay here and I can't leave you. It'll just have to be me and you from here out.

"I'd like to get the things together tonight. We're gonna take and leave early in the morning. We're gonna be limited to what we can carry, so I want you to think about what you want. You can carry that small trunk of your Granddad's, so you decide what you want in it."

Mark asked anxiously, "What about all the other stuff?"

"Just close the cabin door and leave it. I sold Cricket, Ada, and the wagon to Wade Samuel, today. He'll pick them up in St. Jo, tomorrow. He said if we ever come back, we could get them back."

"Now, let's start gathering up what we intend to take."

"Yes, sir," said Mark, as he went into the other room to start emptying the trunk.

It was a real blow to a fifteen-year-old boy to have to leave the only place he had ever known. All that he could remember was centered around the cabin and the surrounding area. But, he had no choice, so he set out to do what had to be done.

He opened the small trunk and set the tray out. He knew the things inside had been collected over a long period of time. He had to make a quick decision of what to keep. He could already feel a lump coming into his throat, but when he unfolded a worn-out piece of cloth and saw what it contained, he couldn't hold back the tears. There was a small iron hoop from an old wagon. It had been his constant companion when he was a little boy. He rolled it for miles around the cabin and down the trails by the creek. He used a special stick that Granddad had carved for him. After Granddad had passed on and he had outgrown it, Granny had quietly laid it away in a "safe place".

Mark contained himself and vowed that he would continue without Uncle Edd ever detecting anything. He couldn't let his mind wander, so he gently placed each item on the bed. When he had emptied the trunk, he took a long look at all the contents.

He started immediately to put back the things he intended to keep.

There were his mother's two dresses. He rearranged the cloth in the bottom of the trunk so he could fold it over them. Next, he put in Granny's "every day" dress. He had put it in the trunk the day he returned from Granny's funeral.

He put her sweater, shawl, and old house shoes snugly beside the clothes. He placed his mother's rag doll on the other side and coiled his Granddad's rawhide rope on the top of the clothes.

At that moment, he thought of his own clothes. He put in the two pairs of homespun jeans, three shirts, and his buckskin jacket. He bit his lip as he thought of how hard Granny had worked to make all of them.

The bottom of the trunk was full and he was ready to replace the tray, when he thought of one more thing he wanted. He ran out to the smokehouse and brought Granddad's drawknife. He remembered how he loved to play with it, when Granddad would allow it.

He shoved it down the side of the trunk; and at that moment, he could see Granny, as plain as day, mixing bread in that familiar wooden bowl. He would not leave without it!

He hurried off to the kitchen, and got the bowl, the "butcher" knife, and the few forks and spoons. When they were firmly stuffed in the sides of the trunk, he replaced the tray on top.

Mark heard Uncle Edd enter the fireplace room, so he went in from force of habit.

"Uncle Edd," Mark said meekly, "is there anything special that you want me to put in the trunk?"

Uncle Edd had consumed several drinks by this time, so he spoke soft and slow. "Son, find room for your Grandma's Bible. That's all I ask."

Mark replied, assuredly, "Uncle, I wouldn't think about leaving it. Have you got everything you want to take?"

"Look it over, son," he answered with a slur.

Mark saw the familiar black "hand bag" that folded together with the two handles at the top. He knew it contained all of Uncle Edd's clothes, his straight razor, his shaving mug, and possibly a couple of extra boxes of metallic cartridges for his Navy Colt 44.

Beside the handbag was the small copper kettle. Mark knew that Edd would not be without it, because he used it to make whiskey. Leaning against the bag was the Sharp's rifle, a breach loading single shot that fired fifty-caliber metallic shells. Edd's hunting knife was on his belt.

"We want to take Granddad's old muzzle loader, don't we?"

"If you want to, boy. There's some shot, caps, and packing in that bag hanging on the rack," Uncle Edd stammered.

Mark knew where it was, so he put the old gun with Uncle's Edd's things and hurried off to put the powder horn and bag in the tray of the trunk.

As Mark started to pack the tray, he noticed that he had not discarded one item from the trunk. In one end of the tray was a large, neatly folded piece of calico cloth. Granny had sent for it, but never did make her dress.

He found the scissors, the thimble, and three spools of thread. Next to the thread was Granddad's straight razor, razor strap, and whetstone. There was the old "Book of Fables" that Granny read to him so many times. He got Granny's Bible, wrapped it in a clean cloth, and placed it snugly by Granddad's watch and pocketknife.

He stood and thought for a moment, closed the trunk lid, locked it, and put the key in his pocket. He pulled it into the other room and placed it with the other things. He then rolled his two woolen blankets into a neat bedroll. Uncle Edd had just finished a large portion of the bread and stew.

Mark entered. He started to suggest going to bed when Uncle Edd spoke. "Son, sit down for a while, there's some things I'm gonna tell you."

Mark lifted his chair from the chimney corner and sat farther back from the fire.

"Boy," Uncle Edd began, "you never was told much about yourself. Very little was ever said about it among me, Ma, and Pa. I think it's time I told you. You've wondered about it on occasions, haven't you?"

"Yes, Uncle Edd, I have thought about it many times," Mark answered.

Granny had talked to him several times, answering most of his questions, but Uncle Edd hadn't known about it. Mark would let him tell his own story.

Uncle Edd poured another short drink and drank it. He sat down, placing his arms on his knees with his hands locked in between and said, "Your real name is McGee. At least, that was your Daddy's name, but you always went by the name of Singletary because you lived with us. I'd just as soon that you keep on wearing that name."

"You see, there was two of us boys. I had a brother, Jim, who was killed when he was thirteen. I was fifteen. I was seventeen when your Mama was born. Ella was her name. I used to bounce her on my knee and got real attached to her. I always made good money and I saw that she got what she wanted. I boarded her over in St. Jo, 'til she got all the book learnin' she could get there. Granny had some book learnin' and she believed in learnin' all you could."

"Well, Ella had hoped to have her own school, someday, but this young feller, Collin McGee, came into the community. She didn't know anything about him, but there were no other young fellers around. I came back off of one of my trips to find out she had married up with him. I didn't like it from the first, but I didn't say anything. I knew I couldn't change it."

Mark reached for more wood, but Uncle Edd stopped him after one stick. "Don't put on too much because we're goin' to bed, 'fore long."

Mark leaned back in his chair for the rest of the story. Uncle Edd began where he left off. "I tried hard to help them in every way, but he was a no-good, shiftless, lazy skunk. In the first place, I gave them a forty-acre plot about six miles across the creek. I helped him cut the logs, build the cabin, and clear three or four acres, so he could get started. I made a trade for an extra mule and told him to just take him and use him. But he didn't do anything. I tell you, he was no good."

"Three times before you was born, I came by to see about Ella and found her alone without hardly a thing to eat. He'd be off on a drunk somewhere, maybe gone for four or five days. I took her home three times, but he'd catch me gone and come back. She'd always go home with him."

"He got so he'd dodge me and wouldn't face me, so I rode by one evening and caught him home. I told him if I ever caught Ella there alone and not knowing where he was, I was gonna beat more hell out of him than he could stand. He promised he was gonna do right. That was about three months before you was expected. He did fairly well for about two months and took off again. I was gone with a load of whiskey and stayed gone for about a week. I was furnishing the tradin' post on the far end of my run. That's when it happened."

Uncle Edd reached over for a bite of cornbread, and Mark remembered that he had not washed the dishes. He could do them later, because, right now, he wanted Uncle Edd to continue.

"You want me to make some coffee?" Mark asked.

"No, no, I don't need any coffee."

"Uncle Edd," Mark said softly, "go ahead and tell me just what happened."

"Well," Uncle Edd started, "like I say, Will was gone, and I was gone, and you wasn't expected for about another month. Your Grandma wanted some things from St. Jo, and your Granddad rode over to get them. He rode an old mare named Daisy. On the way back, he decided to ride by and check on Ella. When he got there, no one answered his call at the gate, so he went on in. You was already here and your mother was almost gone. Your Granddad turned you up where you'd be sure to get air and rode hard as he could to the nearest neighbor, the McAnalley's. They lived about a mile and a half this side."

"Mrs. McAnalley headed for your mother, while Mr. McAnalley went to St. Jo for the doctor. Your Granddad came to get Granny. He threw a sidesaddle on that old mare he had been riding, and your Granny got on and didn't even wait for Pa. Ol' Cricket was a young horse then, not broke too well, but he saddled her and headed out after your Grandma. He overtook her about a mile down the road and they went on over, together."

"Mrs. McAnalley had already taken care of you and made it as comfortable for your mother as she could. The doctor come on out later, but she had already lost too much blood. She passed away about four o'clock the next morning. A good friend of mine, Jade Haynes, knew about where I would be, so he rode up to tell me. He caught me about twenty-five miles up the river. I left the wagon and team with a man I knew there and borrowed his horse. Jade and me got in late that night and we had the burial the next morning. Now, you know why we raised you."

Uncle Edd stood up as if he may be ready for bed, but Mark stopped him.

"Uncle," he said gently, "I want to know what happened to my Daddy."

Uncle Edd sat down again and continued his story. "Will found out what happened before he got back here. However, your mother was already buried. He knew I'd be laying for him, so he never came back. He never saw you. I found out which way he was headed and that's when ol' Cricket really got broke. She was a three-year-old then and as green as they come. I rode better'n two hundred miles on his trail. I learned he was several days ahead of me, headin' for Oregon Territory, so I gave up and came back. When I came home, Ma asked me if I caught him and I shook my head no. She gave thanks to the Lord, 'cause she knew I would have killed him. Your Granddad never even asked about him, so I didn't tell him anything. I guess he died not knowin' whether I killed him or not, 'less Ma told him. Now, that's it, boy. Let's go to bed, for we'll be up early in the morning."

Mark got up and started to bank the fire from force of habit, but Uncle Edd scolded, "No need to preserve the coals. We won't need any after the morning. Go to bed and get some sleep. Don't even bother with the dishes."

Uncle Edd lit a candle and went to the back room to get ready for bed.

There was warm water on the fire, so Mark quickly washed the few dishes. He took some of the cornbread and stew to his dog. He hadn't asked Uncle Edd, but he was taking Hawk for sure. A man had passed through, about a year ago, with the mother dog and three pups and had given him one.

Mark had been fascinated by the odd color. They had a bluish-gray background with black spots. The man had called them leopard dogs.

Hawk would already mind when spoken to and wouldn't let Mark out of his sight.

He returned to the cabin and lit a candle. He remembered that he did not put any in the trunk. He took all the candles that were in the box and found a place for them in the tray of the trunk. He eased into the other room and went to bed.

He lay on his back with his eyes wide open and wondered what it would be like in the "new world." He had been here all his life and had never been anywhere else. Many thoughts of the past filled his mind. He remembered so vividly the little school across the creek. How he loved his teacher, Miss Sally. He couldn't understand why, after his second term, Miss Sally had to leave because she didn't have enough pupils.

He remembered how Granny continued to teach him so he could be a good reader. He thought of the humility of his grandparents, how Granddad raised vegetables to sell the travelers going west, and Granny always trying to save. He knew they didn't approve of Uncle Edd's whiskey business and would have no part of it.

There were so many things that caused that lump to come into his throat. He finally chased them from his mind and fell into a fitful sleep.

CHAPTER 2

Traveling On

MARK'S EYES AUTOMATICALLY OPENED AT five o'clock. He couldn't believe that he was so wide-awake this early in the morning. Hurriedly, he put on his shirt and jeans, and laced his shoes.

He hurried to the kitchen to make coffee, but he heard Uncle Edd speaking to Ada and Cricket in the horse lot. As he opened the kitchen door, he could see that Uncle Edd had already harnessed the horse and mule.

He got to the wagon at the same time Uncle Edd did.

"Morning," Mark called out, "I thought I'd beat you out of bed and have coffee ready, but you're too early for me."

"We need to get off as quick as we can," replied Uncle Edd. "If you want that last cup, you'd better hurry."

Mark took Ada and moved her to the right side of the wagon tongue. He lifted up the tongue and hooked the breast yoke chain. Quickly, he hooked the traces and hurried off to the house to make coffee.

He lighted the kindling in the fireplace, but did not put too much water in the pot so it would boil quicker. As Uncle Edd entered the kitchen, Mark was pouring the second cup of steaming coffee. Uncle Edd reached for his immediately because he liked it just as it was, but Mark always drank his sweet.

As he opened the wooden bucket that Granny always used to put sugar in, Uncle Edd said, "Take that along, boy, if you want to.

We'll find room. I'll tell you what, take that little wooden box she used to put her feet on. Put that sugar bucket, that medium sized skillet and that sack of salt in it, and set it in the wagon. See if you can squeeze that last smoked pork shoulder and that sack of coffee beans in. We may have to cook somewhere along the line."

Mark gathered up everything that Uncle Edd mentioned and proceeded to load the other things on the wagon. Edd helped him load the trunk, and Mark made his last trip to the cabin for the guns.

He was checking over things when Uncle Edd came from around the cabin carrying his big jug from the smokehouse, the ax, and part of a sack of cornmeal.

"Thought we might need that ax," said Uncle Edd, as he buckled on his forty-four.

"Here, Hawk," called Mark.

As Hawk ran up, anxiously wagging his tail, Edd blurted, "What'r you doing?"

"I'm taking my dog," replied Mark sharply.

"You can't take him on that stage. You might as well leave him here," argued Edd.

"I'll take him as far as I can before I part with 'im," replied Mark.

"All right, but I'm afraid it will be harder down the way."

Mark breathed a sigh of relief as he ordered Hawk to jump into the wagon.

"Get in," said Edd. "I'll untie the team."

He climbed upon the seat as Edd untied the lines, handed them up, and climbed aboard. He gave Edd the lines and they were off for St. Jo. The brisk, chilly, September morning caused Mark to pull his old jacket close to his ears. He wouldn't dare look back because that lump in his throat was forming again. Only the jingle of the trace chains broke the silence until they had rounded the bend.

"We're supposed to meet a feller named Gilder in St. Jo," broke in Edd. "We'll get our instructions from him."

Mark knew they would reach St. Joseph in about two hours, so he prepared for a short nap. He climbed behind the wagon seat and rested his head on his bedroll. Hawk snuggled up close to his side, and soon both were asleep.

Edd's deep voice aroused Mark suddenly. "Boy, get up! We'll be there before long and I need to talk to you before we get into town."

Mark sat up and yawned and then realized that he had been spoken to. He scrambled back up to the wagon seat.

"Give me a minute to wake up, Uncle Edd," Mark begged.

"Well, get yourself situated because I want you to fully understand everything I say," Edd said gruffly.

The fresh, chilly air soon had Mark wide-awake. "I'm ready, Uncle, if you are," Mark exclaimed.

"Now, boy, you hear every bit of this," stated Edd.

"I'm listening," whined Mark.

Edd cleared his throat and began. "Boy, I'm packin' about seven thousand dollars. I've saved it for a long time. I realize I can't carry a damn bit of it with me, so if anything should happen to me, it's yours if you work it right. I don't believe anybody will gun a kid, so if I meet my fate, claim me. When nobody is around, get the money belt from under my shirt. Do you understand?"

"I understand," replied Mark.

"Maybe things won't come to that, but I wanted you to know, just in case," stated Edd.

"We'll make it, Uncle Edd, just me and you," assured Mark.

"Boy, I want you to know I love you, no matter what," said Edd meekly.

Soon, they rounded the bend in the road and could see the town ahead. Mark had heard many tales about St. Joseph. He knew this was the starting point for many wagon trains going west.

He had heard Granddad speak about the caliber of people coming through. He had come in with Granddad on occasion, but only long enough to get supplies and get out. He prepared himself to be "seen and not heard" while they were there.

It was just good daylight when they approached the edge of town. "We'll tie up close to the livery stables, 'cause Wade and Gilder, both, will be around there," said Edd.

Mark could see a few wagons had already arrived and a saddle horse or two were tied to the racks. Other than dogs barking, everything was calm. They were the first to tie up at the livery rack.

"Yonder's Wade's horse, over by the boardin' house," blurted Edd. "Let's go over there and see if we can eat."

As they angled across, Mark could see the big bay standing at the rack. Edd opened the door and Mark shyly went in.

"Hello, Edd! Who you got with you?" called out Wade.

"Mornin' Wade," smiled Edd. "Don't know this boy, he's just a stray."

Mark smiled as he went over to shake Jess' hand.

"It's been a while, boy," said Wade. "Believe you're growin' every day.

We can get some coffee now, but the victuals are not quite ready."

The man in the kitchen looked through the door and yelled, "Come on back here, Edd, and get your coffee. I'm too busy to serve you. I'm late!"

Edd returned with two cups of coffee.

"Is ole Mark big enough to drank coffee?" teased Wade.

"He still has to have sugar," laughed Edd.

Mark finally spoke out. "The cooking sure smells good."

Suddenly a dog barked outside the door.

"There's that dog, boy," snapped Edd.

Mark hurried outside, and sure enough, Hawk had followed.

"Go back, Hawk! Get in the wagon," scolded Mark. Hawk turned and scurried back with his tail between his legs. He stopped at the wagon, but Mark scolded again. He grudgingly jumped in.

As Mark returned to the table, the man in the kitchen was bringing a large platter of scrambled eggs and slab meat.

"Help yourself, fellers. There's plenty," said the cook.

"Eat up, boy. It'll be a long time before you get another meal like this," urged Edd.

Mark didn't need urging, for he had not had biscuits like these since Granny died. He stayed busy gorging himself while Wade and Edd ate and made the deal for the team and wagon. He heard Edd say he would take two hundred seventy-five dollars and Wade agreed.

"Wade, I need to find that feller, Gilder, before I let you leave with my rig," Edd stated.

"Take your time, Edd. I'm in no hurry," replied Jess.

Mark had finished, so when Edd pushed back his chair, that meant for him to move.

"I'll pay the cook here and then we'll go over to stables," Edd suggested.

As he paid the bill, Mark and Wade waited by the door. Others had begun to come in for breakfast. As they walked outside, Mark could still feel the chill in the air. They crossed the street and were waiting by the wagon, when Edd said suddenly, "here comes Gilder."

"Sorry, I'm late, Edd. I got tied up," said Gilder as he approached.

"That's alright. It's early yet," replied Edd. "This is my friend, Wade Samuel, and this here is my nephew, Mark."

Mark just nodded as they shook hands.

"Well, Edd, I guess I'd better line you out, so you can be on your way," suggested Gilder.

"I'm not rushing things, but I let Wade have my team and wagon. He needs to be headin' back," replied Edd.

In the meantime, Mark had gone around the wagon and gave Hawk the two biscuits and a piece of meat. He had put them in his jacket pocket at breakfast.

"Well, we can fix that," Gilder said eagerly. "Just set your stuff right there on the ground and let him go. You'll be out of here, quick, because everything is ready,"

As they hurriedly unloaded the wagon, Mark eased around and patted Ada's nose. He quickly turned away, because he knew what could happen. Wade brought his horse and tied him to the back of the wagon. They waved to him as he rumbled out of town.

Hawk stood close as Mark stood by their belongings waiting for the next move.

"Edd, here's the deal," said Gilder. "You are to go by stage from Fort Smith out to the way station in Texas, but I want you to deliver a team and wagon to Colonel Jackson at Fort Smith. You ever traveled that road from here to Fort Smith?"

"Yeah, I rode it horseback about a year ago," answered Edd.

"Well, I'm going to give you two letters," continued Gilder, "one for Colonel Jackson about the team and wagon and the other is for the Stage Master at Fort Smith to identify you as the one I hired. You see, I work for the stage line, but I never pass up a chance to make a little money. Colonel Jackson told me to find him a light hack and a small pair of mules for his personal running around. I found just what he needed, so I'm having you to carry it down. Think you can make it?"

"Sure, we'll get it down there," assured Edd.

"Well, I'll tell ya," went on Gilder. "These little lines backed mules are as gentle as a dog, but they're spirited and can cover the ground. The hack is first-class. It's got a canvas stretched over the bows, just like a big covered wagon. It's real light and you can make good time, maybe less than six days."

"What about feed for the mules," asked Edd.

"Oh, I intend for you to pick up a hundred pounds of corn," answered Gilder. "That'll be all you need. Six or seven pounds of corn at supper, stake them where they can graze overnight and they'll stay fat. Let's go harness them and get the hack. We'll go by the trading post and get what you need."

"Here, boy," blurted Edd, "take this money and go over to the post. See if there's anything you want."

Mark was astonished when Edd handed him five dollars.

"Thanks, Uncle Edd," Mark stammered.

"Go ahead," ordered Edd. "We'll take care of loadin' this stuff."

Mark let Hawk come along as he headed up the street to the trading post. He hadn't had that much money in all his life. He had no idea what he could buy.

One of the first things he saw was the fishing kit. It consisted of a piece of reed cane cut off below the joint to be used as a bottom and a small plug in the top. Fishhooks could be kept inside, and the line wrapped around the outside.

"How much for this?" asked Mark.

"Ten cents," replied the keeper. "There are six hooks inside and plenty of strong line, there."

"I want two of 'em," Mark said shyly.

"What else, sonny?" asked the keeper.

"What is this?" Mark asked as he examined it closely.

"That there, son, is a new kind of fire starter. You take it and drag it across this paper and it lights up, right now," answered the keeper.

"Give me one package," requested Mark.

"Now, sonny, you have to be careful when you light it. Don't smell the fumes," instructed the storekeeper. "You get ten of these sticks and the paper for fifteen cents."

Mark bought a new piece of flint and steel for everyday fires. He paid ten cents for a dozen eggs and twenty-five cents for a coil of grass rope. He paid the bill and hurried back to the things on the ground. He opened the trunk, put the matches inside and closed it. He put the eggs down in the cornmeal so they wouldn't break. He kept the fishing kits in his pocket and put the flint and steel in the cook box.

Mark was stripping the bark off a cedar post for a fire starter when he saw the hack come around the stables. He was astonished at the sight of the rig. He had never seen a pair of such evenly matched mules. They were a dun color with a strip down their back that broke down each shoulder. They were small, but he could tell that they were in tip-top shape. The hack had a canvas top and flowed along like water.

"Boy, did you buy the place out," called Edd as they pulled up beside Mark.

"No sir, I only spent seventy-five cents," replied Mark.

"Well, boy, I guess it's born in ya to watch pennies," teased Edd, as he pulled to a halt. "Load her on and we'll be out of here before you know it."

Gilder and Edd climbed down to help Mark load the hack. Mark climbed into the back of the hack so he could arrange the luggage. The two men lifted the trunk up first. Mark pushed it to the left front behind the seat and put the other things behind it. He left enough room at the rear for the sack of corn.

With this arrangement, it left enough room for a bed on the right side. Mark knew Edd had been drinking and would soon need a place to sleep.

"Let's go by the post to get what you need and you'll be off," said Gilder.

When they pulled up at the post, Edd and Gilder went in the store.

Mark pulled back the canvas at the back and ordered Hawk to get in. The merchant came out with a sack of corn and tossed it into the rear of the hack. Mark moved it into place.

Soon, Edd and Gilder came out. Edd was carrying a sack of onions.

Mark remembered how Edd loved onions.

Edd shook hands with Gilder, assured him of a safe delivery and climbed up. Mark handed him the lines and the little mules plunged forward toward Fort Smith.

CHAPTER 3

Gone Fishin'

I T WAS OBVIOUS THAT THE mules were in shape for a day's work from the way they hit the road gait. The sounds of their small hooves were in perfect cadence.

"Here, boy," Edd grumbled as he handed Mark the reins, "you can drive as good as I can. Just keep them headed down the road. When you get to the big Y about eight miles out, take the right fork."

"Yes, sir," Mark answered.

He knew he would have to take care of things for the rest of the day. Edd took a big swig from his jug, and wiped his mouth with the back of his hand.

Mark wasn't really driving the mules—he just let them have their heads.

They were setting their own pace and eating up the country. It was past light-thirty when they left town, and Mark knew that the first day would be short of their average.

Edd kept tapping the jug, and after about an hour's ride, Mark handed him the reins.

"What 're you doing, boy?" scolded Edd.

"Just a minute," replied Mark meekly.

He climbed over the seat into the back and untied a bedroll. He rolled out a blanket, doubled it, and placed it on the right side of the hack. After placing the pillow and the cover blanket, he climbed back into the seat. "All right, Uncle Edd, when you get tired, your bed is ready."

"I won't need no bed," barked Edd. "We need to cover a lot of territory before dark, but it's mighty thoughtful of you, anyway."

"I thought, maybe, we could take turns," answered Mark.

"Well now, if you are looking for an excuse to sleep, you just crawl over there and lay down," Edd almost shouted.

"Uncle Edd, I'm not sleepy, and I'm not trying to make you sleep. I just wanted you to know you could count on me," replied Mark humbly.

"I'm sorry, boy. I guess I'm a bit touchy. I know I can count on ya, and if I get tired, I'll leave everything to you and bed down," Edd stammered.

"Here, take these lines, I need a drink."

The mules were going in an easy trot at the rate of about four or five miles an hour, so Mark gave them the road. After a while, Edd began to nod. Mark knew he had drunk more than usual, but all he could do was wait. They had traveled about five or six miles, when Edd, without a word, climbed over the seat and stretched out on the bed. Mark relaxed and settled back for a long day.

They had already taken the right fork at the Y, so Mark knew they were headed in the right direction. Hawk began to stir around, so Mark pulled to a stop and let him out for fear he would disturb his uncle. Mark knew he could keep up, so he immediately let the mules resume the road gait.

Hawk checked first one bush and then another, but soon, he was loping along beside the rear wheel. After five or six miles, Mark stopped the team and ordered Hawk up on the seat with him. Hawk sat on his haunches with his tongue hanging away to the side indicating how hot and tired he was.

Mile after mile, the cadence of the little mules' feet meant they were that much farther on their way. Mark knew it was past noon because the sun was farther to the west than straight up. He had already made up his mind to stop at the first stream. When the mules seemed to get faster, he knew that they smelled water. As they came over the rise, Mark could see the creek at the foot of the hill. Old campfire signs made it obvious that this was a favorite stopping place.

Mark pulled off to the right and stepped to the ground. He was more than ready to stretch his legs and get out of a sitting position. He didn't unhook the traces because he knew the mules could easily be backed into position. He unbuckled the hames straps and slid the harness off the mules. He placed it on the double tree. He removed their collars and put on their stake ropes before removing their bridles. They hurried off, side by side, to drink their fill from the cool stream.

After staking the mules in the lush grass, Mark soon had a cooking fire going. While the fire was burning down to coals, he sliced several slabs from the pork shoulder. He boiled water in the skillet to make the cornmeal stick together; and while the meat was frying, he mixed the cornbread. After pouring most of the grease into the grease bucket, he fried the cornbread into small "hoe-cakes."

Hawk was watching every move, in hopes of getting something. Mark had to scold him several times before he got coffee made, but he made sure there would be plenty of scraps for the dog. He emptied the water jug of the lukewarm water and refilled it with cool, clear water from the creek. Edd had been sleeping about three hours and Mark knew he had better rouse him so he would sleep through the night. He climbed up to the wagon seat, reached over, and gently placed his hand on his uncle's shoulder.

"Uncle Edd," he called calmly.

Edd sat up immediately and felt for his gun.

"What is it, boy?"

"Nothing wrong," assured Mark. "It's past dinner time and I thought you needed to wake up and eat."

The canvas flap on the back of the hack was open and Edd could see the bright sunlight.

"I thought it was early morning," groaned Edd. "My head feels like it's bustin' open."

"Come on out and get some cool water and a cup of coffee," coaxed Mark. "You'll feel a lot better."

Edd got a towel from the clothes sack and ambled down to the creek to douse his face in the cool water. Mark quickly poured two cups of coffee and placed the water jug close by. He knew Edd wouldn't eat until he had finished his coffee and sat for a while.

He was getting the small jug of syrup when Edd came up and reached for his coffee. "This sure looks good," complimented Edd. "I couldn't get along without you."

Mark grinned as he brought the syrup.

"Now, you go ahead and eat, 'cause I know you're hungry," encouraged Edd.

"I'll be glad to fix your plate," replied Mark.

"No, I'll eat in a minute. You go ahead," said Edd.

Mark immediately stuffed himself with the fried pork, cornbread, and syrup. He took a piece of the meat and a couple of hoe cakes, and was feeding Hawk, when Edd started to fill his plate. Mark hurried over to pour Edd some more coffee.

"You sure take care of that dog," exclaimed Edd.

"He's a good dog, Uncle Edd," Mark answered. "Granny loved him, too."

"She sure did. She loved him because you loved him and I'm not gonna be the one to separate you," assured Edd. "Here, give him these scraps of meat."

"How far have we come?" asked Mark.

"Between twenty and twenty-five miles," replied Edd. "Them little mules are real dandies," he said as he stood up. "Barring trouble, we can make fifty miles a day."

Edd went to bring the mules while Mark quickly washed the dishes and gathered the utensils. He put the leftovers in the mixing bowl, covered it with a cloth and put it in the cook box. He folded the bedroll and pushed it to the front. He then ordered Hawk in the back. He climbed up with Edd and they were off again.

The first night, Mark insisted that Edd sleep in the wagon and let him sleep on the ground under the wagon. This was a mistake because Hawk slept at Mark's feet. At the slightest noise, he was off and barking. He kept both of them awake most of the night. Edd knew being in a strange place at night caused a dog to become nervous. He told Mark to take his dog and sleep in the wagon and to cut out the noise.

The third evening out, it began to rain at about five o'clock. It wasn't a hard rain, but it looked as if it had set in for the night. They had covered a good forty-five miles, but the mules slowed with the rain. They traveled three or four miles looking for a place to camp when they came to a small creek. They were crossing when Mark saw the old log cabin on the opposite bank.

"Look, we can sleep in there and leave our stuff in the wagon," Mark almost shouted.

"We may have to run the snakes out," grinned Edd.

As they pulled up in front, they could tell it was abandoned. They could also see the evidence of other campers. The old wagon shed in the small lot would make good shelter for the mules. The shutters had rotted off the one window in the end; and when the door was opened, it gave more light inside. It had a puncheon floor (split logs with the split side up) and a clay chimney.

Edd told Mark to unload what they needed for the night and he would unhook the mules. Mark carried in the cook box and both bedrolls. He returned to the wagon to get a candle and some cedar bark to start a fire.

The rain had been a slow drizzle, so he hurried down by the creek to find dry wood under the leaves. He noticed the creek was muddy; and on a slight rise, indicating heavier rain up the country.

As he approached the cabin with the dry wood, Edd came from the lot carrying a rabbit. "Look what I got," he called proudly.

"How'd you catch him?" asked Mark.

"I didn't," beamed Edd, "Hawk did. He ran from under the shed, and Hawk had him before he knew it. Sure will be good for supper."

"I love rabbit," exclaimed Mark as he carried the wood inside.

The rain had brought a dull day, but it was a good while before dark.

Mark told Edd to rest while he cleaned the rabbit and started supper because he had an idea. As Edd went to the wagon for his jug, Mark went to break some dry limbs to dry by the fire. Soon he had a nice fire going, with the wood stacked around the hearth to dry. He went outside and skinned the rabbit. He gave Hawk the head and all the intestines, except the liver and a small piece of the lungs. He kept these pieces for fish bait.

He knew Edd would occupy himself with the jug for a while, so he got the butcher knife, and hurried down to the creek. He looked around and chopped three green poles to stick deep in the mud on the creek bank. Soon, he had them baited and set out. He hurried back to the cabin to start supper.

When he returned, to his surprise, Edd was frying the rabbit on live coals on the hearth. He didn't have any flour, so he mealed it, and was carefully turning it.

"I was going to do that," chided Mark.

"I know, boy, but you're not the only one who can cook," retorted Edd.

Mark noticed the steaming coffee on the far side of the hearth. He was so glad that Edd had only taken an "appetizer" for supper. Hurriedly he set out the cold cornbread and the syrup.

The rabbit was so delicious that Mark almost gorged himself. Edd was proud to see him eat "like he meant it". Mark unrolled the bedrolls and placed the pillows and the cover blankets. Edd let Hawk get settled at Mark's feet before he blew out the candle. Soon, all three were asleep.

It wasn't quite daylight when Mark suddenly sat up on his bedroll. Edd was still snoring. Mark dressed quietly and eased over to the fireplace. He raked back the ashes from the live coals and put the cedar bark and dry twigs on top of the coals. He only had to blow once to get a blaze started. With a few larger twigs and several sticks of extra dry wood, he soon had a roaring fire.

It would be a while before the fire burned down for cooking, so he crept outside to go check his hooks. It was still hazy outside, but he could see the path to the creek. He hurried along with Hawk right on his heels.

Suddenly, he heard water splashing. He looked down the creek bank to the first hook by the small tree growing out over the water. It was pulled far to the left and shaking up and down. He rushed down the bank, slipping and sliding all the way. Straddling the pole, he pushed it away from himself to free it from the mud. By shear force, he dragged the fish up the bank to safety. It was the biggest catfish he had ever seen.

He put his fingers in the fish's gills and carried it higher up the bank. He wasn't disappointed at all to find the baits gone on the other two hooks. He wound his fishing lines around a stick, took his prize catfish, and hurried back to the cabin. Even though the fish was still flopping, Mark put it on the floor just inside the cabin door. Edd was still sleeping.

Mark raked two piles of coals out on the hearth, one for the coffee, and one for cooking. He poured enough water from the water jug to make coffee and placed it on the coals. He cut several more slices from the pork shoulder and placed them firmly in the skillet. The meat was frying and Mark had already mixed cornbread before Edd raised up and wanted to know what was going on.

"I beat you up this morning," boasted Mark.

"You sure did," replied Edd, as he reached for his pants. "I slept like a log! I sure can sleep with a slow rain falling, especially if I'm dry."

"I slept sound, but I woke up early," answered Mark joyfully.

He had hoped that Edd would see the big fish by the door when he went to wash his face, but he didn't notice it. Hurriedly, Mark divided the meat on two plates, laying aside two pieces for Hawk. He began to fry the little cakes of cornbread on one side of the skillet and two eggs at a time on the other side. He was glad he had preserved the eggs in the cornmeal.

Edd's eggs, pork, cornbread, and coffee were ready when he returned from the porch. Mark was taking up his eggs when Edd noticed what a fine breakfast had been prepared. "Boy, you are really splurging this morning with eggs and all the trimmings," he exclaimed. "What's the occasion?"

"Oh, I've got one," replied Mark elusively.

Edd finished eating before Mark, because he got an earlier start. He sipped his coffee and waited for the boy to get through. Mark couldn't hold it any longer. "Uncle Edd," he almost shouted. "Look over there by the door. I caught the biggest catfish I have ever seen!"

Edd turned his head and gasped, "Well, whatta you know! That fish weighs eight pounds, if it weighs an ounce. I didn't know that you set a hook."

"I just set three," cut in Mark. "I used rabbit entrails for bait."

"Man, you sure got a good one," Edd beamed. "We'd better get him cleaned and be on our way."

"You start on the fish. I'll load the bedrolls and the cook box and then I'll help you," suggested Mark.

"That's a bargain," replied Edd as he started for the porch.

Mark washed the dishes, put them in the cook box, and carried it to the wagon. As he went back for the bedrolls, he thought about the wood he had dried by the fire. He carried out the bedding and came back for an armload of dry wood.

"Boy, didn't I see your Granny's old clamp lid jar in that cook box?" called Edd.

"Yes, sir," replied Mark. "I just put it in there. I don't know why."

"Well, I'm glad you did. If we put a little moisture around it, our fish will keep just fine," Edd stated. "Bring it here."

Mark ran to the wagon, got the jar, and eagerly returned it to his uncle. When Mark returned from the lot with the mules, Edd had the fish sliced and packed the jar. He took a wet cloth, wrapped it around the jar, and put it in the cook box.

Mark had both mules backed into place when Edd came to help hook up. Mark ordered Hawk into the back of the wagon and climbed up to the seat with his uncle. Soon, the mules hit their road gait, and the rhythm of their little feet meant progress.

Edd knew Mark had had an exciting night and morning, so he suggested the boy sleep "for a spell". Mark climbed over the seat to the back, rolled out a bedroll, and stretched out. Hawk settled at his feet and Mark was soon asleep.

They passed through a town and a couple of small communities, but Mark never knew it. The sun was high in the sky when he suddenly awakened.

"Why didn't you call me?" Mark asked, as he scrambled up.

"You were doing some good sleeping, boy. I didn't need you," Edd replied.

"How long before dinner time," asked Mark.

Edd took out his pocket watch and looked at it. "It's just ten-thirty. We got an early start this morning."

"Let me herd these mules and you rest awhile," demanded Mark, as he crawled over the seat.

"Well, I won't argue with you," blurted Edd as he handed Mark the reins.

He reached over the seat for his jug.

"I need an appetite for dinner, 'cause that fish will sure be good."

"Uncle Edd, did Mr. Gilder tell you the names of these mules?" asked Mark.

"Rube and Minnie," replied Edd, "and they sure are steppers. We've covered a lot of ground."

"They are well matched and easy to handle," said Mark.

Edd reached for his jug again; and after the second swig, began to stroked Hawk's head and neck.

"If Ma hadn't thought so much of you and that boy, I would have left you," Edd mumbled to himself.

Mark kept the mules at a fast clip as they covered mile after mile.

Edd had gotten into the back and propped himself on one of the bedrolls. He was ready for a good meal!

When the mules picked up the pace, Mark knew water was close ahead. As they dropped down the hill, the small creek came into view. The mules didn't need to be pulled off the road. They almost stopped by themselves, because they knew a cool drink was forth coming. Mark jumped to the ground, dropped the breast yoke, and unbuckled the hames strap in order to lead the mules out with the collars still in place. He immediately removed the collars and led the mules to the creek with the stake ropes. They seemed to drink for minutes before they stopped for a breath and then they drank some more.

When Mark led the mules up the hill, to his surprise, Edd had a fire going with the coffee already boiling.

"That green stick across the top will keep that coffee from boiling over," Edd instructed.

"I'm sure ready for a cup," replied Mark as he proceeded to stake the mules.

When Mark returned to the fire, Edd had already poured the coffee and shuffled down the coals for cooking. Hurriedly, Mark drank his coffee and brought out the fish. Edd insisted that he fry the fish, so Mark brought out the grease bucket, the cornmeal, and the salt. Soon, the aroma of fresh catfish filled the air.

In the meantime, Mark peeled and sliced an onion, set out their plates, and set out the jug of syrup. Hurriedly, he mixed what he thought was enough cornbread. When Edd "took up" the fish, he poured most of the grease into the grease bucket, and began to fry the bread in the remainder. Neither one had to be told the meal was ready. Both of them began as if they hadn't eaten for a week.

"Boy, I haven't had a meal like this since your Granny passed away," commented Edd.

"I was just thinking," said Mark. "Tomorrow is Sunday and Granny always read the Bible to me on Sunday. Will you listen if I read, Uncle Edd?"

"Shore, I will, boy! What do you think I am? I realize my position, but I admire those who love God," answered Edd.

That evening, Mark fixed supper because Edd "didn't feel too good." They made dry camp for the first time. The mules were restless all night, because of thirst. After breakfast, the little mules were ready to move on. They had traveled about an hour and a half when the mules picked up speed. Mark knew water was ahead and he was grateful for the mules' sake. As they stood belly deep drinking their fill, Mark called Edd.

"What is it, boy? Is something wrong?" Edd asked anxiously.

"No, nothing's wrong," assured Mark, "this is Sunday and you promised to hear me read God's word."

Hawk scrambled to one side as Edd crawled over the back of the seat.

"Sure, boy! Sure I promised and I intend to hear you. I believe every word is sacred, whether I live it or not," he replied meekly.

Mark had already taken the Bible from the trunk and had picked the reading. Edd sat in silence as Mark humbly read Colossians 1:13–

and 14, "Who hath delivered us from the power of all darkness, and translated us into the kingdom of his dear Son. In whom we have redemption through his blood, even the forgiveness of sins."

"You make a feller feel mighty small," accused Edd, "but I'm so proud Ma taught you the way. She tried so hard."

Mark could see the moisture in Edd's eyes, but he didn't let Edd know it. The rest of the day passed without incident. They had cold fish and cornbread for supper, a good night's sleep in the open, and were on their way by daylight.

"Boy, we ought to get there before dinner," Edd broke the silence.

"I'm ready," Mark said eagerly. "Is there any place we can get a store-bought meal?"

"Sure is, boy, and I intend to give you the best 'cause I couldn't have made it without you on this trip," bragged Edd.

As they topped the next rise, Fort Smith came into full view. Mark relaxed because he knew that, from there on, someone else could worry about driving the team.

CHAPTER 4

A Few Good Men

A GUARD STEPPED FROM EACH side of the road as Edd pulled the mules to a halt at the gates of Fort Smith.

"A delivery of a wagon and team to Colonel Jackson," shouted Edd as he handed the letter to the guard at his side.

The guard mumbled through the letter and yelled, "Pass through, third building on your left."

Edd clucked to the mules and they darted through the gates. They pulled to a halt in front of the third building.

"Wait here, son. I'll be back shortly," said Edd as he stepped to the ground.

Hawk jumped from the back of the hack into the seat with Mark. Mark put his arm around the dog's neck and calmed him.

"Take it easy, boy. We'll get settled before long." Hawk's eyes glared as he watched every move inside the fort.

Mark was fascinated with the drill team in the open space to the right of the hack. He sat with his arm around his dog, watching the precision drill. He was jarred out of his trance by Edd's voice.

"Boy, we've got the right place and just about time to eat. We'll unload two buildings down to the right and bring the team back here."

Mark turned quickly to see Edd and a soldier approaching the wagon. Mark jumped to the ground and stood humbly. Colonel Jackson was elated with the mules and hack.

"Gilder sure knew what I wanted. Aren't they beauties?" he asked as he viewed the whole.

"They are the best little road mules I have ever handled," replied Edd.

"I'll put them to good use," retorted Colonel Jackson. "Take your gear down there to the way station and tie them here in front of the office. I'll have one of the troopers to take care of them. Thanks again for bringing them down."

"It helped us as much as it did you. We were glad to get the opportunity," replied Edd.

They pulled up in front of the way station and Edd went inside. Soon, he returned with a tall, gray-haired, pleasant looking man.

"Mr. Peoples, this is my nephew, Mark. Mark, this is Mr. Peoples, the station keeper," Edd said politely.

Mark shook hands and nodded.

"Boy, you remind me of my boy, when he was your age," said Mr. Peoples. "He's been gone west for five years now. I'd give the world to see him."

"Let's unload right here on the porch, boy, and get rid of these mules and wagon," urged Edd.

Mr. Peoples helped them unload the trunk, the bedrolls, the cook box, and other odds and ends. Hawk ran around eagerly exploring everything, taking care not to get too far from Mark.

"I've got a place for both of you to sleep," said Mr. Peoples. "It will be tomorrow afternoon before the next stage."

"We'll be grateful to you," replied Edd. "We could sure use a decent bed."

"Take the mules on down to the Colonel and come on back. I'll show you your quarters," promised Mr. Peoples.

Edd climbed up on the hack to carry the mules to the Commandant's office and Mark and Mr. Peoples went inside to the station. Mr. Peoples hurried to the back of the station and returned with a burlap sack.

"Here, boy," he said, "I can see already you'll need a place for that dog to sleep. Just put him at the end of the room on this sack. My boy's dog was a part of him and I can see how you feel toward yours."

"I'm sure obliged to you, Mr. Peoples. He would sure get lost in a strange place," Mark said meekly.

When Edd returned, Mr. Peoples insisted that they have dinner with him at the best place at the fort. Mark made Hawk stay on the sack and closed the room door.

As they approached the frame building, the aroma of frying steak filled the air. Mark read the sign over the door "Meals, Coffee, Whiskey". It was crowded already with several soldiers and civilian men. Some were having dinner and others were drinking at the bar. They took the table in the far corner, and immediately, the waiter was ready to take their order. Mr. Peoples ordered steak with all the trimmings and a pitcher of hot coffee for all of them.

Mark stuffed himself with the good food and listened eagerly while Mr. Peoples explained their assignment. He told them that their station was approximately two hundred miles west of Fort Belknap, Texas, and about fifty miles north of the Concho River. He explained further that it was by an all-weather stream with good facilities because it was usually where the stage stopped overnight to give the driver and passengers needed rest. It was a large station with a barn for storing feed and a corral all made of rock.

They also learned that mules were used west of Fort Belknap and they would have six in their care as theirs was the team change station. Mr. Peoples warned them that it was in desolate territory and frequently hampered by Indians. Edd was confident he could handle the situation and took the job. Mr. Peoples paid for the meal and they started back to the station.

"Boy, you might as well find something to do, because we will be here for a while," Edd said jokingly.

"There's not much for a boy to do around here," replied Mr. Peoples, "but Mark can stay around the station and keep me company."

"He don't talk much," jostled Edd. "I guess he's saving up for a special occasion."

Mark smiled, but kept silent.

"I bet we can find something to interest us," promised Mr. Peoples. "When they reached the station, Mark immediately checked on Hawk.

As he opened the door, Hawk came bouncing to him wagging his tail.

"I plumb forgot that dog, boy," apologized Mr. Peoples. "If I'd thought, I would have had Sam to fix us some scraps. I've got some cold cornbread in the kitchen that will tide him over 'til supper."

"That dog is a lot of trouble," blurted Edd.

"No trouble at all," assured Mr. Peoples. "That boy will need his company away out yonder."

"Do you think the driver will let him ride?" asked Edd.

"They change drivers and Will Hays will be driving out of here," began Mr. Peoples. "I'll see him tonight or tomorrow and I'll bet he gets the boy's dog to his destination."

"I sure will thank you, Mr. Peoples," Mark said eagerly.

"Don't mention it, boy. Come on, let's feed your dog," he said, as he started for the kitchen.

Edd went to the room to clean up, while Mark went to feed his dog.

Mark knew his uncle would spend most of his time at the saloon. Mr. Peoples had already established himself with Mark and gained his confidence. Mark thanked him and called Hawk out of the kitchen door. Hawk gulped down the bread and looked around for more.

"Boy, you stay around here and I'll be back before long," called Edd.

"All right, I'll be here with Mr. Peoples," answered Mark.

"Don't worry about him. I'll keep an eye on him," asserted Mr. Peoples.

Mark brought Hawk inside and ordered him back to the sack in the room.

"Come on in here, and I'll put on the coffee. Let's sit a spell," invited Mr. Peoples.

Mark came in and took a seat on the bench at the kitchen table. He listened intently while Mr. Peoples talked of bygone years. He had lost his wife about eight years back, and his two daughters and his son were scattered over the country. A lump came into Mark's throat as he realized how lonely one could be when he felt like all had deserted him for their own interests.

"Son, how much book learnin' do you have," asked Mr. Peoples.

"I can read fairly well and I can add and subtract numbers," answered Mark.

"Well, I haven't got too much myself, but I always loved numbers. I've got something you need," said Mr. Peoples.

He went into the next room and opened the trunk in the far corner. He rambled through its contents and came back to the table.

"Here is an old slate with a pencil," he said as he handed them to Mark, "and here are two copies of Pilgrim's Progress that will make good reading when you're lonesome."

Mark was so excited he could hardly thank Mr. Peoples. He was always interested in something new to read.

"You can read those later," suggested Mr. Peoples. "I have something else for you."

He took the yellow sheet of paper and unfolded it on the table. Mark could see it was filled with numbers.

"Son, this is a copy of the multiplication tables. Multiplication is simply a short way to add."

"I love to work numbers," exclaimed Mark.

"I figured you did and I believe you will learn these," answered Mr. Peoples.

He explained the process and was pleased because he knew Mark understood.

As they drank coffee, he asked Mark several questions about himself and his family. He noticed that Mark could hardly keep his eyes off the numbers.

"Son, I've got some book work to do. Why don't you go out on the gallery and study those numbers?" he suggested.

"I'd sure like to," replied Mark, "and let me thank you again for the books and the numbers."

"You're just as welcome as you can be," said Mr. Peoples.

Mark went by the room, put the books in the trunk, and hurried out to the porch. He followed Mr. Peoples instructions. He started memorizing the "two's" first and then the "threes." By late afternoon, he knew through the "fives." Mark was reciting them to Mr. Peoples when Edd came noisily in the front door.

"Boy, I just came to check on you," Edd said loudly.

"He's doing real well," replied Mr. Peoples calmly. "He knows his multiplication tables though the "fives."

"If book learnin' was worth anything, he sure would be on top, 'cause he sure is a sucker for it," slurred Edd.

"He's eager to learn and a fine boy, Edd," stated Mr. Peoples.

"Yeah, I ride him a little, but I couldn't get by without him," Edd loudly replied.

"You go ahead. The boy will be all right with me," Mr. Peoples suggested.

"Well, I'm sure obliged to you," Edd called as he went out the door.

Mr. Peoples suggested that Mark take Hawk and look around the fort. Hawk stayed close to Mark as he viewed the surroundings. He watched the busy supply wagon making deliveries and the soldiers going about their daily tasks. He was returning to the station when he saw a company of soldiers gathering in front of the headquarters building. As he stopped, he saw them come to attention, and the bugler began to blow retreat. As the flag was lowered, he stood at attention remembering how Miss Sally had taught him to love and respect the flag.

Mr. Peoples was waiting on the porch when Mark returned.

"It's supper time, son," he called.

"I'll pay for it this time," replied Mark.

"Don't be silly," scolded Mr. Peoples, "put your dog in the house and let's go."

Mark made Hawk go to his sack and hurried out.

The saloon was crowded and a lot louder than before. Mr. Peoples led the way to the empty table at the side of the room. Sam immediately started for their table.

A short, fat man from the bar staggered up and said loudly, "Peoples, you can't bring that boy in here."

"The hell he can't," Sam said as he approached, "and if you want to stay, mind your own business."

Mark was embarrassed, but he tried not to show it. Sam put his hand on Mark's shoulder as Mr. Peoples gave him the order. Mark saw Edd at the table in the far corner. He could tell by the stack of bills that his uncle was winning, because he loved money too well to play very long if he was losing. Mark made as if he didn't notice him. Sam was bringing the platter of steaming steaks when Mark saw a large man come into the bar. Mark guessed him to be about six feet four and 240 pounds.

"There's Will Hays," said Mr. Peoples, "now, when he gets settled, I'll call him over here."

Sam set down the steaks and returned for a pitcher of coffee.

"Son," began Mr. Peoples, "lots of these people drink and I don't approve of it, but I've got to deal with them. Will Hays drinks heavy, but he's good at his word and does his job. I'll just have to accept it."

"I understand," said Mark politely.

Sam returned with the coffee and Mr. Peoples asked him to tell Will Hays to bring his bottle and come to their table. Mark watched Sam as he stopped to talk with Will Hays. He saw Will look in their direction, pause for a moment, and walk slowly toward them without the bottle.

"Peoples, are you asking me to drink in the presence of a boy?" he asked pointedly.

Mr. Peoples said calmly, "Will, I don't mean to embarrass you, but this boy knows what's going on and he needs your help. Bring your bottle and sit down, we'll explain.

Reluctantly, Will brought his bottle to the table.

"Will, this boy is going to Valley Creek station the other side of Mountain Pass in Texas. You know Edd Singletary back there at that corner table? Edd is all this boy has and he has no other choice," pleaded Mr. Peoples.

"Edd Singletary saved my life once," mused Will, "and he's your uncle?"

Mark nodded.

"Well, what's your problem, boy," asked Will.

"He's got a dog that needs to go with him," cut in Mr. Peoples.

"Well, I know all the drivers between here and Fort Chadbourne and I'll bet I can get him there," boasted Will.

"I sure would be obliged to you," said Mark hopefully.

"Will he mind you, boy?" asked Will.

"He minds real good, Mr. Hays," answered Mark.

"You be ready tomorrow evening and I'll get you and that dog to Texas, if I have to put him in the mail rack," promised Will.

"You don't know how I appreciate this," Mark said, as he clasped Will's hand. "I couldn't go without him."

"I understand, boy," said Will, as he started back to the bar.

Mark and Mr. Peoples began immediately to make way with the luscious steaks that Sam had brought.

CHAPTER 5

Farewell to Fort Smith

THE SUN WAS BARELY PEEPING over the horizon when Mark suddenly awakened. He saw Uncle Edd in the other bed and breathed a sigh of relief. As he sat up, Hawk immediately came to him, wagging his tail.

"All right, boy, I'll let you out," Mark whispered.

He eased across the room, and quietly opened the door.

Mr. Peoples' voice startled him.

"You don't have to be so quiet, son. I'm already up, and it looks like Edd will be there for quite a while."

"I was afraid I would disturb you," stammered Mark.

"Not me," bragged Mr. Peoples, "I've been up for quite a spell. Turn your dog out, and come on in for coffee."

Mark let Hawk out the front door, and returned to the kitchen. Mr. Peoples set out a steaming cup of coffee between the cream pitcher and the sugar bowl.

"Help yourself," he encouraged.

"You sure have been nice, Mr. Peoples, and I want to thank you for all you have done for me," Mark said politely.

"Don't mention it, boy. It's not often that I have the company of a fine boy like you. I wish you could stay here with me," replied Mr. Peoples.

"I'd like to," answered Mark.

Hawk scratched at the kitchen door and Mr. Peoples let him in. Mark made him lie down by the door.

"There's Will Hays now," blurted Mr. Peoples as he hurried to the front door. "Come on in, Will. I've got coffee made," he called.

"I need to carry my hoss over to the livery. I woke up and remembered I left him tied to the rack all night," Will called back.

"Hurry, and we'll have you a hot one," promised Mr. Peoples.

Mark saw Will come across the porch, and into the front room.

"You're up mighty early, Mr. Hays, to be making a run tonight," Mark observed.

"Yeah, I forgot that damn horse. I'm going back to bed," yawned Will.

As he sat down on the bench, Mr. Peoples sat a hot cup of coffee in front of him.

"You have breakfast with us first," he demanded, "I'm fixing to fry up some slab meat and eggs, and I've got biscuit dough already made up."

"I hate to be trouble to you, but that sounds mighty good," groaned Will.

"It won't be long," said Mr. Peoples as he started to slice the meat.

Hawk stirred, and caught Will's attention.

"There's a leopard dog!" exclaimed Will. "I haven't seed one in twenty years. Where did you get that dog, boy?"

Mark told him where he got him and asked, "How'd you know he was a leopard dog?"

"We had some of the stock when I was a kid in Georgia. They shore are good dogs, especially with stock. We hunted with them, and worked stock, too," mused Will.

"He's making a good one," bragged Mark, "but he's young yet."

"Just keep workin' 'im. He'll make a dandy," asserted Will.

"Shall we let Edd sleep through breakfast?" asked Mr. Peoples.

"Goodness, no!" exclaimed Will! "He got in fairly early last night. The poker game broke up by twelve, and he must've won five hundred."

"Wake him up, Mark, and by the time he's ready, breakfast will be ready," offered Mr. Peoples.

Mark hurried to the long room and called Uncle Edd.

Edd jumped up immediately and asked, "What is it?"

"It's me, Uncle Edd," Mark said quietly, "you need to get up for breakfast."

"Yeah, I guess I do," yawned Edd. "I'll be right in."

Mark returned to the kitchen and sat down on the bench. Shortly, Edd entered on his way to the wash gallery.

"Mornin', Edd," said Will boisterously. "Feel like somebody put fertilizer in your mouth?"

"That's about it," replied Edd, as he went on to the back porch.

Mr. Peoples was taking up the last egg when Edd came in with a freshened face and his hair combed. Mr. Peoples reluctantly asked Mark if he would say grace.

Mark began immediately. "Dear, Lord, bless the hands that earned and prepared this food. Bless it to our bodies and help us realize the value of thy guiding hand. We pray in Jesus name, amen."

"That's a fine boy you've got, Edd," commented Will. "I don't know if you know it or not."

"Yeah," replied Edd. "A lot of Mama rubbed off on 'im."

Breakfast was finished in silence. The men were lighting their pipes, when Will Hays broke the silence. "Edd, they change stages here. We'll be riding one of those Celerity wagons. The seats fold down, and floor it for a bed. It's light because it has a canvas top. Peoples will pull it around to the front about one o'clock. Put your kettle at the bottom of the mail rack, because you won't change stages before Fort Belknap."

"What about the trunk and the cook box?" asked Edd.

"I believe both of them will go under the seats," replied Will.

"Where will I carry Hawk?" asked Mark shyly.

"Son, get you a short piece of rope and we will tie him to the mail rack.

After he falls off a couple of times, he'll lay down and behave his self," answered Will. "Now, y'all get things loaded, because I'm going back to bed. I'll see you about two o'clock."

"Wait a minute, Will," said Edd eagerly, "give us a little information about how far do you go, and where do we stop."

"I drive from here to Riddles," Will said. "It's about thirteen to fifteen hours, according to the load. We eat supper at Walker's, about three hours out. Y'all be ready when the stage pulls in here."

Edd left with Will and Mark helped Mr. Peoples with the dishes.

"Mark, you will have to make arrangements to feed your dog. It will be hard to get him anything at the way stations," instructed Mr. Peoples.

"We've got a lot of cornmeal left in the cook box. I could make up a lot of corn cakes, if you would let me use your fire," Mark entreated.

"Just help yourself. I have some old cracklings you can have, and an extra flour sack you can put the bread and all in," coaxed Mr. Peoples.

Mark spent most of the morning cooking dog bread. When he finished the last corn pone, Mr. Peoples helped him to put the bread and cracklings in the sack. Allowing two corn cakes and a handful of cracklings per day, along with what they could scrap on the way, they figured Hawk would have enough to make the trip.

It was almost noon when Edd came in. To Mark's surprise, he wasn't drinking. He announced that he was buying the noon meal, and he didn't want any argument out of Mr. Peoples.

"Alright, Edd. I'll let you buy mine," said Mr. Peoples, "but I want this boy to have the best before he leaves."

"I want both of you to have the best," retorted Edd. "I can't thank you enough for taking care of him."

"He's a good boy, Edd, and you just make sure you take care of him, or you'll be hearing from me," returned Mr. Peoples.

"Hugh, he's all I've got! I've got to take care of him," promised Edd.

"Let's go ahead and eat, and have everything ready ahead of time," inserted Mark.

"If you're ready, I am," said Mr. Peoples.

"Well, let's beat the rush, and this time it's all on me," demanded Edd.

They hurried over to Sam's, and were the first ones to order. After dinner, Mark and Edd helped Mr. Peoples push the stage around to the front of the station. The incoming stage was expected to arrive in an hour or so. Edd put his kettle in the bottom of the mail rack and placed Mark's old muzzleloader on the floor beside it. All the mail sacks could be put on top of them. Mr. Peoples helped Mark load his trunk and cook box under the seats. Edd's old Sharps rifle was hooked on the rack inside the stage.

"Come on, Mark. Let's go out to the barn, and find a piece of leather to make a dog collar," suggested Mr. Peoples.

"Don't bother, Mr. Peoples. I've been enough trouble, already," replied Mark.

"No trouble, son," retorted Mr. Peoples. "Besides, you don't want his neck rubbed raw with that rough rope around his neck."

At the barn, they found an old piece of harness strap with a buckle. With a little altering with a pocketknife, it was made into a snug collar for Hawk.

"We might as well catch and harness the horses," said Mr. Peoples. "It won't be long now."

They went through the barn to the horse lot on the other side. Mark was astonished at the size of the horses. There were six of them, four heavy built blacks and two beautiful bays with longer bodies and legs.

"They're fine looking horses," exclaimed Mark.

"In pretty good shape," replied Mr. Peoples.

"Will we use them all," Mark asked.

"Let's just harness four. If we need the other two, we know where they are," said Mr. Peoples.

Mark thought that they would use the four blacks, but to his surprise, Mr. Peoples bridled the bays first. He explained that the bays were excellent lead horses who were always put at the front because of their easy reigning and their ability to step out. The two bald-faced blacks were expert wheelers and never used anywhere else. The other two were used only in the middle or swing position of a six-horse hitch. He explained that Will Hays thought more of the four they were gearing up than any other horses on the run.

Edd was sitting on the porch with his jug and luggage beside him when Mark and Mr. Peoples brought the horses around to the front.

"Edd, did you find anything to go in that jug," asked Mr. Peoples jokingly.

"Got 'er filled up and ready to go," blurted Edd. "How 'bout a snort before I leave?"

"No thank you, Edd. I quit a few years back and I have to lay off completely," Mr. Peoples said convincingly.

Mark could tell Edd had already had a few. They tied the horses to the front rack and sat down on the porch. They hadn't seated themselves before they saw Will Hays coming to the station with his whip and satchel.

"You're a little early aren't you, Will," greeted Mr. Peoples.

"Thought maybe I'd get everything set and help this boy get his dog situated," replied Will.

"That boy is going to wind up walking and the dog riding," grumbled Edd.

"Naw, we'll get 'em there," promised Will.

Edd offered Will a drink and he took a short one. He called Mark to the stage and showed him how the mail sacks would be thrown into the mail rack. He explained that they would tie Hawk up short so he could lie on the sacks, but not get completely out of the rack. He also told Mark that at times, if they' were not too loaded, the dog could ride inside under the seats. Mark sincerely thanked him again.

Mr. Peoples had coffee made and was waiting for Mark. Will sat on the porch with Edd as they didn't prefer coffee just then. Mr. Peoples gave Mark some valuable tips on how to cook and how to cure meat so it would keep, and also what to expect from most of the stage riders. They were finishing their coffee when they heard Will on the porch.

"Edd, I saw the stage come over that rise. Help me hook up these two wheelers," Will requested.

Mr. Peoples and Mark came out to help.

"What about the bays?" asked Edd.

"Just leave 'em tied there. We may have to get the swing horses, if the load is big enough," instructed Will.

Soon, the stage came into clear view, and they could see it had a fourhorse hitch.

"Let's hook up old Buck and Bundy," said Will. "If they can go with four, the load won't be much more."

Mr. Peoples backed the bays to the front of the stage tongue and Edd and Will hooked the traces.

The stage pulled in close enough to the outgoing stage to transfer the mail sacks.

"Well, Jack, you've made another one," called Will.

"Yeah, I got on about two-thirty this morning," moaned Jack, "I sure could use a cup of coffee."

"It's ready," shouted Mr. Peoples, "go on in and help yourself."

There were only two passengers, soldiers going to Fort Belknap. Jack and the soldiers went in for coffee, while Mr. Peoples and Will transferred the mail sacks. Will put Hawk in the rack and tied him up short.

"Son, you can ride up there on top with me 'til we get to Walkers," invited Will.

"Who rides shotgun?" asked Mark.

"Ah, we don't use one on this little stretch. We'll pick him up at Walkers," answered Will. "That'll give you a chance to calm your dog."

Edd was already in the stage when Will yelled it was time to go. The soldiers hurried out, pitched in their baggage, and climbed aboard. Mark shook Mr. Peoples' hand and expressed his deepest thanks. Mr. Peoples embraced him and helped him climb up to the driver's seat. Will threaded the reigns in his fingers and yelled at his team to move out. Buck and Bundy lunged forward and swung left toward the road with the blacks in close pursuit. The stage rolled out of Fort Smith in fine style. Hawk began to jerk on his rope and swing back and forth. He swung himself out of the rack and was hanging over the side. Mark started to crawl across to help him, but Will stopped him.

"Leave him be," Will shouted, "he'll scratch back in and behave himself."

Sure enough, Hawk scrambled his way back into the rack. He looked all around and finally settled himself on top of the mailbags.

"He learns fast," smiled Will.

Mark nodded his approval as the horses raced along at a fast clip.

They were about an hour out of town, when Will yelled, "What in the hell is that noise?"

Mark braced himself and leaned far over the side to look through the stage window.

He raised up and shouted, "All three of them are drunk as a skunk and trying to sing."

A broad grin came upon Will's face as he hollered back, "With a noise like that, we don't need a shotgun rider. They'd scare the devil off."

Mark laughed as he nodded his thoughts.

By the time they reached Walker's station, Edd and both the soldiers were out cold. When Will learned that no passengers were coming aboard, he got into the stage, folded down the seats, and floored the stage for sleeping.

He rolled Edd and the soldiers over to one side and put their bedrolls under their heads. He turned to Mark with a grin. "We'll pick up Chester Teague for shotgun, so you and your dog can bed down when we leave here."

Mark and Will were the only ones reporting for supper, so they got the best of service. The hot coffee, sowbelly, and corn-bread tasted mighty good to Mark. He offered to pay for both of them, but there was no charge for Will because he was the driver. Mark paid his fifty cents and expressed his thanks to the lady who served them.

A short stocky man walked in carrying a shotgun. Mark knew immediately that it was Chester Teague.

"Well, Will, I see you survived another one at Fort Smith," shouted Chester.

"Same old thang," returned Will. "I want you to meet my little buddy, here, Mark Singletary."

"Glad to know you, boy," stated Chester. "Goin' very far?"

"You know Edd Singletary," cut in Will. "He and this boy are gonna take over Valley Creek Station."

"Edd Singletary? I haven't seen him in months," mused Chester. "Where is Edd?"

"He's in the stage with two soldiers, passed out cold," laughed Will.

"I might have known," grinned Chester.

Hawk had been well fed through the generosity of the kind lady. With a new team, they were ready to leave Walker's. As Chester climbed up to the top, Mark and Hawk got into the stage and found a place to bed down. After many miles and several stations, they finally reached Riddle's at daybreak.

Mark awoke as the stage pulled to a halt in front of the station. He quickly got his bearing and realized where he was. Edd and the soldiers were still sound asleep. Mark eased over to the door and stepped down. Hawk jumped out beside him.

Mark was startled at Will's voice. "Wake Edd and those soldiers up, boy. You'll change stages here."

"I'll get 'em up, Mr. Hays," Mark answered softly.

He crawled back into the stage and eased across the stage to put a hand on Edd's shoulder.

"Uncle Edd, wake up! We're at Riddle's," he said softly.

Edd sat up and felt for his gun.

"Everything's alright," assured Mark. "We'll change stages here and you and the soldiers need to get up."

"Alright," groaned Edd. "You go ahead and I'll get 'em up."

Mark went inside with Will and Chester. They were thoroughly enjoying the fresh coffee, corn cakes, and sowbelly when Edd and the soldiers came sleepily through the door.

"Come on in, Edd," Will called, "we're waiting for you like one hog waiting on another."

"I see you are," grumbled Edd as he and the soldiers sat down at the table.

Mark knew it would take lots of food to fill those three empty stomachs. They ate in earnest for quite a while before Will finally broke the silence. "Edd this is the end of my line. I'll take the stage back to Fort Smith about six o'clock tonight."

"I figured you'd drove about long enough," replied Edd. "Wish you could go all the way."

"I do, too," said Will, "but twelve hours straight is a long time to herd those critters."

"I don't see how you keep goin', day in and day out," returned Edd as he pushed back his plate.

The new driver, Short Mitchell, came in, and Will introduced Edd and Mark. He told Short to look after Mark and his dog and to pass the word to the other drivers.

They thanked Will for his kindness, bade him goodbye and boarded the stage. Mark made Hawk lie down in the front corner and stretched out beside him. Edd and soldiers sat up most of the day, but by dark, they were in fine shape to sleep.

Mile after mile, they rumbled along. Each driver was instructed to take care of Mark and his dog. On the third day, just before noon, they rolled into Fort Belknap, Texas.

CHAPTER 6

Half a Ton of Corn

A S THE STAGE STOPPED IN front of the station, Mark could see that Fort Belknap was a thriving place. It wasn't as big as Fort Smith, but it was the largest place west of it. He was to learn later that it had six stores, a blacksmith shop, a livery stable, and three eating-places.

Mark and Hawk were the last ones out of the stage, so the elderly man at the front was already unhooking the team.

"All that want to catch the next stage out, put your things in that one," yelled the driver, pointing to the empty stage to the left.

Mark was stretching his legs when he heard Edd's voice.

"Let's put our things on the porch, boy. We probably won't leave 'til tomorrow."

Mark nodded, reentered the stage, and shoved out the trunk and cook box to Edd.

"Go on in and clean up for dinner, boy. I'll get the rest of it," instructed Edd.

Mark left Hawk on the porch as he entered the station.

"Come on in, son."

He was startled to hear a lady's voice.

"I've got dinner ready and I'll bet you're a hungry, boy."

He looked in the direction of the kitchen, where the voice came from.

"I sure am, ma'am," he stammered to the kind looking elderly lady.

"I'm Mattie Flurry," she said pertly. "Everybody calls me Mattie."

"I'm Mark Singletary," Mark said politely. "I'm too young to call a lady by her first name, so if you don't mind, I'll say Miss Mattie."

"Son, you'd better say Mrs. Mattie," she retorted. "That Miss business went so long ago, it's hard to remember it. I've already out lived three husbands."

"I'm sorry for your heartaches, ma'am," replied Mark, "but to say 'Miss' pays you the highest respect."

"Say what you want, son," said Mattie, "but go on to the back gallery and wash up. Dinner's waitin'."

He had just finished drying his face, when Edd entered the station.

"Edd Singletary!" squealed Mattie as she rushed to embrace him.

"Mattie, it's been too long," mumbled Edd, as he held her tightly in his arms.

Mark was embarrassed, but he pretended not to notice. Suddenly, he realized Edd was talking to him.

"Boy, you don't have to hide your face. Me and Mattie are old friends and our trails have crossed a lot of times."

Mark nodded as he headed toward the front porch. "I'd better see about Hawk."

Hawk was sitting on the porch along with the trunk, the cook box, and the guns. Mark walked out front of the station to get a clear view of the place. Suddenly, he heard Mattie's squeaky voice saying, "You are not carrying that boy out there miles from nowhere to grow up!"

He heard Edd's stern voice, "He's all I've got. Where I go, he goes."

Mark suddenly realized Edd's strong feelings for him and he vowed within himself to stick by Uncle Edd come what may.

Mattie was disappointed because there weren't more folks there for dinner. Mark, the driver, Edd, and Mattie were the only ones there.

Mark ate silently, but thoroughly enjoyed the turnip greens, the hog jowl, and the corn bread that Mattie had prepared.

Edd asked several questions and Mattie gave several sources where he could inquire about the supplies he wished to buy. Mark knew Edd intended to buy supplies here because it was the closest place to Valley Creek to find the things he wanted. The stage line furnished the meager necessities, but Mark knew that Edd had ideas of selling more than the meager necessities.

After supper, the stage driver disappeared, and Mattie showed Mark to the back room.

"This is your room and you can keep your dog right here with you," she said as she hooked the back door. "You, Edd, and me are going to the dance tonight. It's too early for you to turn in."

"I've never been to a dance," Mark replied with embarrassment.

"Well, you're going tonight," retorted Mattie, "I don't intend to leave you here by yourself."

Mark nodded, went to the back gallery, washed his face, and combed his hair.

As they approached the dance hall, Mark could see this place was the center of attention. All the other buildings were dark. Mark's thoughts immediately turned to his Granny.

"There's no good in them places," he could hear her say.

They pushed their way through the crowd to the table in the back corner. Girls were busy bringing bottles and glasses to tables while a large crowd of men were gathered at the bar. A scantily dressed girl took their order and soon a bottle and three glasses were placed on their table. Edd gave her a bill and told her to keep the change.

As the waitress left the table, Edd unstacked the glasses. He set one in front of Mattie, one in front of himself, and threw the third in the corner as hard as he could.

Mattie screamed in amazement, "Edd, what's the matter with you?"

The whole room came to silence, but Edd gave his answer clearly and distinctly. "All hell will freeze over before I'm responsible for that boy having his first drink."

Mark listened to a few of the fiddler's tunes and watched the dancers, but could muster very little interest. At about eleven o'clock, he excused himself, walked briskly to the station, and went to bed.

After breakfast, Mark went with Edd to order supplies. Edd made arrangements for three freight wagons to leave immediately.

Mark listened intently as Edd gave the order: two barrels of flour, four barrels of sugar, two barrels of corn meal, one hundred pounds of salt, two hundred pounds of potatoes, one hundred pounds of coffee, one barrel of lard, three cases of short fuse dynamite, five cases of sharps rifle cartridges and percussion caps, two hundred pounds of dry beans, one thousand pounds of corn, one plow, several types of garden seed, twenty-five jugs, saw, and three water buckets.

"Is there anything else you want, boy?" asked Edd.

"I would like one of those Dutch ovens and a stew pot," Mark said respectfully.

"Throw 'em in," Edd growled at the clerk.

Most of the next day was spent with Miss Mattie while Edd checked out supplies. Mattie talked about how important it was for a boy to be able to read, write, and do arithmetic. She was amazed at how well Mark could do all three.

Mark told her how much he loved his teacher and how his Granny had taught him. Mattie was a good listener and expressed her confidence in Mark's future.

It was late evening when Edd came in. Mark could tell he was bothered and drinking heavy.

"Boy, I'm gonna send you on and come later," Edd said nervously. "I can't get any corn and I've got to wait 'til I can get some."

"Edd, you're not gonna send that boy out there by himself," screeched Mattie.

"Now, Mattie, it won't be that long, and the boy will be settled by the time I get there," replied Edd firmly.

Mark knew his uncle well enough not to argue. He knew Edd would go to any lengths to get that corn.

CHAPTER 7

Texas and Plenty of It

T HE STAGE WAS READY TO leave at seven o'clock. Mark met the driver, Jug Meyers, and the shotgun rider, Bozy Combs.

Jug assured Edd that if the station keeper would not agree to stay at Valley Creek until he got there, then Mark would be carried on to Fort Concho.

There were no other passengers going out of Fort Belknap, so Mark and Hawk would have things to themselves. After receiving strict instructions from Edd, Mark climbed aboard and the stage rolled out.

They made a short stop at Franz station and picked up one passenger. He introduced himself as Mr. Lambshead and explained that he was going to Mountain Pass station to visit a relative.

"I'll put my dog in the mail rack," Mark offered.

"Oh, no, son. He won't hurt a thing here," Mr. Lambshead assured. "Why, that's a Sharp's rifle," he said, as he noticed Mark's guns.

"Yes, sir, that belongs to my Uncle. I told you about him," said Mark.

"I can understand why they use those for buffalo. That's a powerful gun up to five hundred yards," Mr. Lambshead remarked.

At Fort Griffin, they changed teams. Mark was surprised to see them bring out six mules. Mr. Lambshead explained that mules were used even past Fort Concho, because of the rocky and sandy country.

They had a good meal and Mark fed Hawk. The driver told them that they were getting into Indian country, and in case of attack to close the shutters and brace themselves. They crossed the Clear Fork of the Brazos River and headed out through rocky country.

Smith's station was the loneliest looking place Mark had seen on the whole trip. It was a small adobe station house with lots of open territory on both sides. There were a few trees on what appeared to be a small creek at the back. The corral was made of stout poles and appeared to be crowded with mules.

Mr. Lambshead and Mark stepped off the stage just as the station keeper called out to Jug. "Ben quit the station over at Fort Phantom. Came by here yesterday a hoss-back and left them mules. Said he was fed up."

"Did he bring the harness?" asked Jug.

"No, he said it was over there in the Fort powder house," replied the keeper.

"Well, let's unhook these and see if we can't fit out six of those critters, and then we'll spend the night at Fort Phantom. We'll go on to Mountain Pass in the morning," allowed Jug.

"You pick 'em and I'll catch 'em," said the keeper.

Mark and Mr. Lambshead helped to harness the mules; and soon, they were ready to move out. Jug told the station keeper to send word by the next eastbound stage to the district supervisor at Fort Griffin that they needed a keeper at Fort Phantom. All the mules seemed to hit the collars at the same time as the stage lunged forward heading across the open country.

Mr. Lambshead was familiar with this part of the country and kept Mark's attention with his interesting comments. He was in the midst explaining why the little creek they had just crossed was called "Dead Man's creek," when Mark heard Bozy yell, "Indians!"

"Pull your shutter and get on the floor," ordered Mr. Lambshead.

Mark obeyed, as he watched Mr. Lambshead kneel by his window and put his head out cautiously to view the situation. The mules were in a full gallop and Mr. Lambshead had to shout to make himself heard.

"Comanche, Nine of them!"

The next thing Mark remembered was Mr. Lambshead shaking him and asking if he had any ammunition for the Sharp's rifle. Hurriedly, Mark reached into his bag, brought out a box of the paper cartridges and caps, and handed it to Mr. Lambshead.

Mark was wondering why he hadn't heard Bozy's shotgun, as Mr. Lambshead moved back to the window.

"They don't seem to be trying to catch us," shouted Mr. Lambshead. "They're careful to stay out of shotgun range, 'bout four hundred yards back."

"Whoa!" yelled Jug and the stage swayed and came to a stop. "Them devils are up to somethin'. Must be some more up ahead, 'cause they won't get in gun range."

Mark peeked out the window and saw the Indians had also stopped. "They've got somethin' up their sleeve, 'cause Comanche's ain't afraid to fight."

"We'd better pull over by that little draw, unhook these mules, and hole up so we can try to hold 'em off" bellowed Bozy.

"Hold it," said Mr. Lambshead calmly. "They know the range of that shotgun, but they don't know this buffalo gun. Let me get up there on my belly and I might put a scare into 'em!"

Mark looked from the window as Mr. Lambshead climbed to the top of the stage. The lead Indian had a little larger pony than the rest and was standing broadside in the road. As the big rifle roared, it looked as if all four knees of the horse buckled at once. He fell belly down before he rolled over.

The whole war party was taken by surprise, but the fallen rider sprang to his feet. Two riders rushed to pick him up at the same time. He lost little time mounting behind one of them, but the other had to circle the dead pony.

Mark heard the second shot just as the pony was completing the turn. It was evident that it struck him in the stomach. He swayed to the right, tried to straighten, nosed to the ground, and rolled over. The rider scampered to his feet and left the road to the right into the brush.

Mark watched the riders go into the brush far down the road.

"That ol' gun shore spooked 'em," shouted Bozy. "Let's wait here awhile. I'll bet they catch that bunch up front and clear out."

After a while, Mr. Lambshead climbed back down into the stage, and Jug moved on, cautiously.

"That's a mighty powerful gun, son," smiled Mr. Lambshead. "I'll bet those Indians think we've got a ghost weapon, the distance we dropped them hosses."

"I just hope we don't have any more trouble," said Mark.

"I don't think we will," the man replied. "It's not three miles on to Fort Phantom."

In order to help Mark calm himself, Mr. Lambshead kept his interest with the story of Fort Phantom. He said there were several stories about the Fort's destruction, but the real truth was that the soldiers had burned it themselves when they had been ordered to abandon it. He explained that nothing but the rock powder house, the small stage station, and the rock chimneys remained.

They were crossing another small creek when Mark saw the chimneys from the window.

"There she is," said Mr. Lambshead, "we've got about two hours before sundown to find some victuals."

Mr. Lambshead and Mark helped to water the mules in the little creek southeast of the fort. After the mules were released in the pole corral, Jug and Bozy went into the way station and opened a jug. Mr. Lambshead suggested to Mark that they try to find something to eat. Mark was in favor but didn't know where to start.

"Turn that dog loose," said Mr. Lambshead. "I'll bet he can find a cottontail pretty quick."

Mark headed Hawk toward the chimneys and followed slowly. They had not gone far when Hawk began to leap high above the weeds and look in both directions. Finally, he flushed out a rabbit that headed straight for one of the old chimneys.

"He's got one," shouted Mr. Lambshead. "Close in fast."

They found Hawk trying to dig under some fallen rocks against the side of a chimney.

"Take it easy," said the man. "We'll move those rocks one by one and get him."

Mark and Hawk stood guard on the side while Mr. Lambshead removed the rocks. Mr. Lambshead pulled the rabbit from under the rocks and gave him a chop behind the head with his open hand.

"There's another one," yelled Mark as he saw movement under the rocks.

The second one was secured in short order. They made a circle on through the chimneys and got two more before returning to the station house. Jug and Bozy came out to help skin the rabbits and Mark went to the stage to get his cook box. Hawk stayed behind to get his share as they skinned and cleaned the rabbits. Mr. Lambshead was washing the big iron pot that was left at the fireplace when Mark returned.

When Mark set out the contents of the box, Mr. Lambshead was overjoyed.

"Why, this boy has got enough meal for bread and flour to make a stew," he exclaimed.

"Here's coffee, too," said Mark. "I'll let you be the cook, so help yourself."

While Mr. Lambshead prepared supper, Jug and Bozy threw several bundles of fodder to the mules. They had made a hard day from Smith's station and had a twenty-mile day coming up. They viewed the area for any sign of Indians before coming in.

The two drivers had their bedrolls and Mark assured Mr. Lambshead that he had enough for both of them. Edd had not taken his. After a fine supper of rabbit stew and cornbread, they made ready for bed.

All the guns were loaded, including Mr. Lambshead's forty-fours and Mark's muzzle-loader. They barred the door and bedded down for the night.

CHAPTER 8

A Man of Property

I
T WAS STILL DARK, WHEN Mark woke to the smell of coffee. He sat
up and looked around the room.

"You about ready for coffee, son," came Mr. Lambshead's voice
from beside the small fire.

"I sure am," said Mark, as he sat up reaching for his clothes.

"Thought I'd better stir up something early," the older man
said. "Jug wants to be off by day break."

Mark was pouring his coffee while Mr. Lambshead called Jug
and Bozy.

The warmed-over stew and cornbread was not the best breakfast, but it was filling. The coffee was a lifesaver as far as Jug and Bozy
were concerned. Mark was proud that he had contributed to their
comfort. For fear that it would ruin, the rest of the stew became a
meal for Hawk.

Guns were buckled on, and the stage loaded before the mules
were harnessed. Jug, Bozy, and Mr. Lambshead did not seem to be
worried about Indian trouble, so Mark felt better. When the six-mule
hitch was all in place, Mark, Mr. Lambshead, and Hawk all bedded
down on the stage for a little more sleep.

The stage ran west for about a mile and a half parallel to the
Clear Fork of the Brazos River, and turned southwest just west of
where Mulberry creek joined the Clear Fork.

Mark catnapped for a while, but soon opened the shutter and looked out. The early sunlight on the rolling hills and the few cedars along the creek made a beautiful sight. Mark's mind drifted back home, but he quickly found something else to think about. He strained his eyes for any sign of Indians, but no movement of any kind could be seen.

Suddenly, Mr. Lambshead aroused from his pallet and looked at his watch.

"My goodness," he exclaimed. "We've been traveling for hours. We're almost there."

"I don't really know where we are," smiled Mark.

Mr. Lambshead looked out the window and assured Mark that the station was just over the rise in the road. Mark was not surprised that the station was built of rock because all sizes could be seen scattered over the hills.

Mr. Lambshead greeted his brother warmly as they stepped to the ground. Jug explained their delay as he unhooked the mules. While the new team was brought up, Mr. Lambshead asked Mark into the station to meet his sister-in-law.

After being introduced to Mrs. Lambshead and the Negro cook, Dee, Mark went out back to the stage to check on Hawk. He was fascinated by the huge timbers on the front and back doors and by how large the fireplace was. He wondered what the station at Valley Creek was like.

The six sleek mules were ready to go and Mark bade good-bye to the fine folks at Mountain Pass. Mrs. Lambshead invited Mark to come over on the stage and spend a few days when it got lonesome. Both men shook his hand and offered help, if needed.

Mark felt hollow inside when he suddenly realized that Hawk and himself were the only passengers and would soon be in a strange place; a place they would have to stay, whether they liked it or not.

Traveling was rougher as they were getting into country that was not as flat as what they had traveled through. They hit full speed going down a hill, but slowed almost to a walk as they topped the next one.

Suddenly, the stage stopped, and Mark looked out the window. The road ran into a small creek, turned upstream on the rocky bottom for approximately twenty yards, and came out on the other side.

They had stopped to let the mules drink in the stream.

"Boy, do you want to ride up here for a while?" shouted Jug.

"Yeah, come on up," encouraged Bozy.

Mark made sure the stage door was shut and climbed on up.

"Well, boy, you'll be where you're goin' in an hour or so," yelled Bozy.

"It sure is a God forsaken country."

Mark smiled and nodded. The mules were slowed to a steady pull going uphill when Jug shouted, "Looka thar! That's a paint jackass."

Mark looked to his right and saw five donkeys a short distance from the road. Three were dark brown, one was mouse colored, and the jack was reddish brown and white.

"You don't see many of them," said Bozy, "but he's shore all donkey!"

"The rest of them are jenny's," replied Jug.

The jack advanced toward the mules, but Bozy cracked his whip in that direction. The jack turned and trotted back to his herd.

"I've never seen donkeys that small," Mark remarked.

"Them are Mexican burros," explained Jug. "None of 'em are more'n ten or 'leven hands high. People brought 'em up from Mexico and they run wild all over these plains. That's the first paint I ever saw."

"He's got him a small harem of jennys," shouted Bozy. "None of these mustang studs wanted them damn jennys."

They had just rounded the bend in the road that sloped down into Valley Creek when they startled a paint mustang mare with a mule colt in the road. The colt cleared the draw to the right by four feet, but the crippled mare stumbled and rolled over on her back as she slid to the bottom.

Quick as a flash, Bozy was off the stage, and dropped his lariat around the mare's neck. Jug brought the mules to a stop, and Bozy ascended the slope and tied the mare to the axle of the stage.

As the rope tightened and the mare staggered up the slope, it was obvious that she had been broken to lead.

"That was a good hoss in her day," said Bozy. "She was probably ham strung by some drunk Indian with a lance."

It had all taken place so fast that Mark could hardly believe what had happened. The mare walked as if her right back leg was made of wood as they continued down the slope to the way station.

"Thought maybe you'd want that mule colt out here," said Bozy. "It'll give you somethin' to do."

Mark suddenly discovered the white mule with the long ears and grayish brown spots.

"He'll follow this mare right into the pen," said Jug, "and he's all yours."

Mark was so excited he could hardly talk at the thought of a mule all his own.

"You mean," stammered Mark, "I can have that mule colt?"

"You can have the mare, too. We shore ain't got no use for 'em," said Jug, "and besides, we gotta make up some time."

Ned Brackin, the station keeper was surprised to see the stage come in leading the crippled mustang. He had a fresh team ready and Jug quickly explained while they changed the mules. Ned led the tired mules into the corral and Bozy followed with the mare. The colt scampered around the stage and dashed through the gate into the pen.

"We saw a paint jackass back up the road," said Bozy. "That's got to be his colt."

"I'm sure it is," replied Ned, "because that mare can't run with a herd of mustangs."

Ned promised Jug and Bozy that he wouldn't leave until Edd got there, so they unloaded Mark's things on the porch. Hawk was happy to get out of the stage and was busy exploring the whole place. As he warmly expressed his thanks to Jug and Bozy, Mark was delighted to learn that he would see them the following night. The eastbound stage stopped at Valley Creek for supper. Jug yelled at the mules and they were off.

Valley Creek station was just one large room with a fireplace at one end. It was constructed of rock and had a huge front and back door like the station at Mountain Pass. Ned had hung a large canvas over one of the joist to partition off his sleeping quarters from the dining area. This part of the station had a rough dining table on one side, with shelves and a smaller table close to the fireplace.

Ned had coffee on the coals and poured two cups as he motioned Mark to a chair.

"I'd better see about my dog," Mark said politely.

"There ain't a thing he can hurt," returned Ned. "Just sit down and relax, 'cause I know you are give out."

Mark learned much about Valley Creek in the short while that he and Ned drank coffee. He learned that the rancid bacon and wormy cornmeal supplied by the company was of very little value. He learned that the Indian raids were about over, as they did most of their raiding in the spring and summer, and usually "holed up" for the winter. He learned that there were fish in Valley Creek and that deer roamed the area.

After coffee, Ned showed Mark around the place. The station was part of the rock wall around the corral. At one end of the corral, there was a shed with bars across the front in which fodder was kept for the mules. Next to the fodder shed was a smaller crude shed made of poles.

"That's my chicken house," said Ned. "I have a few hens and three or four roosters. The ones that stay in the house at night do fairly well, but the ones who steal their nest off get caught by the coyotes."

Mark noticed a small sow slide under the gate with six piglets following.

"Oh, you've got some hogs," Mark exclaimed.

"Yeah," replied Ned. "I've got another sow with five pigs and a boar around here somewhere. "I've also got an old nanny goat."

"Do you intend to carry them with you?" asked Mark.

"Lord, no," blurted Ned." I can't. I thought maybe I could make a deal with you and your uncle.

"I've only got four dollars," stammered Mark.

"Give me that four dollars and everything here belongs to you," encouraged Ned.

Mark handed over the money and shook Ned's hand on the deal.

Ned showed Mark how to strap the water kegs to one of the mules and get water from the creek. Mark was astonished at the huge gourd dipper Ned used to fill the cans. He was happy to learn that Ned had grown the gourd and had several more in the station. He was shown the best fishing holes and given instructions on how to catch the big ones.

Bedtime didn't come any too soon as it had been a long day. Ned called Hawk inside and barred the door. With a feeling of security inside the rock station, Mark faded off to sleep wondering of the whereabouts of Uncle Edd.

CHAPTER 9

A Birthday Present

NED WAS ALREADY STIRRING ABOUT the fireplace when Mark woke the next morning. He insisted that Mark stay in bed, but to no avail. Mark was ready for breakfast and went over to help Ned hurry it up. Coffee was already boiling in the big pot in the corner of the fireplace and Ned gave Mark the big skillet to fry the rancid bacon.

"That damn bacon is already spoiled before we get it," Ned growled, "but that's all the company will furnish."

"I can eat anything this morning," smiled Mark, "even if it is a little tainted."

After frying the bacon, Mark started to scramble the eggs when Ned stopped him. "Here, cook this potato in that grease before you cook those eggs. It sure helps the taste."

Mark cut up the potato, fried it, and warmed the hard tack bread before he scrambled the eggs. It all tasted mighty good to a hungry boy.

Hawk was eager to get outside and explore the place. He jumped a cottontail rabbit not twenty yards from the station and chased it to the pile of rocks to the left of the corral. Ned showed Mark how to use a green limb to get a twist in the rabbit's skin to pull him out of the hole. Before thirty minutes time, they had four cottontails.

Jug and Bozy came in about ten to six, with one passenger. Mark had prepared supper by himself to show Ned that he could do it. The stage folks ate like horses and praised Mark's ability to smother rabbit and fry cornbread.

Bozy promised to have the blacksmith in Fort Belknap make a bit and bridle that would fit the little mule. Mark promised to mark the days that they would be there and to try his best to have a good meal. As Jug and Bozy pulled out of sight, Mark took a long look at the station that would be his home "right out in the middle of nowhere".

After breakfast the next morning, Mark asked Ned if he knew where to get worms to use for fish bait. Ned explained that, unless it was immediately after a rain, it was hard to dig worms. It was easier to catch grasshoppers. He showed Mark how to take a brushy limb and swat them as they hit the ground. He had a good supply of bait before he turned in for the night.

Mark had just finished cleaning the seven catfish he had caught that morning when he heard the wagons coming. He stood at the front of the station and watched the three freight wagons come down the slope to the creek. He was thrilled to see his Uncle Edd on the first wagon.

As the wagons pulled to a halt, Edd dismounted and approached Mark with open arms. Without shame, Mark embraced his uncle and held him close.

"Boy, I hated to send you on like this, but I knew you could make it," whispered Edd.

"I'm glad you did, Uncle. Everything has worked out fine and we're gonna make it," assured Mark.

"Son, I couldn't have hand-picked a better partner. You bet we're gonna make it," stated Edd as he patted Mark on the back.

He convinced Mark and Ned that nobody aboard was hungry, as they had eaten breakfast at Mountain Pass. Mark knew that nobody could be hungry that quick after eating a breakfast cooked by Dee. The coffee pot was the center of attention for the next hour.

The drivers of the freight wagons were eager to unload, so Edd ordered a system of unloading. The wagons pulled to the front of the station and Edd directed where each item was to go. The two barrels of flour, four barrels of sugar, two barrels of cornmeal, and one hundred pounds of salt were placed in the corner of the station. The two hundred pounds of potatoes, three cases of short fuse dynamite, and ten sacks of corn were placed in the barn with the fodder. One hundred pounds of coffee, two barrels of lard, and two hundred pounds of beans were put in the corner of the sleeping quarters. The rifle and pistol ammunition and the garden seed were put under Mark's bed. The rest was left on the front porch for later.

The wagon drivers unharnessed the horses and fed them in the corral. Mark knew they would stay all night before starting back, so he must do his best to make them feel comfortable. Before he could start cooking dinner, Edd had opened a jug. Before too long, it was evident that neither of the drivers, Edd, or Ned would need anything to eat for a while. They drank and told tall tales until all of them fell asleep on the bunks early in the afternoon.

Mark walked out into the bright sunshine of the late September day. For the first time, he began to really notice the surrounding countryside. About a half mile to the southwest of the station, there was a hill rising up from the rugged plain. It was not a large hill, but large enough to notice from several miles away. In turn, someone on top of it could monitor the activity of the area for many miles. It also served as a wonderful landmark to use in returning to the station from hunting or exploring.

Mark decided to climb the hill and look his new home over. He called Hawk, picked up the old muzzleloader, and started for the hill. In less than a half hour, he was standing on top.

As he looked the country over, he noticed several things to remember. North of the station, he could see that the creek split into two forks. He noted that the station was built where it was so the stage could make one creek crossing instead of two. To the west, he saw the great grazing land. To the south, he could see scattered hills on the horizon, similar to the one he was occupying. To the east, the country seemed to have more trees, especially along the creek.

He noticed a herd of about a dozen animals that he guessed were buffalo. He had heard about them and had them described to him, but had never seen one. He thought they would taste better than the rancid bacon and he was anxious to tell Uncle Edd about them.

He decided that this would be his special place. It was a wonderful place to observe his surroundings, but it also was a quiet place to think and work out plans and problems. He even named it. He decided to call it Sentinel Hill.

Mark started back to the station, as it was getting late in the afternoon.

He knew that if they were going to have supper, he would be the one to fix it. He was feeling much more at home after his little excursion, and his mind was whirling with the things he wanted to tell Uncle Edd.

When he arrived at the station, all the men were still asleep. They wouldn't even know he had been gone, if he chose not to tell them. He built a small fire in the fireplace and began preparing to fry the catfish he had caught that morning. The smells of frying catfish and boiling coffee filled the house and the men soon began to stir.

Ned sat up and said, "That coffee smells like fine perfume, 'cause my old tongue feels like it needs a shave!"

Edd got up and walked out the back door to the washstand. He splashed water on his face and drank from the dipper that hung by the door over the water bucket.

"Boy, I didn't mean to put this all off on you," he said earnestly.

"That's all right, Uncle Edd," Mark grinned. "I know you needed to check your eyelids for pin holes."

Everyone laughed and one of the teamsters said, "Edd, that boy knows you inside out!"

As sunset painted the western sky, they ate a fine meal. All of them ate until they could hold no more.

Ned said, "I'm so full, I feel like a big ol' hog just looking for a place to lay down." It had been a full day and it did not take much encouragement for them all to get ready for bedding down for the night. No one even mentioned the jug and Mark was relieved. They barred the big doors and they all slept like dead men.

The next morning, Ned told them that the freighters had offered him a ride back to Fort Belknap and that he was going to accept. After hitching up the wagons and loading Ned's few belongings, Mark and Edd shook all their hands and offered their appreciation for the kindness they had received.

Ned said, "Edd, that boy is a keeper. You are lucky to have him. You take care of him, or you'll answer to me!"

Edd returned, "You don't have to tell me! I don't know what I'd do without him. In fact, this is a special day for him, and I'd like y'all to be witnesses to it. He don't realize it, but today is September 26, his birthday. He's sixteen years old today."

All the men congratulated Mark and patted him on the back. Each one offered some advice, or a wish for a bright future. Mark blushed at all the attention, but politely thanked them all for their friendship. He said, "Granny always said that a man was rich if he had good friends."

As the wagons topped the rise, Mark and Edd watched them disappear. Their dust was still drifting off toward the northeast when Edd said, "I've got you something special for your birthday. Let me go inside and get it and I'll be right back."

When he returned from the station, he was carrying a box that was hinged on one side.

Mark asked, "What is it, Uncle Edd?"

The reply came back, "Well, open it, silly! You think I'm gonna spoil the surprise?"

Mark opened the box, and found a revolver inside. The pistol was over a foot long, and when he picked it up, he found it weighed over three pounds. There were two barrels on the handgun, and a cylinder revolved around the lower barrel.

He said, "I've never seen a pistol like this one."

"No, I don't suppose that you have. I got this one special from a gunsmith in Fort Belknap. It was manufactured by a fellow named Krider in Philadelphia, but it was invented by a man named Le Mat out of New Orleans. They call it a 'Le Mat Grapeshot Revolver.' That bigger barrel in the center of the cylinder is a short shotgun. The other nine chambers hold 40-caliber bullets. The lever on the hammer is used to select the barrel you want to fire," was Edd's reply.

"I thank you very much," said Mark respectfully. "That's a lot of gun to be carrying around."

"Son, I know it's heavy, but it's what we call a horse pistol. You keep a scabbard for it on your saddle, and when you run into trouble, you have it close at hand. For close up work, I'd always keep that hammer lever on the center barrel for the first shot."

"Uncle Edd, I'd never want to use it on somebody!" blurted Mark.

"Son, I know you try your best to go by the Good Book, just like your Granny taught you. I know you quote the Ten Commandments, including the one about "Thou shall not kill," but I want to remind you of a story that your Granny used to read to you. It was the one about that youngster called David that fought that giant with a slingshot. He hit that big man right between the eyes, and then cut his head off with the big man's sword. He had the Good Lord's help, because he was defending himself, his people, and what was right. I got this for you in case you ever have to defend yourself, your people, or what's right."

Mark nodded and then asked, "Why won't people just leave you alone, and let you live in peace?"

"I don't know, boy. Your Granny always said that it seemed like God's people were always having trouble with the Philistines. David fought 'em. Samson fought 'em. They even stole the Ark of the Covenant one time. It seems like we're always gonna have Philistines, and we need to be ready."

"Well, I shore like it, Uncle Edd," Mark beamed. "I can't wait to try it out."

"I can't see why now ain't a good time," laughed Edd. "I'll teach you how to load it, and we'll try her out."

They spent the morning learning the mechanics of the pistol and the feel of how it shot. One of the most important things they learned was that the shotgun barrel cut a swath like a small cannon. It was so short that "scatter gun" didn't seem to be descriptive enough.

Edd said, "Son, I need to give you a few rules to always remember. The first one is: Don't point this pistol at no one without pulling the trigger. When it is necessary to point it at somebody, the talking is over. The second one is: Don't ever point or shoot at somebody because it is your choice, make it be their choice."

After a midday meal of scrambled eggs, bread, and coffee, it was time to look over their situation and make the station fit their personalities. They needed to organize the barn to make care of the horses, harness, feed, and water all to have no wasted motion. The station building was to be arranged to make service to passengers more convenient and the defense of the structure the highest priority.

Uncle Edd instructed, "Mark, the most important thing we have to always take care of is water. I brought two empty barrels with me with good wooden lids. We need to keep them inside the door and we'll fill 'em both with water. When we use all the water in one barrel, we'll haul water to fill it up. Then we'll use the water from the other barrel. By alternating the barrels, we'll always have at least a full barrel of fresh water inside the house in case of attack."

Mark asked, "Do you reckon we'll have trouble with the Indians?"

Edd replied, "I hope not, but we need to be prepared. If they won't start nothin', we shore won't."

"Ol' Hawk will help us keep a sharp eye out," suggested Mark.

"He'll be a help, that's certain," replied Edd. "I guess all that trouble gettin' him here was worth it."

As the sun started to sink behind Sentinel hill, they went inside to fix their evening meal. After cornbread, coffee, and some left over catfish, Edd said, "Boy, you'd better put a big pot of beans on to soak. We'll have folks to feed every other day and you can just keep adding to it as it runs low."

"Is beans all we're gonna feed 'em?" wondered Mark.

"Goodness, no!" huffed Edd. "But if all we've got is beans, that beats a swift kick in the pants."

Mark smiled at the mental picture of all the passengers lined up in a row to receive their swift kick and scurried to soak the beans.

They checked on the stock, banked the fire, bolted the door, and went to bed for their first night as the masters of Valley Creek Station.

CHAPTER 10

Entrepreneurs

THE NEXT MORNING, THEY BOTH were awakened by the crowing of four different roosters. Edd snorted, "No more hens than I've seen around here, we don't need that many roosters. You wanted something besides beans, we'll make dumplin's out of a couple of those knot-heads."

"I'd sure hate for the coyotes to get the other two before my hens hatch off in the spring," replied Mark.

Edd thought for a minute and returned, "I guess you might be right. Here I am trying to get you to think ahead and I'm trying to go off half cocked. They'll taste just as good in the spring, but I'll have to get used to all that noise in the morning."

Mark grinned, "Sometimes, you wouldn't get up if I set off a cannon in the yard."

Edd had to smile. His eyes lit up as he said," Oh, that's right. I need to get my still situated."

Mark knew that his uncle didn't want him to have any part of dealing with his liquor business, so he left Edd to his own devices. He salted the pot of beans, added some jerky, and put it on some coals to cook slowly.

Edd went down toward the creek and walked along toward the south. He found an area that was fairly level and was almost solid flat rock. He knew he could build a place to cook off his mash without the danger of starting a prairie fire. It was shielded from view of the station by a small bluff and a stand of prickly pear, keeping the stage passengers from knowing his business. He set about gathering the tools and materials to build a lean to against the bluff to keep his stash of jugs, both full and empty.

While Edd was consumed with his whiskey enterprise, Mark began to look for a place to plant his garden. He knew that if he planted a garden, he would have to keep his livestock out of it. Hawk would keep the varmints like deer and 'coons chased out, but that old goat and the hogs could mess things up in a hurry. He decided that he would have to build a rock wall around it. If he used the corral as one side, he would only have to fence three sides.

Mark had noticed that the horses in the corral had a habit of going to the same area in the corral to have their bowel movements. This resulted in there being a large collection of horse apples in one spot. By locating the garden spot just across the fence, he could shovel fertilizer across the fence a couple of times a year.

About noon, Edd came walking up from the creek to see what Mark was doing. When Mark explained, Edd said, "You've put some thought into things, son. I'm proud of you, but it's gonna take a lot of rock to fence that space. I need some rock, myself. Why don't we rig up a slide with a pair of the mules and work together?"

"We don't have anything to make a slide out of," said Mark.

"Sure, we do!" said Edd. "We'll cut a couple of small trees to make the runners out of and taper them on the ends. Then we'll attach small logs across them, with a little space between the logs. That way, we'll gather rocks that won't fall through the cracks, but won't roll off because they are resting in the cracks."

"You sure are wise, Uncle Edd," said Mark.

"Son, that ain't wisdom, just experience," grinned Edd.

"Uncle Edd, it will be cold weather soon and we'll need to butcher some of these pigs in the early spring. Do you think we ought to gather enough rock to build a small smokehouse?"

"We might as well, while we are at it," replied Edd. "That should be enough to keep us busy for a spell. Let's not dream up anything else 'til we finish what we've laid out."

They went into the station to fix a meal. Edd looked through the supplies for a bucket of molasses he had brought with him, while Mark made Johnny cakes and coffee. Mark added water to the bean pot and put more coals under it. This was a chore he would repeat many times in the following months.

The afternoon was spent with the ax, a crosscut saw, and a mule. They pulled the logs they cut up to the station yard to be made into the slide the next day. Then, they began to prepare for their first stage to reach the station.

"Mark, if you'll go in and fix a big pot of coffee and check on your beans, I'll pen up the team for in the morning. You can fix whatever else you might think of," Edd offered.

"All right, Uncle Edd," returned Mark. "I'll fix some cornbread and I'll cut up one of those onions you've got hidden."

"Now, those onions are for special occasions, because they are hard to come by, this far from civilization," barked Edd.

"This is an occasion," said Mark. "It's our first effort as serving customers."

"Well, I guess it is, at that," Edd smirked. "Do your best, Boy."

Mark went inside and stirred the beans. They had been on the simmer all day and the beans were nice and tender. The juice had thickened up and the aroma was inviting. He mixed his cornbread, heated some lard in the Dutch oven, and poured in his mixture. He took a shovel of coals from the fireplace and put it on the hearth. He set the Dutch oven on the coals and shoveled about twice as many coals on the lid. The bread was ready in a few minutes, so he set the hot pan off the coals and dumped the lid. He left the bread in the hot Dutch oven to keep it warm.

The stage came from the south and crossed the creek just before sundown. There were two passengers. One of them, a Lieutenant William Ballinger, was returning from Camp Stockton to a new assignment in Washington. He had a lot of spit and polish in his bearing, but was pleasant enough. The other was a character who called himself Clear Fork Jack.

Jack said he ran an "eatin' joint" up at Fort Belknap and he was thinking about moving to Grape Creek.

"Things are a little rough up at Belknap," he said.

"Most of the hard cases in the country seem to pass through that place."

Jack walked with a very noticeable limp in his right leg. Mark asked," Did one of those hard cases mess up your leg, Mr. Jack?"

"Mark!" barked Edd. "Please excuse the boy. He ain't learned to mind his own business, Jack."

"It don't bother me," said Jack. "But, boy, some men would shoot you for asking questions. I think you need to know, 'cause it might save you from making the same mistake I did. You see, I was keepin' company with this Mexican gal and she found out I was slipping around behind her back. She came with a shotgun with the intentions of shooting off my manhood. I saw her at the last minute and turned and took the blast in my hip. I was laid up for six months and nearly died. I'll be a cripple for life because I was running with the wrong crowd and then didn't treat them right. Son, take it from somebody that knows. Stay on the straight and narrow."

"I'm ashamed for my manners, sir," Mark apologized. "I appreciate your kindness and your advice."

"Think nothing of it," returned Jack.

The driver was a capable hand named Ross Vinson. He was soft-spoken, but very good with the mules. He chewed tobacco and the juice trickled down the crease from the corners of his mouth down on to his chin. His dry sense of humor soon made folks forget about his appearance.

Slick Newton was the shotgun guard. He was a nice enough fellow and seemed easy to get along with. However, he was sporting a big black eye.

When Slick went out behind the corral to relieve himself, Ross said, "Boy, I know you want to ask about that eye, but you already learned your lesson. I'm gonna tell you without you asking. His wife gave that to him this morning before he left the house!"

Ross laughed loudly and walked off, leaving Edd, Mark, and the passengers to wonder if he was joshing, or telling the truth. The hot coffee, beans, cornbread, and molasses were eaten with enthusiasm; and Jack told Mark to come see him if he ever needed a job as a cook. The next morning, Edd did the cooking chores, while Mark helped Ross get his team hitched. Ross complimented the boy on his quiet manner with the mules and gave a few small suggestions on saving steps.

He said, "Young'un, don't be in too big of a hurry. Pay attention to detail, and it saves problems, later. Always learn to do things right and the speed will come."

"I'll try to remember, Mr. Ross," he promised, "I sure thank you for giving me some pointers."

"Just call me Ross, boy! You're doing a man's job and don't have to back up from nobody," asserted the older man.

"Thank you, just the same, sir. My Granny always said that to get respect, you had to give it where it was due," was the earnest reply.

Ross had a twinkle in his eye and said, "Well, call me anything you want to, except late for supper."

As soon as a quick breakfast was eaten, the stage pulled out, headed east. Edd showed Mark how to notch the runners for the slide, in order for the lashings to be off the ground. This way, the lashings wouldn't wear through from dragging across the ground. By the time the sun was straight up, the slide was ready to be put to use.

After a quick bait of beans, Mark dutifully added more beans and water to the pot.

Edd chuckled, "You catch on quick."

The two men hitched a pair of mules to the slide and started north along the creek.

Edd said, "Let's not load any rocks until we pass enough for a full load. There's no sense in making these mules pull 'em both directions."

"That's sure makes sense, Uncle Edd. I guess we had better take the east fork of the creek, so we won't have to cross it."

"Who told you that the creek forked?" asked Edd.

"Nobody. I saw it from Sentinel Hill," he replied.

He pointed to the southwest.

"Did Ned take you up there?"

"No, sir," he answered. "I went up there while y'all took a nap, the day you came in with the freighters."

"Sprout, I'll make a deal with you," Edd started. "Don't ever go anywhere without either telling me, or leaving me a message. We'll put your slate up on the mantle and you can write on that. If you'll do that for me, I'll do it for you."

"Sure, Uncle Edd," Mark blinked. "I didn't think there was a problem."

"It ain't that, boy. A man can sure get in a jackpot, real sudden like, and it helps when your backup knows where to look for you. This old country can sure be unforgiving."

"I understand. It will keep us from worrying, until it's time to worry."

"Yeah, there ain't no sense in fretting when you don't have to," Edd smiled.

As they walked around a bend in the creek, they flushed four mallard ducks off a small pool.

Edd said, "I 'spect some smothered duck and gravy would go good over some of your cornbread. You ought to ease down here in the morning with Pa's old muzzleloader. Get set and let your dog flush 'em up. They are hard to kill sitting on the water because their feathers lay flat and shed the shot. When they just raise up off the water, you might get more than one with that old scatter gun."

"I think I had better, before we turn into beans," Mark teased.

"As many of these rocks as we've got to gather, you might get to appreciate that the beans sort of cook themselves!" Edd chuckled.

They hauled four loads of rock to the still and then called it a day. Mark suggested that could enlarge a hollowed-out place in the bluff and wall off the front. This would make a good storage area for the jugs and not require as many rocks to construct it.

"Boy, you're always lookin' and thinkin', ain't you? It'll help keep 'em cool, like a root cellar, too."

"Uncle Edd, we might build our smokehouse the same way."

"I was thinkin' the same thing! Let's see how this works out and go on from there."

The next morning, the westbound stage rolled in about the middle of the morning. They had had an early breakfast at Mountain Pass, and Mark knew he couldn't compete with a meal cooked by

Dee. He did have coffee, Johnnycakes and beans for anyone who wanted them.

Jug and Bozy were glad to see Mark. They told him the news from Fort Belknap and gave him greetings from the Lambsheads and Dee.

When the stage rolled out with a new team, Mark and Edd took care of the spent team, ate a quick bite, and continued their rock hauling chores. Edd suggested that they use every other day to haul wood and buffalo chips with the slide to get ready for cold weather. "We can scope out where the loose wood is while we are gathering rock and go back and get it the next day."

For the next few weeks, the work settled into a routine. The storage cellar for the whiskey business was completed, as well as a small smokehouse. Work on the garden fence could be done throughout the winter, as they wouldn't plant anything until spring.

There were always a couple of extra mules in the corral that were spares to be used when one of the teams came in with a lame or injured animal. Edd and Mark picked one out that was gentle and could be ridden and worked.

The managed to keep him in the corral and sent the other out when a spare was needed. He had a habit of snorting when he spotted something unfamiliar and so they called him "01' Snuffy".

Mark used Snuffy to bring in wood. He put the harness on him and rode him down the creek. When he found a big limb that had fallen out of a tree, he would hitch it to the mule and drag it back to the house. When he had dragged several in, Mark and Edd would cut it up into firewood lengths and stack it against the rock wall of the station. This added to the wood that they brought it with the stone boat.

On his trips down the creek, he noticed several trees with green balls in the foliage. When he asked Edd about them, Edd said, "Those are pecans, boy! After frost, we'll try to beat the varmints to 'em."

"What will we do with them," asked Mark.

"We'll take a bunch of 'em over to Dee and she'll show you what to do with 'em," grinned Edd. "When you bring limbs from those trees home, we'll put them down by the smokehouse. They will do well, since we don't have any hickory."

"What are we going to put in the smokehouse, Uncle Edd? My shoats seem to be a mite small, yet."

"Well, we need to jerk some venison," replied Edd. "I guess it's about time for you to kill your first deer."

"I've hunted lots of game, but the deer were hunted pretty hard around the old place. How do you go about killing one and how do you handle the carcass?" questioned Mark.

"Son, you butcher one just like you do a calf or a goat. You've helped do that enough and you've helped with enough hogs to do that in your sleep. If you can't get a clear shot at his neck, shoot him behind the shoulder. Give him time to expire and then cut his throat and let him bleed out. If you are close enough to the house, come and get me. If you are not, gut him and load him on ol' Snuffy. He may snort enough for the whole woods to hear him, but he'll pack him in," Edd observed.

"Uncle Edd, what about killing a buffalo? I've seen some from up on Sentinel Hill."

"You've noticed a lot from up on that hill! You'll have to take me up to your watching place." said Edd. "A buffalo is a sight more work than a deer, and Snuffy can't bring one in unless we make more than one trip. Those shaggy beasts can be real disagreeable, too. Let's steer clear of them unless we have planned ahead and are working together."

Late that evening, Mark killed two ducks as they flew off the creek just below the fork. When the stage came in at noon, the next day, the passengers were treated to duck and gravy over cornbread.

Ross Vinson told Mark, "You keep cookin' like that and you'll make somebody a good wife."

Mark laughed and replied, "You keep talkin' like that and all you'll ever get is beans."

The next morning, Edd announced that he had run off his first batch of whiskey. He said, "Let's take some of that wood from those crates the supplies came in and build us a bar in here."

"Uncle, I thought I wasn't going to be involved in your business."

"Son, you are just selling what we would sell if someone else made it," Edd noted.

"These passengers always want something to cut the dust."

"Ain't there always trouble in a place that sells spirits?"

"Not always, but that's why I want a bar. You need a place to put your pistol close at hand," was the reply. "You never know who's going to stop by a stage station, liquor or not."

"Well, all right, if you say so. I just want you to know, I have my doubts about it," said Mark. "Let's get all our work done, so I have time to read my Bible this evening."

Edd didn't reply, but he knew he had been jobbed. He could feel it just as plain.

By the last week of October, the bar was in operation, meal preparations were becoming routine, and fall was in the air.

CHAPTER 11

Cold, Hard Facts

T HE NIGHTS WERE COOL AND the days pleasant when Edd suggested that Mark needed to start working with his mare and mule colt. They got a rope on the mare and found that she settled down quickly. She had evidently been a fine mount before she was crippled.

They made a halter to fit the mule colt and Edd managed to get a rope on him by dropping it across the mare's back. Then the fun began! He might as well have put that rope on a coyote. After an abundance of squealing and bucking, that colt fell on his side. Edd shouted, "Get your knee on his neck, and pull his nose up. He can't get up, if he can't get his nose down. Hold him down and I'll get the halter on him!"

When the halter was secure, Edd said, "Let him up! We'll tie him to a post and he can fight himself and get tired enough for us to do something with him."

When the colt was attached to the post, he pulled back as hard as he could. Edd joked, "As tight as he pulls that rope, we need to name him Pulltight."

Mark said, "That sounds good to me, and I guess we can call his momma 01' Gimpy."

Edd chuckled, "It's a funny thing how critters get their names."

After about thirty minutes, the colt had discovered that if he let the rope get some slack in it, he was much more comfortable.

Mark put a loop of rope on the hind end of the mule and untied him from the fence. When the colt pulled back on the halter rope, Mark pulled on his hindquarters and forced him to step up and make the halter rope slack. It didn't take long for the colt to start leading in a halting manner.

Mark worked his way down the halter rope until the mule could smell of his hand. By moving slowly, he was able to rub Pulltight on his neck.

Edd coached, "Let him wear that halter and drag that rope. He'll step on the rope enough to make his nose tender and he'll be easier to handle. Now, rub his neck, talk real nice to him, and walk away. You always want to quit on a good note, when you train an animal."

After a few days, Pulltight would let Mark walk up to him without having to step on the dragging lead rope. Mark was able to take the halter off and then was able to halter him by placing a lead rope around his neck to put the halter back on.

After each session, he made sure to feed Gimpy and Pulltight so it was a positive experience. Gimpy soon warmed up to Mark and generally became a pet. Her demeanor helped Pulltight to become more gentle and he learned quickly.

One day about noon, Jug and Bozy came through with the stage. Mark served them beans, cornbread, and hot coffee. After the meal, Jug mentioned, "Now I ain't complaining about your cooking, Mark. I just want you to know, we noticed that the deer and other critters sure are on the move. Next time we come through, a good venison roast sure would taste good."

"I've been thinking about doing some hunting," returned Mark. "I'll see if Granddad's old rifle will kill a deer."

"If it's that same old gun that knocked that horse out from under that Comanche, I should say it will kill a deer," Bozy affirmed.

Jug said, "Just be aware of the weather, Mark. These critters are on the move for some reason and we might get a norther 'fore long."

They shook hands with Mark and Edd, mounted the coach, and rolled out of sight.

Mark washed up the dishes and said, "I think I will go up the west fork of the creek and try to kill a deer."

Edd nodded his head.

"I thought you might ease off hunting. Ride Ol' Snuffy. He can carry in whatever you kill, and if you come up empty handed, you won't have to walk. Take enough rope to tie your kill to the bellyband and hang your traces on the hames. You won't need a saddle, which is a good thing. We ain't got one."

Mark tried to keep a straight face and said, "Are you sure you'll be all right until I get back?"

Edd smiled and counseled, "Be sure to take a coat, it might turn off cold."

Mark rode Snuffy up the creek, crossed below the fork and rode up the west fork. About mid-afternoon, he tied his mule to a small oak tree where a draw ran down to the creek. He went up the creek about two hundred yards and sat down on a fallen tree in some oak brush.

After about an hour, he saw a doe easing down the creek from the north.

She kept looking behind her and taking a few steps along. Mark noticed some movement behind her and saw a big buck trailing the doe. He was smelling her tracks and looking straight ahead. He was intent on the doe.

Mark eased the Sharps into position, and when the buck was directly across the creek, he pulled the trigger. The buck dropped instantly. Mark crossed the creek, and found he had hit where he had aimed. The buck's neck had been broken, and no meat was wasted. Uncle Edd would be proud. Mark cut the deer's throat, as Edd had instructed, and went for his mule. When he returned, he took a flour sack from inside his rolled-up coat. When he had gutted the deer, he put the heart and liver in the flour sack to take home.

Snuffy wasn't sure he wanted to carry the carcass, but Mark led him off in the creek by the deer. This enabled Mark to pull the carcass over onto the mule instead of lifting the carcass up to throw over the mule. With lots of soothing talk, and after lots of snorts from Snuffy, the buck was tied in place. Mark brought the mule out on the west side of the creek, as the traveling on that side was easier.

Mark started to turn for home and the wind picked up out of the north. Immediately, the temperature began to drop. He took his coat off the mule and put it on. He thought about the weather helping keep the meat fresh as they tried to preserve it.

He was pretty proud of himself as he led the mule with the rifle under his arm. He had just reached the fork in the creek when Snuffy looked across the creek, threw up his ears, balked, and snorted real loud.

Mark looked across the creek and looked a Comanche brave right in the eye. He knew it must be a Comanche because he was dressed like the ones Mark had seen on the stage. At that moment, he remembered that he had not re-loaded the rifle. The next thing that Mark realized was that the warrior was not alone. He was leading a horse pulling a travois. There was a person on the travois and another walking along beside the horse. There didn't seem to be enough furs for the three for the cold that was now howling in from the north.

The brave was carrying a lance, but Mark could see that his bow was not strung and was in his arrow quiver with his arrows. Mark could sense that the little group was in some kind of trouble.

As the warrior stood and stared at him, Mark held up his hand and slowly leaned his rifle against a tree. He tied Snuffy to the tree and walked back to the buck. He pulled out his butcher knife and cut a hind leg off the carcass. He plunged his knife in the dirt, wiped it on his leg, returned it to his scabbard, and started across the creek with the meat.

As Mark came out of the creek, the Comanche pointed the lance in his direction, and stepped between Mark and the travois. He said something to the person on the other side of the horse, and Mark saw that it was a girl when she came around to meet him. It was a white girl!

When she spoke, it was in somewhat halting English. She said, "He wants to know what it is you want."

Mark said, "You looked like you could use the meat. I want to give this to you."

She spoke in Comanche to the warrior and he spoke back.

She looked at Mark and asked, "Why would you offer us a gift?"

Mark replied, "I believe it's what the Good Lord would have me to do."

She again conversed with the warrior and informed Mark, "He wants to know if your Great Spirit is the same as his."

Mark answered, "I reckon so. The Good Book and Granny said that there ain't but one."

After she had relayed the message, Mark asked, "If you are in trouble, is there some other way I can help?"

She seemed to ask permission for something from the warrior and he nodded.

She began to tell of their situation. "We have been up north visiting his wife's relatives and she had a new baby while we were there. We stayed longer than we should have so she could have the child, and we could travel south to the Antelope band of the Comanches. Screech Owl is a noted warrior in that band. After we started the trip, his wife, Meadow Lark, has become quite ill. He is afraid she will cross over into the next world and she has no milk for their son."

Mark interrupted, "How do you come to be with these people?"

She said, "I am his wife's slave. He saved me from death and brought me to her when his war party attacked and killed my family five winters ago. His wife has been kind and treated me almost like a daughter."

Mark said, "Tell him that there are no women at our stage station, but I have a wet mare. We can save the baby with mare's milk. My mare has a bad leg and can't travel, or I would let you take her with you. If you will stay with the baby, he can get his wife home and return with means to care for the child. You tell him."

After she spoke to Screech Owl, he looked for a long time into Mark's eyes. He lowered the lance and stuck it into the ground. He then went to the travois and the two parents talked back and forth for several minutes.

When he stood up, he walked up to the girl and Mark. He looked into Mark's face, and spoke through the girl. She said, "Meadow Lark wants the child to live and she says he cannot make the trip. She fears that he is so weak he will freeze before you can get him to your lodge, for she has nothing warm to wrap him in."

84

Mark took off his coat and handed it to the warrior.

He said, "I'm strong enough to make it. It's not far."

Screech Owl continued and the girl translated, "You speak of the Great Spirit and I believe I see him in your eyes. I make this hard decision. I will leave my child and my wife's slave in your care. When you hear the sound of the screech owl, it will be me. I will return for what is mine, and if it is not here, I will take what is yours. If you speak the truth, you will need not fear the Comanche."

Mark looked deep into the eyes of Screech Owl and said, "I speak the truth. Get your wife to safety and come back for the others. They'll be here."

Screech Owl spoke to the girl and she took the coat to the travois. She knelt down by the sick mother, wrapped a tiny babe in the coat and came over to Mark. Mark told her to wait and he crossed the creek to get Snuffy.

He said, "No sense in you wading the creek, the station is on this side."

When he untied the mule and turned around, the warrior and his travois were gone.

Mark looked at the girl and the baby. He knew he needed to get them to shelter, so he said, "We'll talk later. Let's get that baby in where it's warm, and get some milk in its belly."

In about half an hour, they walked up in front of the station.

Mark yelled, "Uncle Edd, I need some help."

Edd looked out the door of the station in surprise. He shouted above the wind, "Looks like you found more to haul home than a deer."

Mark nodded, "If you'll do something with that buck, I'll get them in the house by the fire. I need to get some milk from Ol' Gimpy to feed that baby. I'll tell you the whole story when we get things settled."

Edd replied, "You can bet I want to hear it. Get 'em inside! We'll talk later."

Mark hustled the girl and the baby inside. He said, "Make yourself at home. Feel free to do anything you need to for yourself or the little one. I'm going to take this cup and see if I can get some milk for it to eat."

As Mark started for the corral, Edd hurried over from where he was pulling a rope over a gate brace to hang up the deer carcass. He asked, "How are you going to milk that mare?"

Mark said, "Well, I hadn't thought that far ahead. I guess I was just gonna play it by ear."

Edd said, "Tie her head to the shed post in the back corner next to the rock fence. We'll push her around where her good hind leg is next to the fence and tie her tail to the other shed post. She can't kick you with that bad leg."

Mark asked, "How do I tie her tail to a post?"

Edd returned, "You remember how I showed you to tie a rope to Cricket's tail when you were teaching your dog to lead?"

When Mark nodded, Edd continued, "Tie a rope to her tail just like you did then. Tie the rope to the post just like you would tie a horse's head to it, but take out all the slack. She'll have to stand up there and behave, or pull her tail out by the roots."

Mark grinned at his Uncle's ingenuity and asked, "Do I need to help you hang up that buck?"

Edd shook his head, "No, I'll pull him up on that gate brace with Snuffy. I'll just jerk the hide off of him and pull him up high so nothing will get him tonight. We'll cut him up in the morning."

Mark nodded, "You might bring in enough for us to cook tonight."

Edd smiled, "Backstrap it is!"

Mark followed Edd's instructions and they worked like a charm. Gimpy had become quite gentle and she didn't put up much of a fuss.

Mark got a cup full of milk from the mare and felt relieved that the colt had not already gotten it all. He decided he would separate the colt from the mare and turn them together after he milked her each time.

Mark walked carefully into the house with the milk, just as Edd was coming in with some venison.

Edd asked, "Which one of us is going to cook, and which one is going to try to feed that baby?"

The girl spoke shyly, "I know not how you will get the baby to drink, but I can cook the meat."

Edd looked at her, and for the first time, he saw that she was a white girl. He stared in stunned silence for a moment and then said, "Sure, girl. You cook, and we'll figure something out."

Mark scratched his head and asked, "How are we going to do this?"

Edd said, "Well, I got me an idea. Go get that whiskey bottle I brought from Fort Belknap. You know, the one that's still got about a swig in it."

Mark bellowed, "You ain't gonna give the little darlin' whiskey!"

Edd laughed, "No, I ain't, but pour what's in the bottle into a cup. We can't let liquor that's traveled so far go to waste. Get some hot water out of the kettle on the hearth and wash out the bottle three or four times. Be sure to get all the smell of whiskey out of it."

Mark started over to where Edd slept and questioned, "How will we get it to drink from a whiskey bottle?"

Edd said, "We're gonna take one of those gloves that spit and polish soldier came through here and left them on the table. We're gonna cut the thumb out of it. We'll take some of that string you saved from the flour sacks for fishing line and tie it real tight around that thumb slipped over the neck of the bottle. Then, if we punch some holes in the end with your Granny's sewing needle, we'll have us a nipple."

Mark was impressed with his Uncle's ability to think quickly and to decide on a course of action. He quickly gathered the items Edd had mentioned.

When he poured the whiskey into the cup, he grinned and said, "You can't drink until the baby does."

"Fair enough," Edd agreed. "Just put a few holes in that nipple. We can always punch more, but we can't un-punch any. Don't pour but about half of the milk in the bottle, we don't want to feed it too quick and tear up it's little stomach."

Mark looked over at the girl at the fireplace.

"Is this baby a boy, or a girl?"

Quietly she said, "It is a man child."

Edd said, "Well, I guess we can start sayin' him instead of it."

When they had the contraption put together, Edd picked up the little boy from where he lay wrapped up in Mark's coat. The baby started to fuss when it was taken from the warmth of the bundle. Edd poked the nipple up to the little mouth and the baby turned his head away, so Edd tried again. The child kept turning his head and fussing and wouldn't take hold of the makeshift nipple.

Mark could see that Edd was becoming frustrated, but Mark couldn't see anything that he would do differently.

Shyly, the girl asked, "Would you let me try?"

Edd was relieved and returned, "I don't know why not. I ain't winnin' no prize."

The girl took the baby in her arms and held it to her bosom in the natural position for nursing. She walked over to the cup with the remaining milk in it and dipped the end of the nipple in it. When the baby started to nuzzle at her bosom, she offered the nipple. He tentatively sucked at it, and when he got the taste of milk, he took it hungrily.

Edd's voice got low and tender, "Look at that young'un eat. His little stomach thinks his throats been cut."

Mark started to stir around fixing a meal for the three of them. The venison was already broiling over coals, so he put the bean pot on to heat.

He started mixing up cornbread batter and making coffee.

While Mark and the girl took care of their chores, Edd made sure enough wood was brought in for a cold night.

When the baby finished eating, he snuggled up and went to sleep. The girl wrapped him back up in Mark's coat, and laid him close enough to the fireplace to stay warm. Mark put the food on the table and set out plates, forks, knives, and cups.

He motioned for the other two to sit down, bowed his head and said, "Dear, Lord, we are truly thankful for this food and all your blessings. Guide us to do the right thing by these that we are trying to help and help us always to look to you for strength and answers. In Jesus name, Amen."

Mark looked at the girl and said, "Help yourself, ma'am. Ladies first." She shyly replied, "I would wait, if it's all right."

Edd said, "Suit yourself, girl," and began to put food on his plate.

The girl sat for a few minutes watching the two as they dished up their meals and as they began to eat. Shyly then, she did as they had done and mimicked their use of forks and knives. She tentatively tasted the coffee and did not pick it up again.

After they had eaten in silence for several minutes, Edd asked, "Does somebody want to tell me what the hell happened out there?"

"Uncle Edd," Mark said gently, "Granny said you don't use that kind of language around a lady."

Edd looked at Mark with surprise in his eyes. It seemed he wanted to be offended, but then his eyes softened and he said, "Sorry, ma'am. I guess I forgot my manners. It's just that something like this doesn't happen every day, and y'all ain't told me a solitary thing since you came marching up in the yard."

Mark started, "I'll tell you what I know."

He related the events that had brought them back to the station. In thinking about what had happened, he got up from the table, went over to the sharps rifle and re-loaded it.

A knowing look came into Edd's eyes and he observed, "Got a little excited, did you? That's a good lesson learned. Getting too excited to take care of the details can get you killed in this country."

Mark turned to the girl and said, "I never even asked your name. What do we call you?"

"The Comanches call me 'She who watches,' but my momma called me Jess," was the quiet reply.

Edd put his hand gently on the girl's arm.

He hesitated and then asked, "I know you have been with the Comanches for a long time, but do you remember if there was more name than just Jess?"

She was silent for a short time and then she said, "I remember that my name is Jesse Louisiana Behannon. My daddy would hug my neck and call me Jesse Lou."

She got a faraway look in her eyes and no one spoke because they all were trying to deal with lumps in their throats.

Mark stood up to do the chores with the remaining food and dirty dishes and Edd said, "Well, we had better make a few decisions. The first one is where are we going to put Jess and the baby for sleeping arrangements."

Jess said, "Since the night is cold, let the baby sleep with me. We are not used to beds, so let us have some blankets close to the fireplace."

Edd said, "That's fine with us, if it's all right with you. Now, what about taking care of his needs when he soils himself?"

"I have that skin bag full of soft grasses to line his covering. We can take out the soiled grass and put in clean."

Mark said, "I'll help gather some more, tomorrow."

Edd asked, "Now, do you think he has enough milk for tonight?"

Jess nodded, "He has been getting along with much less than this, but as he gets stronger, we will need more at a time."

Edd said, "It's been a full evening. We've got lots to do in the morning, including a stage coming through. We ought to go to bed."

He carried the kettle over to the washstand outside the door and poured hot water in the basin. He added cold water to suit him and said, "Jess, you can wash up first."

Jess again said, "I would wait, if it's all right."

A knowing look accompanied his reply, "Suit yourself, ma'am."

After Mark and Edd had washed up and Jess was at the basin, Mark asked, "Why won't she go first?"

Edd answered, "I 'spect it's got something to do with Comanche customs and she's living up to her Comanche name, she who watches. She's not asking silly questions, she's watching how we do it."

In a little while, the door was barred, and everyone was sound asleep.

CHAPTER 12

Visitors

A WEEK PASSED AND THINGS were settling into a routine. Gimpy was not causing a lot of problems milking her, but Pulltight was sure raising a fuss about being separated from his ma. It was a chore to milk the mare several times a day to feed the baby boy. Jug and Bozy came through on a run and Edd explained their situation.

Jug whistled low and said, "I've heard of that Screech Owl. He ain't nobody to fool around with. If Mark got away with his hair, it's a pure miracle."

Bozy added, "Yeah, Mark sure needs to keep his word, or there ain't no way you need to stay here."

Edd said, "Well, we sure need to take care of that baby and I don't know if we can keep milkin' that old crippled mare."

Jug lifted his eyebrows and said, "Fidel and Consuela have goats over at the Fort Chadbourne Station and they might trade you a goat to milk."

Edd brightened up and offered, "Mark's got an old nanny goat that's not milking, I might could trade her and a couple of shoats for a wet nanny."

Bozy said, "I don't particular want to haul no hogs, but if they're small enough, I guess you could tie 'em in a tater sack apiece and throw 'em on top."

Jug said, "We can cross tie that old goat on top where she can't fall off either side. Edd, you go with us to do the trading and you

91

can come back with Ross Vinson. You might have to hold a pistol on him, but he'll bring you back the next day."

They all had a good laugh about what a joke it would be on Ross. He was always amused at someone else's frustrations, perhaps it was his turn in the barrel.

Edd noted, "I don't know if I want to leave Mark here alone."

Bozy said, "Seems to me he made out with Screech Owl without you the last time and Comanches ain't much for lying. If Screech Owl was intent on mischief, your presence wouldn't help anything. You'll just be gone a day and you'd leave Mark by himself to take care of your whiskey business."

Edd blushed a little and said, "I hope I wouldn't leave him in danger, Bozy."

"I didn't mean no offense," said Bozy, "I just meant the boy can handle himself."

"I'd have to talk it over with Mark. It's his stock I'd be trading around," Edd said.

Jug blurted, "Well, get to talking! Catching and hauling livestock ain't exactly on our schedule. It's only fifteen miles over to Ft. Chadbourne, or I wouldn't consider it at all. Hurry up, or your gonna think you're dealing with Ross Vinson."

Everyone laughed. Edd went inside the station where Mark and Jess were cleaning up after the meal. He explained his idea to Mark, and Mark readily agreed.

Edd asked, "How are we going to catch these critters real quick?"

Mark said, "I can catch that nanny goat with a little bait of corn at the barn. After we get her tied, I'll take some of these scraps from the table and lure the hogs inside the rock corral. If you, three men, can block the gates so they can't get out and scatter, I think I can pick out a couple of the little ones that Hawk can help me catch."

Edd said, "That's good thinking, but we had better get at it. Jug and Bozy are ready to roll."

The goat was not hard to catch, and after circling the corral a couple of times, they had a little gilt and a little boar both in their sacks. They got them loaded on top of the stage and were ready for the stage to depart.

Edd said, "Mark, you and Jess keep a sharp look out. Stay close to the station and I'll be back late tomorrow evening. Ross Vinson's run will stop for the night, you remember."

Mark shook Edd's hand and said, "Don't worry, Uncle Edd. Screech Owl probably hasn't had time to get back yet. If he does come, I've kept my word. He struck me as a man who would keep his."

Edd looked Mark deep in the eyes and said gently, "I know you are getting attached to Jess, and it will be hard to let her go back to the Comanches."

Mark looked determined and said, "I intend to talk straight with Screech Owl to see what can be worked out. I didn't deceive him when we spoke before. I don't intend to deal any way but straight."

Edd said, "Don't push him too far. I know he should owe you for saving his child, but their customs ain't ours."

Mark returned, "He probably won't come, but if he does, I'll be very respectful."

Edd smiled, "That's right, boy. To get respect, you've got to give it!"

Mark grinned, "You'd better get on the stage, they're raring to go. You'd better get some more than a goat, as much of my stock as you're trading off."

Edd climbed up on top to help with the critters and yelled back, "A nanny goat might not be all I bring back."

The stage crossed the creek and disappeared down the trail toward Ft. Chadbourne. Mark took care of the stock and Jess took care of the chores in the station. When Mark finished milking Gimpy, he brought in the milk to feed the little one. At sundown, Mark put the bar behind the door. He had brought in plenty of wood for the night and the water barrel was full just inside the door. He checked the load in the Sharps and made sure his big revolver was in its place under the bar.

When he took down his Granny's bible, Jess asked quietly, "What is this thing that you look at every night?"

Mark said, "It's a Bible, Jess. Don't you remember anything about a Bible?"

Jess was silent for a moment and then said, "I remember that we had one in our wagon, but I never learned what to do with it."

Mark asked, "Jess, did anybody ever teach you to read?"

She replied, "I guess we moved around enough that there never was any time for such. Would you show me what you are looking at for so long?"

"Sure, I will," he replied. "These marks are what we call letters, and the way they are put together makes up words. When you put the words in the right order, they tell a story."

Jess thought a moment and then said, "The Comanches paint pictures on rocks and hides that tell a story."

Mark commented, "Well, I guess it would be about the same thing. You'd have to learn to read the pictures like you learn to read words."

She asked, "Would you tell me one of the stories?"

He returned, "I'll read you one of my favorites."

He turned to the second chapter of Luke and began to read the story of the birth of the Christ child.

When he read verse 6, "And she brought forth her firstborn Son, and wrapped Him in swaddling clothes, and laid Him in a manger, because there was no room for them at the inn."

Jess injected, "Well, at least he didn't have to eat mare's milk for supper."

Mark grinned.

He continued to read through the story about the shepherds and then asked, "Do you understand?"

She said, "There are some words I don't know."

He said, "Stop me when you hear a word you don't know and I'll try to help you with the meaning."

After they had discussed several words like Savior and angels, she settled down in her place close to the fire with the baby. Mark went to his bed and blew out the candle. After an uneventful night, Mark woke up to the smell of coffee and bacon. He hurried to get up, a little embarrassed that Jess got up before him.

Mark spent the morning staying close to the station. He was a little uneasy and was watchful for the return of Screech Owl. Hawk ran two different cottontail rabbits into holes in the rocks and Mark twisted them out with a green stick. Hawk enjoyed the entrails and a fine meal was enjoyed in the station.

Jess and Mark had begun getting things ready for the stage to lay over for the night as it was expected before suppertime. Around two-thirty, Mark saw two riders approaching from the direction of Sentinel Hill. They both wore greasy buckskins, carried rifles, and wore the knives that were fashioned after the one Jim Bowie had made popular. They were mounted on common mustangs, led a packhorse, and were leading a beautiful dun and white paint stallion.

The men rode up to the front of the station and Mark invited them to step down. When they did, he told them they were welcome to put their stock in the corral and wait for supper.

Mark said, "The east bound stage will be along, 'fore long. They will lay over for the night, and you're welcome to stay."

The lanky one of the pair grinned a half grin at the other one and said, "I believe we'll just do that, sonny."

Mark said, "Help yourself," and went into the station.

Jess met him at the door.

She looked a little worried and asked, "Do you know these men?"

Mark replied, "I've never seen them before."

"I fear that they are trouble. I know that the stallion that they led in belongs to Jackrabbit, a close friend of Screech Owl."

"We'll be careful until Uncle Edd gets here. I noticed that they came from the direction of Sentinel Hill and they may have been watching the station."

Mark knew that men like these would want to cut the dust from their throats, but he didn't want them to get drunk and be hard to handle. He knelt down behind the bar to put some of Edd's jugs out of sight while Jess was feeding the baby. He was out of sight when the two men entered the station.

When they entered, the lanky one asked, "Cagle, where'd that damn kid get to?"

The tone of his voice caused Mark to pause where he was, and to remain still.

Cagle drawled, "I ain't got a clue. Maybe he's gone to get wood or vittles."

The other stated, "Well, we'll catch him when he comes in the door. I didn't know we'd find a place like this to ransack. Look at this little squaw gal! We'll cut that kid's throat, knock that papoose in the head, and have our way with this gal until we get tired of her. We'll ambush that stage when it rolls in and see what kind of treasure it has to offer."

Mark was kneeling behind the bar and there on the shelf under the bar was the big revolver. He remembered that Uncle Edd had told him to always fire the big barrel first. He also remembered that you didn't point it at someone until you were ready to shoot. He adjusted the lever on the hammer, swallowed the lump in his throat, and stood up.

"If you think we'll go down without a fight, you're mistaken! Get your outfit and rattle your hocks on down the road!" He held the revolver with both hands about waist high and pointed it at the floor about half way between the two hard cases and himself. There was a tremor in his voice, but he was obviously serious.

"What have we here?" 01' Lanky exclaimed. "Cagle, I believe this pup thinks he can kill two grown men with that funny looking contraption."

Cagle was a step behind the other man and a little to his right. He grinned at the thought, and swung his rifle around. The quick movement of Cagle caused Mark to flinch and the center barrel of the Grape Shot revolver spoke. The buckshot struck the stone floor and flattened into the shape of coins instead of balls. They ricocheted into the men like a fine billiard shot. One of the shot tore into Cagle's throat since he was farther away. He gurgled in his own blood as his life drained away and his heels drummed on the floor. 01' Lanky was struck in the belly and the chest. The only thing he said was "A shirt tail kid!" He moaned and breathed no more.

Mark was frozen in place. He couldn't believe what had just happened. He had accidentally pulled the trigger. Here were two men dead and he had killed them!

Jess broke the silence, "You are a mighty warrior. I have never heard of anyone who kills two at a time."

"It was an accident. I didn't even point the gun at them!" he stammered.

"Then your medicine is strong and it was the hand of this God that you tell me about," she observed.

Mark sat down and Jess brought him a cup of coffee. When his hands stopped shaking, he drank it down and calmed down. He got up and set about dragging the men outside. He covered them with blankets from their own bedrolls and cleaned up the gore inside the station.

Jess put her hand on Mark's elbow. When he turned to look at her, she quietly said, "I know you are troubled by this thing, but it was not your choice. We still need to be ready for the stage to come."

Mark set his jaw and nodded. They set about preparing a meal and doing the chores. The only times that Mark paused in his work were when he had to walk past the two bodies.

The shadows were beginning to lengthen when they heard a shout and a crack of a whip from the top of the rise. The stage came rolling in with a cloud of dust. Ross Vinson worked the reins with Slick Newton on the seat beside him. Edd was on top of the coach with two goats cross-tied so they wouldn't fall off.

Edd had a big grin on his face as he yelled, "Come help me get your livestock off the top of this coach before Ross shoots us both, boy!"

Mark went over and took the first goat in his arms. Edd said, "Tie her to the gate post and come take this young billy. I made a good trade for him as I didn't want to have to make this trip again. Now, we'll have a fresh nanny a couple of times a year."

Ross had stepped down off the coach and was looking toward the front of the station house. His tone was serious as he spoke to Edd. "You'd better quit crowing about them goats, and look over here to more pressing matters."

Slick took the young goat from Edd, and Edd was quiet as he climbed down. He went over to the bodies and pulled back the blanket on Cagle.

He covered his face once more and looked at the other corpse. When he looked at the second face, he looked at it for what seemed a long time. He had a strange expression when he returned the blanket and stood up. No one spoke, and the silence was overwhelming.

Ross Vinson was the first to ask, "What happened, son?"

"I shot 'em, but I didn't mean to! They were planning on killin' us and ambushing the stagecoach," blurted Mark. "I told 'em to leave and they made fight. That pistol Uncle Edd gave me went off, and killed 'em both with one shot. I wasn't even pointing it at them, I was pointed at the floor!"

Edd said, "Looks to me like that pistol was the best thing I ever gave you. I would have hated for you to fight these Philistines with a jawbone!"

Slick had tied up the goat and walked up to hear the conversation. He suggested, "We can chew on the particulars after dark. We need to get these two in the ground, we don't want to leave them just laying around."

Edd agreed, "You're right. Let's put the saddles back on their horses, so we can tie them across the saddle. The diggings easier on the high bank across the creek."

When a place had been selected, two graves were dug. The two bodies were placed in the graves wrapped in their blankets. The entire population of Valley Creek Station gathered around. This included Edd, Mark, Jess, the baby, the two stage employees, and one passenger.

When Mark asked if anyone was going to say anything over the departed, no one spoke for a long moment. The passenger, a Mr. Michael Levens from around Grape Creek, said quietly, "Son, why don't you take that Bible you are holding and read the Twenty-third chapter of Psalms? When you finish, I'll pray over them."

Mark nodded his appreciation and began to read the passage. He read it with emotion, as it was plain that he took the deaths of the two very hard. When Mark finished, Mr. Levens stepped forward with his hat in his hands. He bowed his head and began, "Dear, Lord, we pray for the souls of these two varmints. They were up to no good when Your providence took them from this earth, but we don't have to tell you that. We know that You will give them whatever mercy they have coming. We do pray for this boy, Mark. Help him to know that he did the right thing and that it was Your hand that called down judgment. We give you the glory in all things. In Jesus name, amen.

Mark raised his head, and looked Mr. Levens in the eye. "Thank you, sir. You don't know how much that means to me."

"Think nothing of it, son," the man returned.

Edd stepped up and suggested that Mark and Jess return to the station to get a meal on the table. When they had gone across the creek, the remaining men filled in the graves and piled rocks on top of them.

Slick drawled, "I reckon you've started a grave yard. I hope you don't have many customers."

Ross grinned, "You might have to lay out a bigger space if that kid keeps killin' 'em two at a time.

Edd looked at Mr. Levens, "Sir, I thank you for trying to ease Mark's pain. I sure didn't know what to say and you said a mouthful. I admit that I fail to credit the Good Lord like I should and I can see that His mighty hand was on that boy's shoulder.

"It's pretty plain that that youngster has been taught about the Lord," Levens noted.

"The same good woman tried to teach me. I just didn't listen as good as he did," smiled Edd.

After a good meal, primarily prepared by Jess, Edd coaxed, "Mark, what exactly happened."

When Mark had completed the details of the encounter, Jess shyly spoke. "These men will be hunted by the Comanches. That stallion is a favorite horse of Jackrabbit, a close friend of Screech Owl."

"That could mean trouble if they track them here to the station," added Slick.

"The more people there are here, the more likely they'll come in fightin'," Ross ventured. "We'll pull out at daylight and maybe this little gal can explain what happened."

Mark allowed, "There won't be any arguments over the horse. They can have him. We don't need a stallion around here with as many horses that pass through these corrals."

Jess quietly said, "We will get a colt out of him, anyway."

Mark asked, "What are you talking about?"

She told him, "Since they have been turned together, he has mated with Gimpy several times."

"I never saw that." he exclaimed.

"You were not watching, your thoughts were far away," she said softly.

Ross stood up and spit tobacco in the fireplace.

"What did you say the Comanches called her?" he asked.

His eyes glinted with humor.

Edd answered, "She who watches."

Ross chuckled, "They don't miss much, do they?"

Mr. Levens laughed, "Looks like she don't, either."

After the cleanup chores, Mark milked the new nanny goat for the first time. She didn't give a great deal of milk, but Ross said if they fed her good and handled her gentle-like that she would do better.

Edd said, "If you have to milk her three times a day, it will beat having to fight that mare."

The baby didn't seem to have a problem switching to goat milk. He had become very attached to the bottle they had rigged up for him. Edd mentioned that he hoped the fingers from the Lieutenant's gloves held out until Screech Owl got back.

They all prepared for an early start the next morning. The men respectfully left a place near the fire for Jess and the baby, while they made down their beds across the room. The room was soon quiet, except for the sound of someone using a crosscut saw in the vicinity of Slick's bed.

Mark jumped up early to do his chores and found that Jess was already slicing bacon. He mumbled to himself and shook his head. She said nothing, but her eyes twinkled.

When the stage was ready to roll, Mr. Levens took Mark by the hand and shook it. He was sincere when he said, "Mark, you're a good man. You have nothing to hang your head about. You did a man's job when you saved the lives of everyone here. I'm very proud to know you and I hope that I can have the privilege of calling you my friend."

"Thank you very much, sir," the boy said. "It is my honor that you consider me worthy. Your kindness has meant more than I can say."

"I'll be coming back through in a couple of weeks on the way back to Concho. I'll be anxious to find how things turned out," Levens offered and then he said in a low voice, "Do what you can to help the little gal. She's a priceless treasure."

"I will, sir. I have been thinking about what to say to Screech Owl. I don't know if I can work something out, but he seems to be reasonable." Mark had a determined look on his face when he said, "The Good Lord has pulled me through this far, and I'd appreciate it if you would pray for my success."

"I'll certainly do that! Good day to you all."

With a wave of his hand, he climbed in the stage and shut the door.

Ross spit and hollered, "See y'all in a day or two. You mules step up, now!"

As the stage started to roll, Slick grinned and waved with his hat. In a short time, all that could be seen of the stagecoach was a dust cloud.

After the goat was milked and the other morning chores done, Edd asked Mark to come down to the still and help carry the full jugs to the dugout.

Mark looked surprised and answered, "I'll help because you asked me, but you know I don't hold with that business."

Edd's eyes softened and he spoke in a low voice, "I know, boy, but I would consider it a personal favor."

Mark looked at his uncle with an expression of adoration. "You know I would do anything for you, Uncle Edd."

Jess was through feeding the baby, and without speaking, she set about to get things in order for the next stage to come through the following day.

When the two had reached the still, Edd turned to Mark and said, "I didn't mean to deceive you, but I won't ask you to carry this whiskey. I got you down here so we could have a private conversation."

"Well, go ahead and talk, Uncle Edd. I'm listenin'."

"I don't know how to put this to soften the situation, so I'll just come on out with it," Edd started. "We haven't talked through the problem of Jess going back to the Comanches. I really don't see how just you and me can keep 'em from taking her, if they are of a mind to."

"I know, Uncle Edd," the boy said earnestly. "I've been giving it a lot of thought. I spoke man to man to Screech Owl and I agreed to help him on his terms. I'm bound to keep my word, but I may be able to trade with him."

"What do you think you have to trade with? I don't think he'll want a hog or a milk goat," Edd said.

"No, sir. I was thinking that the paint stallion belongs to them anyway. I would give that to them as a gift. Also, the horses that belong to those two dead men, along with their weapons, would already belong to the Comanches if they had caught 'em before they got here. I would give those as a gift."

"Wait, son! You can't be giving guns to the Comanches!"

"I wouldn't give them more ammunition than the men had with them and they would have had them anyway! If it will help get Jess's freedom, I won't hesitate," Mark replied.

"Well, if you give all these as gifts, what have you got to trade?"

"That's where you come in. I don't want to trade whiskey because I would be going against my beliefs. I would, on the other hand, like to take the saddlebags of those two coyotes and fill one with salt and the other with sugar. Jess says they value salt very highly. If she can persuade them to taste the sugar, we might have a chance," Mark remarked.

Edd was lost in thought for a moment and then nodded, "It appears to me that you have been building this plan for quite a spell. I can't say if it will work, but it's shore worth a try."

"Then you won't mind if I take the salt and sugar?"

"Mark, you know you can have anything I've got and welcome to it," was the sincere reply.

He thought for a moment, raised his eyebrow, and asked, "Are you gonna give 'em both of the saddles?"

"They don't seem to use saddles. I thought we might need those around here. If we ever have to make a run for it, it would be nice not to ride bareback," Mark answered.

Edd nodded approvingly. "I'm gonna quite worrying. You're a step ahead of me at every turn. I guess I need to quit calling you boy."

"Uncle Edd, you can call me boy all my life. I don't expect to ever get too big for my breeches around you," Mark said humbly.

CHAPTER 13

Resolution

THE NEXT MORNING, IN THE gray light just before the sun peeped over the hill, Jess spoke to Mark in a low voice. "Screech Owl has come. I heard the call of a screech owl from the direction of the creek."

Edd scrambled up, reaching for his weapons.

Mark said calmly, "Uncle Edd, there won't be any need for that. I expect him to keep his word, so I'll be keeping mine."

Jess picked up the little one and followed Mark to the door. When he took down the bar, she followed him outside. Mark walked to the center of the station yard and stood looking toward the creek. The Comanche seemed to materialize out of thin air and walked toward the three. He seemed to look much more fierce than he had looked when last they met and then Mark realized the man was painted for war.

Mark was the first to speak. "Jess tell him that I have kept my word. Ask him why he comes to me painted for war?"

Jess relayed the question and listened to the response. "He says that he sees his son is alive and well and that he is thankful. He does not come to make war on you, but on the men who ride those horses in the corral."

"Tell him he is welcome to dig 'em up and make all the war on 'em he wants," Mark said quietly.

Jess grinned slightly and began an excited conversation with Screech Owl. They talked back and forth for what seemed to Mark a long time and Jess said, "He says you are a better warrior than he counted you and he says he knows of no warrior who kills two at a time. He says the men who rode those horses killed his friend Jackrabbit and stole his stallion. He thanks you for killing them."

Mark said, "I am honored by his confidence. Tell him I wish to return the stallion to Jackrabbit's family. I also make him a gift of the two horses. Tell him it is my great pleasure to return his son, safe and healthy."

When Jess had relayed the message, the Comanche nodded his understanding. Jess handed the little boy to his daddy and Screech Owl raised his left hand.

At the signal, a squaw walked out of the brush by the creek to take the baby. At the same time, twenty mounted braves topped the rise on the other side of the creek.

Mark hesitated a moment and then said, "Jess, ask him about his wife."

When the Comanche had answered her inquiry, she turned to Mark with tears rolling down her cheeks. "He says that Meadow Lark has crossed over."

Mark felt a lump in his throat because he had been a new baby without a mother. He said, "Ask how he can manage to raise the baby without a ma."

She talked quietly with the man for a little while and finally said, "The woman who took the baby is Cactus Flower. She was Jackrabbit's wife. She will come to live in the lodge of Screech Owl as his wife. She needs to be taken care of and she will nurse Little Horse along with her new daughter."

Mark asked, "Who is Little Horse?"

Jess answered, "That is what he will call the baby because he survived on the milk of a mare."

Mark grinned, "Don't tell him about the goat or he'll want to call him Billy."

Jess nodded her agreement.

Mark looked at the man, and said, "Jess, tell him I want to talk trade."

After the exchange in Comanche, Jess said, "What have you got to trade?"

Mark said, "Tell him that it will take a couple of trips to bring out my trade goods and that when he sees me carrying weapons that they are to use for trade. I'll be right back."

He left Jess explaining the situation, and strode quickly back into the station. He found Edd peeking out the door, with every weapon in the place loaded and within reach. Mark picked up the rifles and knives of the two dead men, along with a small amount of ammunition for each one.

When he had returned to the yard and placed the items on the ground, he went back for another load. He took the saddlebags he had filled the night before and took them to the trade area. He opened the flaps on both sides of each one and tasted the contents of each one. He then motioned for Screech Owl to do the same.

Screech Owl tasted from each pouch and nodded without changing his expression. He spoke to Jess and urged her to interpret.

Jess started, "He knows what you have to trade, what is it that you would trade for?"

Mark looked the Comanche in the eye and said, "Jess, tell him I want to trade for you."

Jessie's eyes got wide. She looked at Mark for a long time and then she lowered her eyes and turned to Screech Owl. She very humbly said a few words in his language. Screech Owl was silent for what seemed like an eternity. He motioned to two braves to come and get the trade goods while he sent three more to retrieve the horses from the corral. When they had finished, he stepped up in front of Jess and Mark and spoke loud enough for everyone to hear. When he had made about a one-minute speech, he took Jess' hand and placed it in Mark's hand. A brave rode up leading his horse, and Screech Owl mounted and disappeared over the ridge with the rest of the Comanches.

Mark finally thought to close his wide-open mouth and then asked, "What did he say, Jess?"

"He said he would trade," she said simply.

Edd had eased out of the station, still armed to the teeth. He had not said a word all day.

The first thing he said was, "I ain't tellin' nobody about this, 'cause they'd call me a liar!"

Jess looked at Edd and softly suggested, "You can put away your weapons. They have gone back to their village to mourn their dead."

He blinked sheepishly at the two youngsters, nodded, and turned back toward the station house. As he walked, he said to himself, "Scariest thing I ever saw and a couple of kids handled it without a hitch."

Jess turned to Mark and asked, "Now that you have traded for me, what will you do with me?"

Mark looked at her with a tender expression and said earnestly, "I didn't trade for you. I traded for your freedom. It's not a question of what I will do with you. The question is what will you do with you."

She was silent for a few moments and then said, "I will need to think on that, because I didn't see this coming."

"Take all the time you need. Uncle Edd and I will help you do whatever you decide to do," he promised.

Edd called from the door, "Are y'all gonna stand in the yard all day, or come on in and help rustle some breakfast?"

When they sat down to eat, Mark insisted that they give thanks. He bowed his head and prayed. "Lord, we thank You for this food and that we are alive to eat it. We know we owe all we have to You. We ask that You continue to watch over us and that You watch over Little Horse, who we have all come to love. Help us to keep a peaceful situation with the Comanches because we know Your hand is in all things. Bless our plans as we help Jess. In Jesus name we pray, Amen."

Edd grinned, "I don't know if you're speaking for me about loving that kid. I threatened Ross Vinson and wrestled those goats back from Fort Chadbourne. Now the kid's gone and we've still got to milk that goat."

"I can milk the goat now that I am not watching Little Horse," Jess offered.

"We'll probably need to let her go dry, before long. She'll be having her kids in the spring," Edd noted. "By next summer, the young billy will be old enough to sire some more."

"I've been craving some milk gravy, like Granny used to make," Mark added. "If the chance ever comes, I'm hoping to get us a milk cow."

"Well, ain't you the business man," Edd teased. "Before you trade for something else to feed, you'd better figure out how to feed what you traded for this morning."

Mark beamed, "That's why I need the cow."

Jess had watched the two as they jobbed each other with twinkles in their eyes and she knew how much each respected the other.

She said, "I thank you for what you have done for me. I saw what happened to Comanche women when they had no man for their lodge. They could not make it without someone to hunt for them, and they became a burden to the chief and the rest of the tribe."

Mark thought for a moment and said, "Jess, God put you in this situation. It sure wasn't our efforts, or abilities, that caused things to work out the way they have. Think about all the accidents that linked up to put you here. I accidentally killed a deer. I accidentally met y'all at the fork in the creek. I accidentally had a wet, crippled mare. I accidentally shot those two owl hoots. How does all that come together without the Good Lord's hand in it?"

Jess quietly returned, "It was no accident that you gave control to the Great Spirit with the first thing that you said to Screech Owl."

Edd cleared his throat, but it still broke a little, when he got up from the table and said, "I need to check on the horses."

He hurried out the door.

Mark smiled at Jess after Edd departed and said, "I guess he got his blood to pumping real early. He ain't even had his coffee yet!"

"I did not even think about eating," she replied. "We need to fix breakfast."

"Let's don't go to a lot of trouble. Maybe just bacon and coffee will do," he suggested. "I want to get busy to stir up something special for when Jug an Bozy roll in on the westbound. We need to celebrate your freedom."

"What does that word mean?" she asked.

"Westbound?"

"No, celebrate."

He thought for a minute and said, "It means to do something you don't do all the time because you are happy about something that happened. I want us to have lots to eat because we are happy that you are with us."

She asked, "Do you mean like the Comanches do when they have a big kill on the buffalo hunt?"

"That's just what I mean," he nodded. "We need to have us a feast."

They set about making a quick breakfast and cleaned up after meal.

They told Edd what their plans were and he was excited to help. He offered to do all the chores with feeding the stock while they put their party together.

Jess told Mark that she had heard turkeys down the creek toward the pecan trees that grew along the banks.

She said, "If you can get a turkey, bring some of the nuts. We will use them to cook in the bird." Edd said, "Hey, that gives me an idea. I'll kill and pick that oldest rooster and we'll boil him. We can make dumplings out of him and I may have a use for some of the broth."

Everyone set about doing the regular chores in record time. They were all excited about their individual contributions to the occasion. Jess milked the goat and put the milk aside to be used in the meal. She took the ax and went down by the creek to find a green sprout to use for a spit in the event Mark got the turkey.

Mark brought in plenty of wood for the fireplace. He made sure that the fire was stoked with a couple of large chunks that would burn down into good coals for cooking. He loaded the old muzzle-loader with shot, took a bag for the nuts, and set off up the creek in search of a turkey.

Edd borrowed some of Mark's fishing line and made a loop with it similar to a rope for catching the mules. He spread it into a circle about the size of a skillet and set it down next to the corral fence. Then he took some of his precious corn to sprinkle in and around the loop. When the chickens gathered up to eat the corn, he waited until the old rooster stepped into the loop and pulled the string. He caught the rooster by the foot and then chopped his head off with his bowie knife.

Edd had cleaned the chicken, put it in a pot, and covered it with water. He placed the pot on some coals on the hearth so it would simmer slowly. He retrieved one of his precious onions, sliced it very thin, and then chopped it into small pieces and put that in the pot. In about an hour, Mark returned carrying a gobbler and a bag of nuts.

Jess showed Mark how to place each nut on a flat rock and tap it gently with another rock to crack the shells without crushing the nuts. She took charge of cleaning the bird while Mark shelled out the nuts. Eventually, Jess put the bird on the spit with the nuts inside to cook as her Comanche mistress had taught her.

Before the stagecoach was due, Edd took the chicken out of the broth to cool. It was so tender, the meat fell from the bones. He then took flour, lard, salt, and hot water and made a dough. He spread flour on the bar and put the dough on the bar. He mashed it out as flat as he could with his hands.

Edd seasoned the broth with salt and took a couple of cups of broth and set them aside. He brought the rest to a boil while he cut the dough into small rectangles. He threw these into the boiling broth one at a time until the dough was all in the pot. When the broth thickened to this satisfaction, he took the pot off the coals. He deboned the chicken, took the skin off, and chopped the meat. He stirred the chicken into the dumplings and set the pot close enough to the fire to stay warm.

Edd looked at Mark and said, "I've seen your Granny do that a thousand times."

Mark asked, "What are you going to do with that other broth?"

Edd replied, "Y'all get the turkey ready, and I'll show you."

By the time Ross came driving the coach into the yard, a feast of roast turkey, chicken and dumplings, beans, and cornbread were ready.

Edd said, "I won't be long with the last thing."

He put some lard in a skillet to get hot. He stirred in flour and salt and stirred it to keep it from scorching. He poured the broth and an equal amount of the milk into the mixture and stirred it until it was thick and smooth.

He said, "Mark, there's that milk gravy you've been craving. You can put it on your turkey or your cornbread."

Mark observed, "I will probably put it on both!"

The trio, along with Ross, Slick, and three passengers, ate until they were stuffed.

Ross remarked, "Y'all keep cooking meals like this and you'll give Dee a run for the money."

Edd's face lit up and he said, "That reminds me. I need to ride over and visit with the Lambsheads about something. I'll saddle Ol' Snuffy and ride over tomorrow. These two have proved they can handle things without me."

CHAPTER 14

On a Mission

THE NEXT MORNING, AFTER THE stage rolled out, Edd caught Snuffy, and saddled him. He called Mark and Jess over and said, "The next stage is not due until tomorrow evening. I'll be back before then. Keep a sharp eye out, and let's not have no additions to the graveyard. I'm a little nervous about leaving after what happened last time, so you look after each other. You have plenty to eat, so don't wander off by yourselves and get in any trouble. I have all confidence in you."

"Are you going on whiskey business?" Mark asked.

"No, I've got other fish to fry. I'll talk to you about it when I get back. I'll see you tomorrow."

When Edd had ridden out of sight, Mark said, "He said he had other fish to fry. That reminds me, I didn't give Hawk those chicken entrails so he won't get a taste for chicken blood. It's too cold to sit and fish, but we can set some lines."

Jess returned, "You will need to teach me about such things, but I would like to learn."

They spent the morning cutting poles and setting lines in the spots Ned Brackin had pointed out.

When Snuffy came single footin' into the yard at the Lambshead's, Edd was cordially greeted. He had not pushed the mule to keep up with the stagecoach because he intended to ride him home in the morning. The meal had been eaten and the stage had already departed. Mrs. Lambshead instructed Dee to find something for Edd to eat.

Dee replied, "I got deer stew and cornbread left and the coffee is hot."

Edd said, "I appreciate anything. The drivers and the passengers all say that if Dee fixed it, it's worth fightin' over."

The black woman smiled so big, her eyes squinted. It was one of those smiles that lights up the whole room. The Lambsheads sat at the long table drinking coffee while Edd concentrated on the meal.

When Edd finished his plate, Dee asked, "You want some mo'?"

Edd said, "I'd like to, but I don't have no more room. I thank you."

When the meal was cleared away, Mrs. Lambshead asked, "Are you headed east on business?"

"Well, I'm on business, but I'm as east as I'm goin'. I came for some counsel from both of you," he said sincerely. "We've had some things to happen that I ain't shore just how to handle."

Lambshead asked, "You mean the girl you rescued, or the killings we heard about?"

Edd furrowed his brow and said, "Both, as a matter of fact."

Mrs. Lambshead suggested, "Since they are two different things, let's take one thing at a time. As far as the killings go, the drivers tell me that it was an accident. They say the boy was doing the right thing and the men more or less caused their own deaths. Any advice we would have won't bring them back."

"Ma'am, that's shore a fact. The advice I need has to do with something I would ask you to keep in strictest confidence. I don't want anyone to know before I decide what course of action to take."

Lambshead looked at his wife questioningly, and she nodded her agreement.

He said, "You can be assured that we will keep your information to ourselves."

"The word of you good people is a comfort. The problem is that one of the two men killed was Mark's father. Mark never knew him and I'm wondering if I should tell him."

The couple sat in stunned silence. Lambshead finally broke the silence when he turned to his wife and asked, "Darlin', what do you think?"

She looked thoughtful for a moment and replied, "That is not something you make a snap judgment on. I think we should pray about it, discuss it together, sleep on it and give Mr. Singletary our answer in the morning."

"Is that agreeable to you, Edd?" Lambshead asked.

"Of course, it's agreeable. I'm asking for free advice. You should be able to give it on your own terms," he answered. "While you are talking and praying, consider the other problem."

"Explain the problem," advised Lambshead.

"This little gal that Mark rescued has been with the Comanches for years. She ain't got nobody and nothing except the Comanche clothes she's wearin'. She's stuck over yonder with two bachelors. I can't teach her what a woman can, even though she's smart as a whip and watches every detail. I'm afraid some knot-head will come through on the stage and say something about her, and Mark has already killed two men defendin' her."

"I thought the killings were an accident," exclaimed Mrs. Lambshead.

Edd's voice became low and sincere, "They were, but Mark feels mighty responsible for that little gal. If some fool riles that boy just right, the next time might not be an accident. Seems like once you've taken a life, the next time it don't give you quite as much pause."

Lambshead observed, "I think the world of that young man and I don't think he's that kind. However, I know a kid's neck starts to get thick about the time he start's shavin', and he has a tendency to bow up like a young buck. We'll think on it and give you our thoughts in the morning."

The rest of the day was spent in doing the regular chores around a stage station. The two women were busy in the house, while the men checked the shoes on the mules. Harness was looked over and mended and the stock was fed and watered.

The Lambsheads had two milch cows. The cows calved at different times of the year, which enabled them to have a cow-milking most of the year. They also had a couple of milk pen calves to butcher during the year.

The milk pen calf they presently had was a spotted heifer.

Edd asked, "Where is your bull?"

Mr. Lambshead answered, "There's lots of wild cattle around. Since we always keep the calves penned, the cows always come in to be fed and milked. They always seem to find a bull at the right time."

"Don't that get dangerous with these wild bulls hangin' around?"

"Well, you know an ol' cow don't stay in season but a few hours. Sometimes a bull will follow the cows right up in the yard, but if he wants to be too much of a nuisance we nail his hide to the barn. There's plenty more around for next time."

Edd grinned, "They say true love is a powerful thang."

Lambshead laughed out loud, "Don't you know it!"

Edd offered, "Mark's got some young shoats that are getting fat on the mash from my still. He's been wanting a milch cow. We might trade some pork and some buffalo for that heifer when she gets big enough to butcher."

"That might be some welcome variety in our vittles. I'll discuss it with the missus and we'll work it out when the time gets right."

The evening meal was not only filling, but a pleasant visit as well. Dee served the meal and was about to take her plate to a table in the corner.

Mrs. Lambshead said, "We count Dee as part of the family and she generally eats with us. We don't want to offend you, Mr. Singletary."

"Mrs. Lambshead, this is your house. As a guest, I shore won't be offended at the way you see fit to run it. I can't see why somebody who would eat somebody else's cooking would be offended to eat with the same person at the table. Dee is most welcome as far as I am concerned."

"Thank you, sir. You are a gentleman," Mrs. Lambshead stated.

"Well, I don't know if l have ever been accused of that," Edd grinned.

Dee sat down at the end of the table. She smiled at the others and ate her meal in silence.

After supper, Mrs. Lambshead and Dee did the kitchen chores. They then sat close to the fire and Mrs. Lambshead handed the family bible to Dee. To Edd's surprise, Dee opened the book and began to read aloud, "The Lord is my shepherd, I shall not want."

Lambshead looked at Edd and said, "Mrs. Lambshead has taught Dee to read. She practices every night and we go to bed with God's word on our hearts. It kills two birds with one rock."

"Mark does the same thing with Jess. It don't just teach her to read, but it seems to be helping her to relearn the language. They seem to have long discussions about what the reading means."

Lambshead approved, "I'm glad to know the Bible is a guide with the Singletarys."

Edd returned, "Well, Mark is the bible thumper around our outfit. My mother took great stock in it and instilled its importance to Mark."

"Well, you may not want people to know it, but I see that she instilled a lot of it in you, too. Sometimes when you try to fool others, you are just fooling yourself."

Lambshead got up with a knowing smile and went out the door in the direction of the outhouse. Edd looked after him and thought to himself that, if women were going to be around Valley Creek, they would need an outhouse. After they went to bed, Edd could hear low talking coming from the Lambsheads' sleeping quarters. He could not hear the words, but he could tell it was earnest discussion. They were still talking when he drifted off to sleep.

The next morning at breakfast, talk was kept to a minimum until all had eaten. Mr. Lambshead started the discourse. "We are not people to run get in other people's business, but we are also not people to turn down a request for help. We are honored that you would ask our opinions in matters that will affect these young people for the rest of their lives. We want you to know that this is only advice and we won't be offended if you see fit not to follow it."

Edd exhaled as if a burden had been lifted. "I know I put you good people on the spot, and I am sorry for that. The drivers all respect you, and Mark has sung the praises of your brother on the trip out. I see that you are wise people who know how to work. You are good managers and you care about those around you. Most of all, I am impressed that you base your decisions on the Good Book. All those traits describe how my folks were, and if I had them to go to for advice, that's where I would go."

Mrs. Lambshead looked at her husband and he nodded to her to speak. "I am so glad that you mentioned God's word, because that's where our advice comes from. Since the first problem you asked about was telling the boy about his father, I would like to address that first."

Edd said, "Go right ahead, ma'am. I'll be glad to listen."

She began, "The eighth chapter of John tells us that Jesus said, 'ye shall know the truth, and the truth shall set you free.' We think that the problems with Mark knowing will be much smaller now than if he finds out later that you kept it from him. The truth will set you free of the burden, as well as it will set Mark free from wondering what ever happened to his father."

"You don't think the burden of knowing he killed his Pa will be too much for him?"

"We think he needs to be assured that he didn't kill those men. They killed themselves! They made the choice, Mark didn't."

"That's sound advice. I'll think real strong on it," Edd nodded. "What do you think about the other situation?"

"That's a little tougher row to hoe," said Mr. Lambshead. "We did a lot of talking about what might be the right thing. If she has nowhere else to go, it would be like throwing her to the wolves to try to send her back east. She only really knows Comanche ways, and people would eat her alive."

The woman asked, "Do you think Mark loves her?"

"I really don't think there is anything like romance involved," said Edd. "I think he loves her more like a sister, but that don't mean something more won't come about."

Mrs. Lambshead pressed on, "What about the girl? Is she in love with Mark?"

Edd looked thoughtful for a moment and said, "I wouldn't say in love, but more like totally devoted. I don't know if it's out of gratitude exactly, but she thinks he's top of the mark."

"Do you think she would come stay here for a while so Dee and I could teach her some things a woman should know? We could work on her clothes, teach her to cook like white folks and talk to her about things that are decent and proper."

"That's a very generous offer, ma'am. I don't mean to let our problems spill over on to you. I don't know if she would come."

"Do you think she would come if Mark asked her to?"

"She might. I s'pect she would do just about anything he asked her to do, but I still don't want to push this off on you."

"Mr. Singletary, we looked to the Book for our advice on this problem, also. It tells us about a man who was concerned enough with his betrothed bride's reputation and welfare that he was going to put her away without people knowing. God helped him to know that she was good and that he should stand by her. That man was Joseph, the earthly father of Christ and he did stand by her. I know this girl is not in the same kind of trouble that Mary was, but the Good Lord has helped us to know that she is good and she needs us to stand by her."

"Well, I guess you don't need to hit me with an ax handle. I am most grateful for your offer and I will try to enlist Mark's help. We can send word back and forth with the coaches and I'll let you know what I get done," Edd concluded. "I want you to know how much I appreciate your hospitality and advice. My folks always said that good neighbors are a treasure and they were shore right."

Edd saddled Snuffy and came to the front door to bid everyone farewell.

He said, "Thank you all, again. I'd like to ask for just one more thing before I go. Dee, could I have just one more of them smiles?"

Her eyes squinted and she grinned from ear to ear. He had already won her respect, and the suggestion just added to her fondness for the man. He started southwest along the stage road for the half-day trip.

Back at Valley Creek Station, Mark and Jess had started the morning by checking their fishing lines. They had been rewarded with four catfish. One of the fish was about a five pounder. They cleaned them and left them in some water to keep them cool.

They would make a nice meal when the stage rolled in later in the day.

Mark asked Jess if she would like to climb Sentinel Hill with him and look around the country. He suggested they might be able to see Uncle Edd on his way back from the Lambsheads. Mark was very curious about what his uncle's business had been. Jess agreed to the trip. She told Mark that the Comanches used the hill as a landmark and that they hunted buffalo on the other side of that hill. She said that they camped on the headwaters of another creek that flowed in a different direction than Valley Creek.

Mark said, "Yes, Ned Brackin told me that we are just to the east of a divide in the country. On this side, the creeks and rivers flow generally south to join up with the Colorado River. On the west side, the springs and the creeks flow in a general northeasterly direction into the Clear Fork of the Brazos. It joins the main Brazos northeast of Fort Griffin and then the Brazos flows south to the sea."

"What is this east, and west, and south that you speak of?"

"These are words that describe where a place is located from another place. East is where the sun comes up in the morning. West is where it goes down in the evening. Where I found you is north up the creek, and Screech Owl took his wife to the south," Mark explained.

Jess thought for a moment and replied, "These words will be useful in telling each other where we are going."

Mark grinned, "Yes, very useful."

"Say the words telling where we go to the hill," she instructed.

He was impressed with her hunger to learn.

He pointed south and said, "That way is south and that way is west. You put them together to tell the way to the hill. That way is southwest."

She seemed to think this over for a moment and then nodded her head.

"Let us go," she said simply.

"Alright, let's take us some water and something to eat. We can eat lunch while we are looking at the country. We'll come on back in time to meet Uncle Edd and get ready for the stage."

In less than an hour, they had climbed the hill. As they looked to the west, they saw a large dust cloud with dark movement at the front edge.

Jess asked, "The buffalo move to the south?"

Mark was impressed by the sheer numbers of the buffalo, but he was equally impressed with how quickly Jess could grasp an idea. They sure do!" he said. "We'll talk to Uncle Edd about trying to get us some."

"I will prepare for the hunt," she said as a matter of fact.

"You don't intend to kill one, do you?" Mark was surprised at her statement.

"No. I must do something with it after it is killed."

"How many should we take?"

She paused and then replied, "Two would be enough for one hunt."

Mark nodded and said, "I'll talk to Uncle Edd and we'll see what we can do."

Toward mid-day, as they were eating, Jess looked to the east. She pointed toward a tiny figure down the road in the direction of the station.

"Do you think that is Uncle Edd?" she asked.

"I reckon so," Mark answered. "We'd better start on in to meet him."

When Edd rode into the station yard, the two young people were waiting for him.

He stepped down from the mule and said, "My belly button's rubbin' against my backbone. What's for dinner?"

"How 'bout bacon, eggs, and Johnnycakes," Mark asked.

When Edd nodded, Mark offered, "You take care of your mount and we'll whip some up for you."

"Ya'll ain't eatin'?"

"No, sir, we already ate up on Sentinel Hill," Mark replied. "We saw something west of here we need to talk about."

Edd started loosening his latigo and returned, "Alright. I've got something to talk about myself. Stir up them pots and I'll feed this knothead."

When Edd had finished eating his meal, he took his cup of coffee and pushed back from the table. "Well, spill it. I can see ya'll are like a couple of worms in hot ashes waiting to tell me."

"There's a big buffalo herd just west of us," Mark blurted.

"Now, that is some news," Edd noted. "Maybe we can ease off over there and get us a little meat."

"When we saw them, Jess said she would come and prepare for the hunt," Mark said.

"Does she intend to hunt?"

"She said she needed to do something with it after we kill it."

Edd's face lit up and he said, "That's right. I expect she has helped with more than one buffalo hunt, and she knows a whole lot more about it than we do. Jess, you tell us what you need and what we need to do. We are always trying to teach you and now you can teach us."

Jess nodded her head once.

Mark said, "Jess says that two will probably be enough for one hunt."

Edd looked at Jess and asked, "Do you think we can handle three? I have some trading to do with the third one."

"If you are not going to try to dry the third one, we can do this," she said simply.

"We won't keep the third one. We will send it to the Lambsheads on the eastbound stage. When we kill hogs, we'll send them one of those. I'm making you a trade for your milch cow, boy."

"That would be a welcome trade. Was that what you wanted to talk about?"

Edd said, "Among other things, but that's enough for right now. I think we need to see what we need to do about this hunt, and we need to make ready for the stagecoach. What are we going to feed them, tonight?

Mark said, "We already have a big mess of catfish cleaned. We won't need to fool with the meal until later."

Edd observed, "Well, you two have been productive while I've been gone."

The two men looked at Jess and she asked, "What is productive?"

They both laughed and Mark said, "He means we have been busy doing good things."

She smiled and said, "Let us do more of this productive."

Edd said, "Ma'am, you just tell us what to do."

Poles were cut and the limbs trimmed from six of the cedar trees in the area to make a travois for each of three mules. Canvas from an old wagon sheet was stretched and pinned to cover the frames with sharpened pins made from the cedar limbs.

When she was asked what they would wrap the meat in, Jess answered, "The buffalo will give us that."

Knives were sharpened. Guns and ammunition were checked. Plenty of rope was packed for tying down the loads. All of the supplies needed were stacked neatly just inside the station door.

Mark inquired, "Which mules are we going to take?"

Edd suggested, "Why don't we pick three from the ones coming in this evenin'? They'll already have most of the rough worked off, and we sure don't want no fresh snuffy mules for this job."

Mark said, "We'll use our two saddles on two of them and I'll ride the other one bareback. We can ride them while they pull the travois."

Jess said quietly, "I will ride bareback. That is the way I have ridden for a long time."

"It's settled, then," Edd said, "we'd better get ready for the west-bound stage."

When the stagecoach rolled into the yard with Bozy at the lines, there were two passengers along with Slick as well. One was a whiskey drummer wearing a plaid suit named Breeden. The other was a scout for the US Army on the way to Camp Stockton. His name was Ringo Smith.

After a meal of catfish, cornbread, and beans, Smith noticed, "I see it looks like you are preparing for a hunt of some kind."

Edd said, "Yeah, these youngsters saw a big herd of buffalo just to the west yesterday and we thought we would try to get some meat."

"Ya hunted many buff?" asked Smith.

"Naw. This will be the first," quipped Edd.

"How many do you plan to get?"

"Well, we thought about three. Two would be plenty for us, but we would like to send some east to the next way station."

Smith chewed on that for a moment and said, "Sounds reasonable, but it will be lots of work for the first time. It takes some know how to save that much meat."

Edd acknowledged, "I am sure of it, but we have an experienced hand with us. This little gal has lived with the Comanches and this ain't her first trip to the ball."

With a knowing look, Smith said, "I thought that dress was Comanche.

How did she come to be here?"

Edd said, "It's a bit of a story, but get you a cup of coffee and I'll tell you about it."

The two men sat down at the table alone and Edd related the incidents.

After hearing the story, Smith exclaimed, "Screech Owl is a powerful warrior! If you survived meeting him, that's a miracle. It's unbelievable that you have him in your debt."

Edd said humbly, "I have learned to let that boy have a lot of rein.

Everything that happened to make that story the truth, he did it. He'd tell you that it wasn't him, it was the Good Lord."

Smith said, "Sounds like to me that the boy is wiser than you realize."

Edd agreed, "Well, I ain't much of a bible banger, but he's fast bringing me around to it."

Smith said, "Let's get back to your hunt. If it won't offend you, I may can tell you a couple of things to help you. Those buffalo are dangerous and nothing to take lightly."

Edd was eager for the advice. "Fire away. Daddy always said a man don't get too old to learn."

Smith pointed to the items stacked by the door. "I see you have a Sharps 50. That would be the one to use. If you can get ahead of some of them, come up a draw within shootin' distance of that gun. Don't get too close. There's a chance you can get all three before you spook the herd."

"Makes sense," Edd observed.

"Don't pick buffalo in the middle of the herd. Find the plumpest, youngest ones on the edge so that when the herd spooks, your kills don't get trampled into dust."

Edd said, "I can see that."

"Buffalo have kind of an armor on their ribs. The Indians shoot them or spear them behind the ribs pointing toward the heart and lungs. Pick animals facing not quite straight away from you. You need to kill them out right because a wounded buffalo is powerful mean."

"I never would have thought of those things. I thank you very much,"

"I've got faith in you. With those two, and the Good Lord, you've got plenty of help," Smith said with a twinkle in his eye.

After the dust settled in the yard from the departure of the coach, the three hunters brought the supplies from the station and lashed them on one of the travois. With eager anticipation, they rode to the southwest toward Sentinel Hill to get a good look at the task ahead."

CHAPTER 15

The Meat of the Matter

F ROM THEIR VANTAGE POINT ON top of Sentinel Hill, the three hunters could see the vast herd stretching from northwest of their position for miles to the southwest. They noticed a draw to the south that seemed to begin not far from the herd and ran to the east to intersect with Valley Creek. They decided to follow the stage road until they reached the draw, then travel up the draw to the west.

When they had traveled up the draw to within about a quarter of a mile from the herd, Jess said, "I will stay here with the mules. When you stop shooting, I will come to you."

Mark and Edd took their weapons and eased closer to the herd.

Mark said, "Uncle, you do the shooting. I'll stand by with loaded guns in case we need them."

"That's good thinkin', son. If we do this quiet and easy, we may come out smellin' like a rose."

They were able to get within two hundred yards of the edge of the shaggy animals. Edd rested the Sharps on a big rock, and picked out his first target.

He lined up his shot and said, "Here goes," and pulled the trigger.

There was a fat cow on the edge of the herd, with no calf following her.

She folded immediately on her legs and didn't even kick. The nearest of the herd picked their heads up and looked around; they sniffed at the air and then went back to grazing.

Edd's next shot dropped a young bull that had been driven out to the fringes by some of the larger bulls. He bawled when he fell, and kicked his hind legs for a few seconds.

Some of the older cows were beginning to get noticeably nervous. As they started to move away, Edd shot a yearling heifer that was fatter than a town dog. When he fired that third shot, the nearest of the herd bolted. This started a chain reaction; and soon, it sounded like thunder as the main herd began a rush to the south and west.

When the dust started to settle, Jess appeared with the mules. One of the mules rolled his eyes and snorted at the smell of the buffalo blood. They unhooked the travois and stretched a rope between a couple of small trees to tie the mules.

Jess began the task of skinning the cow where she fell. Edd and Mark did what she told them, but basically tried to stay out of her way. When she had the topside of the carcass skinned, she spread it on the ground so they could flop it over to skin the other side. They tied the four legs together and threw the rope across the carcass. They attached the rope to a saddle horn, and gently rolled the carcass over where it was resting on the hide.

When the carcass was completely skinned and rested on the spread out hide, Jess told them to take two mules to pull the heifer closer. She then repeated the process on the fat heifer.

When she had skinned out the heifer, she began to quarter out the carcass. She had the two men carry the cuts of meat and place them on the half of the cow's hide that had no meat on it. This included the tongue, liver, and sweet breads. She took the bare-backed mule and hooked up his travois. The hide from the heifer was placed skin side up on the travois with half of the hide hanging over on one side.

All of the cuts from the heifer were place on the travois, along with a hindquarter from the cow. The loose hide was folded over the load and it was lashed into place.

The process was repeated for the bull. After he had been rolled over, the travois could be attached to both the saddled mules. All the meat was placed on one travois until the hide from the cow could be placed on the other travois. The two men were more helpful as the process went along, and they could see what Jess was doing. "She who watches" had learned her lessons well. They harvested the three animals without the meat touching the ground. Jess suggested that they build a fire and broil some of the liver before they started back.

Edd said, "I 'spect it is getting along toward time to eat. I never would have believed that we would have this much done by mid-day."

As they approached the station, they noticed the sky was blue and dark to the northwest.

Edd said, "There's a norther coming. That will help us do something with this meat before it ruins. I wonder where we can put it to keep the varmints out of it."

"Why don't we hang it from the rafters in the barn? It will stay cold and the hogs and Hawk can't get to it. We'll be able to bring it in a piece at a time to do with it what we can," said Mark.

"That's a good plan," said Edd, "we can get Jess to teach us some more."

They hung up the meat, with the exception of some of the back strap. Mark seasoned it, rolled it in some flour, and fried it in some lard. The fire felt good with the norther blowing in; and with full stomachs, they wasted no time in going to bed. It had been a very productive, but exhausting outing.

The next morning, Jess was up early. She had coffee ready by the time the men stirred and breakfast was started. She was anxious to get to the task at hand.

Jess sent Mark out to bring in one of the tongues and she started a stew to cook slowly for when the eastbound came through. They brought in a quarter off the buffalo cow and started cutting it in strips to dry in the smokehouse. Many people, both white and red, made it through the winter on buffalo jerky.

When the stagecoach stopped, all those aboard enjoyed the stew. It had cooked slowly and was very tender with a thick broth. It was no trouble to talk the driver into carrying the meat from the bull to the Lambsheads. He said, "I can just imagine what Dee will do with some of this."

They spread the hide from the bull on top of the coach, flesh side up. They stacked the meat on the hide, pulled the sides up to cover the meat and tied the bundle firmly.

Edd said, "Tell 'em we'll send something else over when we kill shoats."

When the team topped the rise headed east, Mark asked, "You fixin' to give one of my shoats away?"

Edd said apologetically, "Oh, I forgot to tell you. I ain't givin' this stuff away. I traded for your milch cow."

Mark beamed, "That's a blessing. God is good!"

"That reminds me," said Edd. "I need to tell you the rest of the news.

Let's all get out of this cold and talk over a cup of coffee." When the two men went in the station, Jess was cleaning up the meat cutting area. She called Hawk to the door and gave him a large leg bone. He took it around on the south side of the building to get out of the wind.

When they all were seated, Edd began, "I asked the Lambsheads to give me some advice on a couple of things that affect you two. I want to talk about Jess, first."

"I am listening," Jess said with a little fear in her voice.

"Don't be afraid of what I am going to say. I hope you know how fond Mark and I have become of you and how much we depend on you. We want you to know that we will always be here for you. Now, I want you to know that you ain't done nuthin' wrong and you ain't got a thang to be ashamed of. What we are talking about fixin' has to do with other people's problems."

"You spent a lot of time with the Comanches and you learned a whole bunch of good things from them. I am so grateful for what you know about dealing with those buffalo. What I'm trying to say is, your time with them wasn't all a bad thing. I know that Screech Owl and his family treated you more like family than a slave. I want you to think back to the two men who Mark had to shoot. Do you remember what they called you?"

Jess replied, "Yes, they called me a little ol' squaw gal."

Edd said, "That's right. Do you remember that Ringo Smith knew you had been with the Comanches?"

"Yes," she said.

"Do you know the reason for this?"

"I think it is because I do not appear as the white women who ride on the stagecoach," she answered.

"I think you are right," said Edd. "Now, the women on the stage are usually wearing what we call traveling clothes. There's no call for you to dress in fancy clothes like that, but you might need to dress more like the white women in this part of the country."

"You are not pleased with how I look?"

"No, it ain't that! It's just that some white men will not be as respectful as Ringo Smith. You know what those two owl-hoots were planning. I just don't want Mark to have to shoot nobody else over their unruly ways."

"I have nothing else to wear and I don't know how to make the clothes like white women wear," she said with a lump in her throat.

"Don't you worry about that," Edd reassured, "I wouldn't have brought up the problem if I didn't think I had a solution. There are two good women at the next way station. Their names are Mrs. Lambshead and Dee. Dee works for Mrs. Lambshead. They have agreed to let you come over and use your skills as 'She who watches' and learn how to dress and cook like a white woman.

That doesn't mean you need to unlearn anything the Comanches taught you. Those are good things to know. You know how to get along with the Comanches. Now, you will know how to get along with white people."

Mark blurted, "I don't want her to leave us!"

Edd said with a knowing look, "I don't want her to leave us, either. It ain't like she's leaving forever. She's just going for a visit, and then coming home."

Jess asked in a very small voice, "Is this my home?"

Edd put his hand on her shoulder and said, "It is for as long as we live here. That is, if you want it to be."

"If it would make things better for you and Mark, then I would go."

"I'm glad you'll go. You'll like the folks over there, and they will be good to you. I want you to understand, though. This ain't for me and Mark, it'll make things much better for you."

Mark got up from the table and went back to his sleeping area. He opened the old trunk and began to look into the contents. Shortly he returned and handed two items to Jess.

He said, "I had forgotten about these. I want you to have them. They were my mother's."

Her eyes shone as she looked at the two dresses, but then she said, "I could not take your mother's clothes. For you to keep them, they must mean much to you."

"My mother died shortly after I was born. It would mean a lot for me to see them worn by someone. Lying folded in a trunk, they give off such an empty feeling," he said sincerely.

Edd said, "I knew his mother. She was my sister and I can tell you that she would be very pleased if you would take them."

Mark added, "I'll bet that those ladies over there will help you make them look like they were made for you."

"But I have no gift for you in return," she said, remembering Comanche custom.

"Seeing you wear them will be my gift," was his reply.

"It's settled then! When we get this buffalo dried, I'll send word. We'll make the arrangements then," Edd said.

Jess asked, "Do we have more to talk about, or can I start on the meat?"

Edd paused and then said, "I need to tell Mark something. It ain't a secret, and I ain't trying to keep something from you, but I think that Mark might like to hear it first by himself."

"I will take strips to the smokehouse to begin to dry," she said.

She got up and went about her tasks.

"What is it, Uncle?" Mark asked.

"I want you to know that I have studied about whether or not to tell you this for a spell now. I went to get advice from the Lambsheads because I had argued with myself about the problem.

I just couldn't decide whether the good outweighed the bad or the bad the good."

"I'm starting to worry, Uncle Edd. It's not about Jess, is it?"

"No, son. It is about you."

Mark said nervously, "Well, please tell me. I would rather get it out in the open."

Edd began, "Alright, here it is. Do you remember that no account that you shot that you called 'Old Lanky?'"

Mark said meekly, "How could I forget?"

"Well, I recognized him. I knew him seventeen years ago," Edd explained. "His name was Collin McGee."

Mark sat in stunned silence. After nearly a minute had passed, he finally spoke passionately. "Do you mean that I killed my own father?"

"Son, I've told you all along that you didn't kill those two. They killed themselves," Edd said emphatically.

"I know you said that, but I pulled the trigger!"

"Would you have done that if they had not gone for their weapons?"

Mark agonized, "No, sir. The fact remains that it was my gun and my hand."

"Would you rather they had done what they had in mind?"

"No, sir, I wouldn't," Mark said as he got the point.

"Let me tell you this," added Edd, "if I had ridden up and found him, it would have been a situation of him or me. I had chased him across the continent with every intention of killing him and he knew it. When he saw me, he would have gone for his weapon. It wouldn't have mattered whether that was still my intentions or not."

"Uncle Edd, what would have been your intentions?"

"Mark, I really couldn't say. If there had been time to think it through, I might have spared him for your sake. I just don't think there would have been time to think it through," Edd returned.

"Maybe that's what I need is some time to think it through," said Mark.

"I wouldn't be surprised," said Edd. "You might want to talk to Jess about it. She was there, and that little gal is wise beyond her years."

"I'll study on it," said Mark.

By the end of the day, they had lashed together enough racks in the smokehouse to dry the buffalo meat. By the end of the second day, all the meat was either in the smokehouse or hanging in the barn rafters to be cooked fresh in the next few days. If the weather turned off warm, they could dry the rest.

These tasks were accomplished mainly due to the efficiency of Jess. She worked at a steady pace and didn't waste motion. It was obvious why the Comanches had given her such a name. She not only watched, she remembered what she had seen.

In the coming days, Mark brooded over the news he had received from Edd. Though he was quiet, Edd didn't crowd him, and Jess acted as if there was no difference. It wasn't only the news about his father, but the prospect of Jess leaving that was a burden on his heart.

Jess tried to do the things she needed to get done before her trip to the Lambsheads. She tried to do things that would make her missed while she was gone. She didn't realize that she would be greatly missed, even if she didn't do anything. Edd sent a letter with the stagecoach to the Lambsheads telling them that Jess had agreed to come. When the next coach westbound came through, they sent word that she would be welcome as soon as she was ready.

Edd called the two-young people into the station to tell them the news.

He said, "I guess we can send Jess over on the next eastbound stage to the Lambsheads. They say she will be welcome as soon as he is ready."

Mark had a pained look on his face. "Are we just going to send her over to people she has never met?"

Edd said, "I really hadn't thought about it that way. How do you think we should do it?"

Mark said, "Why don't you let us ride two of the mules over? I could introduce her and help get her settled. When I ride back, I could lead the other mule."

Edd grinned, "Well, I know it would be asking a lot of you, but if you insist. I know this would all be for her sake."

Mark blushed, "You're jobbin' me. I can feel it just as plain."

Edd chuckled, "Aw, I have to give you a hard time, some times. I really think it's a good idea. We'd all three probably be more at ease if it is done that way."

Two days later, word was sent with the eastbound that Mark and Jess would arrive before night.

The two saddled up to begin their half-day journey.

Mark said, "Uncle Edd, I'll be back tomorrow before supper."

Edd said, "Ya'll be careful. Mark, don't forget your pistol. Jess, if you run into Comanches, use Screech Owl's name."

The two riders looked apprehensive as they rode their mules up the road to the east. When they topped the rise, they turned and waved goodbye to Edd. He watched them until they were out of sight.

CHAPTER 16

A Flower Blooms

WHEN THE COUPLE RODE INTO the station yard at the Lambsheads, Mr. Lambshead was standing at the corral. He recognized Mark, and said, "Welcome! Y'all step down."

Mark greeted the man warmly, "Hello, Mr. Lambshead. I'm glad to see you. I would like to present Miss Jesse Behannon. We call her Jess."

"I'm honored to meet you, Ma'am," said the gentleman.

Mrs. Lambshead, followed by Dee, came out of the station house.

Mrs. Lambshead said, "Well, hello, Mark! It's a pleasure to have you visit. Who is this you have brought to us?"

"This is Miss Behannon, Ma'am," Mark returned. "We thank you very much for having us."

"It's very nice to meet you, dear," Mrs. Lambshead stated. "I would like for you to meet Dee. Dee, this is Miss Behannon."

Dee smiled one of her eye squinting smiles as the young girl said, "I am called Jess."

Dee said, "We gonna get along fine."

The lady of the house said, "Put up your mules and bring your things in the house. Dinner will be ready in a short time."

After a meal of fried chicken, hot biscuits, and white gravy, Mrs. Lambshead said, "We want to thank you for the buffalo you sent over. The variety to our meat sources is quite welcome and the stage passengers certainly enjoy it."

"We'll be sending some pork as soon as we get some room in the smokehouse," answered Mark.

Mr. Lambshead said, "There's no big hurry. Your heifer won't be weaned for a while, yet. We need to get her gentled and broke to lead so you can take her home, when it's time."

Mark's face lit up.

"I'd love to see her!"

The man said, "Well, let's go!"

Mark asked, "Will you be alright, Jess?"

Dee inserted, "You men's go ahead and get out from under foot. We need to get to know each other, anyway."

The men rose from the table and went out to the corral. When they looked into the stall under the barn, a red and white heifer about two months old bawled at them.

Mr. Lambshead said, "Every time she see's somebody, she thinks it's time for her mama to come feed her."

"Where is her mama?" asked Mark.

"We milk her and let her calf suck in the morning. We turn her out to graze and she comes in at milking time. We have another dry cow with her and we feed them a little morning and evening. We keep them penned during the night."

"Well, that baby's a good heifer. I'm glad Uncle Edd made a trade," Mark mentioned.

Mr. Lambshead agreed, "It was a good trade for us both. We brought that milk stock with us when we came out here. You would be hard pressed to locate one like that, but we will realize a lot more meat out of the trade than butchering her."

"Uncle Edd says it's a good trade when both parties are satisfied."

Mr. Lambshead laughed, "That's shore true! I have made a few where I wound up unsatisfied!"

When Mark stood close the pen, the heifer timidly eased up close to sniff at him. He eased his hand out to touch her and she drew away just out of reach. He said, "She doesn't seem like she will be too hard to tame."

Lambshead supported the idea. "Dee helps some with the milking and that heifer will let her scratch her. When we milk after a while, we will drop a rope on her and start her education."

Mark said pleasantly, "I'll look forward to it."

Inside the station, the women were warming up to each other. Jess was hesitant to speak much because of her language skills. Her long stay with the Comanches had caused her to be more fluent in Comanche than she was in English, but the amiable manner of the other two ladies dispelled some of her hesitance. Dee had somewhat of an accent herself and that helped to ease Jess's feelings.

Dee noticed the bundle of clothing Jess had brought with her. "What you got in de bundle, girl?"

"I have some of Mark's Mother's dresses. I have not worn them," Jess told them.

"He must think a whole lot of you if he gave you some of his fambly treasures. Let's have a look at 'em and then we'll have a look at you in 'em," Dee bubbled.

Mrs. Lambshead was much more dignified, but still said enthusiastically, "Yes. We certainly should see what we have to work with."

Jess untied the bundle and handed a dress to each of the women. It was obvious that the dress she handed to Dee was the dress she wore for every day chores, and the other was for more special occasions.

Dee said, "Theys a mite big for you, but I'm sho we can take 'em in to fit."

Mrs. Lambshead added, "Yes, we should have no trouble having one ready before supper. Let's get first things first, though. Dee, start heating water for a bath. I'll tell Carson to bring in the tub."

After the tub had been placed in the Lambshead's bedroom and was filled with warm water, the two women looked at Jess. She looked back with the expression of a startled antelope.

Dee smiled at Jess and asked, "Ain't you ebber had no bath?"

Jess said, "I wash myself in the creek. I remember my momma bathing me in a tub, but it is a dim memory. I'm not sure I can fit in the wash tub like she had me to do."

Katherine Lambshead instructed, "You don't have to sit in the tub. Stand in the tub, take this gourd dipper, and pour the water over you. Lather up with the soap and then pour more water to rinse it off. When you get finished, dry off with this clean flour sack. Dress in these undergarments. Dee and I will come in and help you with your dress and your hair. Do you understand, dear?"

Jess replied, "I have one question. What are undergarments?"

The two women looked at each other in slight astonishment before Dee replied, "They's clothes you wear under your dress. The one goes over your head like a dress, and the other you put on one leg at a time. This little bow here goes in the front. Mrs. Lambshead gave these to you from her own clothes."

Mrs. Lambshead said, "Yes, Jess. Ladies always wear undergarments. While you are with us, we'll make you more."

By the time the men came in from their afternoon chores, Jess was dressed in the blue dress that matched her eyes. Her hair had been washed, brushed, and put up in the same style as the older woman.

Mark walked in the door and thought someone else had come to the station. After a moment, he realized that it was Jess. All three women laughed at the look on his face.

Jess said, "I looked in a looking glass for the first time in a long time. I did not know the girl looking back."

Mark nodded, "I'll bet Screech Owl wouldn't know you either."

"I wouldn't let them burn my doe skin dress. There may come a time we need to skin more buffalo," she said.

"Did you help skin and dress the buffalo you sent us?" the white woman asked in a surprised voice.

"She didn't help. We did. She did most of the work, and showed us what to do," Mark interjected.

"Well, what y'all sent over here was expertly done. I nailed the hide to the barn. It will make a fine buffalo robe," said Carson Lambshead.

"Looks like we won't be doin' all de teachin' while you stay here," said Dee.

"I don't want to skin a buffalo while I am dressed like this," said Jess.

Katherine Lambshead returned, "That is a point well taken, dear."

After the evening meal, Jess and Mark walked out by the corral. Mark showed the heifer to Jess, and said, "When your stay is finished, I'll try to halter break that heifer so we can lead her home."

"That will be good. I hope you don't have to take the heifer, and leave me here," she said quietly.

"I won't leave you this time, if you don't want to stay," he said flatly.

"I would go with you, but Uncle Edd says I need to learn to be a white woman. I will do this so I will not bring trouble on us. I am interested to see how I will learn to be a white woman from a woman with black skin," she said innocently.

Mark laughed out loud. "That's a good question! You wait till I hit Uncle Edd between the eyes with that one. I think what he meant was for you to learn to be a lady."

"Tell me what is a lady," she asked.

He said, "I guess I have never had to think much on that. It seems to me that when people talk about a lady, it has to do with respect. She knows how to act in a respectable manner. She knows her place when it comes to dealing with the men folks, but she demands that they know theirs in dealing with her. She has dignity, and honor."

"If that is what it means, I have known many Comanche ladies."

"I see what you mean," he said. "I can understand that 'respectable' can mean different things in different places."

"I will try to learn what it means to Uncle Edd," she purposed.

"I agree with Dee that you may not be the only one getting taught," Mark mused.

Jess said, "If you are going to have a milch cow, I need to learn to milk one."

"We'll do that chore together in the morning, if you like. About the only difference between milking a cow instead of a mare or a goat, is that there are four spigots instead of two. Oh, and a good milk cow will let you sit on a stool to do the chore."

"This I would see," she said.

The next morning, the two had a good time getting the milking chore done. Jess learned that sometimes you had to feel instead of just look. It's hard to see how firmly someone is squeezing.

Dee fried buffalo steaks for the midday meal. After they ate, it was time for Mark to start for home.

Both Jess and Mark had looks on their faces that were both pained but resigned.

Mark said, "If you need me to come to you, send word by the stage."

Dee patted him on the back and said, "You come on back and visit when you can. We'll take good care of her, and she'll learn all we can teach her in two shakes of a lamb's tail."

Mark took the lead rope of the spare mule, stepped up on 01' Snuffy, and headed west at a ground-eating trot. He would be back at Valley Creek before time to make supper.

As she watched him fade from sight, Jess resolved to herself to learn all she could. She also decided that the heifer would be gentled and leading before Mark came back for her. It would be her gift to him in return for the dresses.

When Mark rode into the station yard, Uncle Edd was in the corral feeding mules. He said, "Glad to see you, Mark. Did you have to peel Jess off that mule when you got over to the Lambsheads?"

"No, sir. I think she prob'ly took it better'n I did."

Edd had a knowing expression when he said, "I know. I miss her myself, but she'll be back soon. It's like your Granny always talked about schoolin' being a good thing. Jess is over there learnin'. It ain't from a book, but it's learnin' just the same."

"I know, Uncle Edd. Seems to me, though, that she might already be smarter than some of the rest of us. She asked me a question that I don't think you can answer," he said with a twinkle in his eye.

"Just what might that be?"

"She asked me why we took her to a woman with black skin to teach her to act like a white woman," Mark said.

Edd removed his hat and scratched his head.

"Now that's a question most of us wouldn't have even thought about. Besides always watching, she sure knows how to ask the right questions," he said. "How are we going to answer that?"

Mark said, "I thought about it all the way home. Dee seems to have really taken a shine to Jess. I believe that by the time she comes home, it will have sort of answered itself. Jess already decided that you don't have to be white to be a lady."

Edd wrinkled his brow as he digested what the boy said. In a moment he said, "You know, I've seen plenty with white skin that weren't. I guess in genteel circles, your Granny might not have been called a lady. You and I both know that she was a lady to the bone."

"I believe those are the kind of lessons she will get from Dee and Mrs. Lambshead," Mark was convinced.

"And I 'spect she ain't the only one around here with a head on her shoulders," Edd encouraged. "You might want to go in and start stirring up something for the stage passengers. They should be rolling in here, soon.

When the stage rolled up, Jug and Bozy were on the box. Bozy set the brake and they both climbed down.

Bozy said, "Mark, I've got something in the boot that Matty Flurry sent to you. Come on over here and get it."

"What is it, Bozy?

"Come on over here and look, man!"

Jug had retrieved a stick with thorns on it that had its root ball wrapped in a small piece of canvas. When he handed it to Mark, the boy asked, "What is it?"

Bozy answered, "Why, it's a rose bush. Ain't you ever seen a rose bush?"

"Granny had two, but they were much bigger than this. Why would Mattie send me a rose bush?

Jug chimed in, "Because she heard about Jess living with y'all and she said a place needs a little color when there are women folks around!"

"Where should I plant it?"

Edd said, "Well, if you want it to be seen, plant it on one side of the front door. You need to put it where you can watch it, or those goats of yours will work it over. That's why your Granny wouldn't have a goat."

"I thank you, sirs, for bringing it. Would you tell Miss Mattie that I appreciate it very much?"

Jug and Bozy said that they would.

Edd said, "Dig you a hole to plant it in; and when you fill it up, mix your dirt about half and half with mule droppings."

Bozy said, "Yeah, and every year give it another dose o' them droppings. Keep it watered and you'll have more roses than a church yard."

Jug said, "Ya need to watch them thorns, too. Between the mule droppings and the thorns, if you want your world to turn up roses, ya gotta take the good with the bad."

Edd said, "I reckon that's what we're having to do right now with Jess."

Mark said, "Yes, sir. I just wish we had her by the door where we could watch her."

"Edd, Mattie wanted you to know that things are getting a little thin since the soldier boys went back east in December. She says she don't know how long she can stay before she has to move toward Ft. Worth. If thangs don't work out there, she may go on to Austin."

"Things have sure started to get restless since that Lincoln fellow went and got himself elected President," Edd spat. "All the soldier boys worth their salt have been called back east. Most of the ones left ain't too chili red hot for nothin'."

"I know it," exclaimed Jug. "The stuff I see in the newspapers that come through in the mail tells me that Mark ain't the only one dealin' in fertilizer. They're nearly comin' to blows in the halls of Congress."

"That may be all that's up there, a bunch of bloomin' idiots."

Bozy said solemnly, "I sure hope them blooms don't produce no fruit."

CHAPTER 17

Two Birds with One Rock

J ESS STARTED HER EDUCATION AT Mountain Pass Station with her two teachers helping her to alter the dresses that Mark had given her. They wanted to destroy her Comanche dress, but Jess would not hear of it. She explained that she had made it herself and she might need it to wear when she skinned another buffalo.

Dee said, "I see dat. If I wuz gonna skin a buffalo, I wouldn't want to do it in my good clothes." She grinned her special grin, and added," I 'spect that would be better than in no clothes."

They all laughed at the thought.

True to her Comanche name, she watched closely to everything. She noticed the vessels and utensils that the women used when they cooked. She vowed to make bread and biscuits like Dee, as the Singletary men lived on cornbread. She noticed how many coals to use on the bottom and the top of the Dutch oven.

Dee said, "You got a good mem'ry, but you might want to write some of these thangs down."

Jess said, "Mark is teaching me to read, but I don't know how to make the marks."

Dee asked, "You mean you can read writin', but you can't write readin'?

"That is true," acknowledged Jess.

"Well, how is Mr. Mark teachin' you to read?"

"We read in what he calls 'the Bible' before we go to bed," Jess said.

The black woman smiled and said, "That's how Miz Lambshead taught me. I still read the Good Book every night. When I got the readin' part down, then she taught me to draw what she calls letters. I'll write thangs down for you, and we'll work on your writin', too."

"When you read, will you teach me?"

"I'd be proud to, honey," Dee assured.

Katherine Lambshead came into the station and said, "Dee, Carson has a fire built under the wash pot. Why don't we show Jess how we wash clothes? I imagine it is quite different from the way she's used to doing it."

The three carried all the things out that they would need. It was quite an undertaking using the washboard, lye soap, and lots of hot water.

"How is this different from the Comanche women?" Katherine Lambshead asked?

Jess reported, "Most of the things they wear are made of leather. Their beds are of buffalo robes. Water makes them stiff. Most of their cleaning is shaking or beating the dirt out. They rub their leather goods with buffalo fat."

The older woman questioned, "How do you wash things at Valley Creek Station?"

"Mark and Uncle Edd usually wash their own clothes in the stream using a rock as you use this washboard. We go by ourselves down the stream to wash our bodies, we do not use a tub."

Dee said, "I bet things get a little ripe during cold weather."

"It does not compare to a winter teepee," Jess replied.

"No, I expect it does not," inserted Mrs. Lambshead. "We won't worry about how you have done things. Instead, we'll teach you how a lady does things."

As the day progressed, the women exchanged ideas about the daily chores of thriving on the prairie. The Mountain Pass women knew about making soap, while Jess could explain about jerking buffalo meat. Jess knew about medicinal plants, while Dee knew about sewing up severe wounds. It soon became evident that this was more of an information-sharing period than a simple teacher and student relationship.

When the Lambsheads excused themselves for the night, Dee pulled out the Bible for her evening reading. Before she started to read, Jess mentioned, "They treat you well for a slave."

Dee looked up from the book and said quietly, "I'm not a slave. They gave me my freedom and my papers."

"Mark told me that you are their slave," Jess replied.

"That is what we let people think," Dee informed. "This part of the country ain't a good place for a free black woman all alone. Folks who enjoy my cookin' and my comp'ny wouldn't have no truck with me if they thought I was an 'uppity nigger".

"If they gave you your freedom, then you once were their slave?"

Dee answered, "Yes, Miz Lambshead inherited me from an aunt. She treated me like fambly from the start. She taught me to read, and at the same time, she taught me about Jesus. After I was baptized into the Lawd, she gave me my papers. She waited 'til I could read 'em before she gave 'em."

"Why would she treat you as family if you were a slave?"

Dee gave her special smile and said, "That's what we'll read about tonight. We'll read the book of Philemon."

Jess gave a wide-eyed look.

"The whole book," she asked?

Dee said, "This book is only one little ol' chapter, but it says a mouthful."

Jess sat beside Dee at the table. With the light from the lamp on the page, Dee followed the words with her finger. She would read each verse slowly in order for Jess to recognize the words, then she would read it faster so the meaning was clearer.

When they had read the whole book, Dee said, "The 'postle Paul told this Philemon feller to treat Onesimus like a brother. He also told Onesimus that he owed Philemon, and for him to ack like a brother. He didn't just 'splain to slave owners, he talked to slaves, too."

"Meadow Lark treated me more like a daughter than a slave," Jess remembered.

"I 'spect you acted more like a daughter than a slave," Dee speculated. "Did you ever notice the difference in the way these men treat the mules who act like they want to mind and work and the ones who roll their eyes and act silly?"

"Yes, some of the drivers like the ones who need scolding. They say they have more spirit. Bozy likes the ones who quietly do their job," Jess said.

"Thank about the kind of men they are. The ones who like to cuss and use the whip wouldn't treat no slave like fambly," Dee observed.

"Mark and Uncle Edd treat me more like family than a slave," Jess stated.

"Well, why wouldn't they? You ain't a slave!"

"I am Mark's property. Mark gave gifts to Screech Owl, and I was Screech Owl's gift to him," Jess explained.

"This Screech Owl feller didn't just give that gift to Mark. He knew that baby wouldn't have made it if you hadn't helped Mark to save him. That trade let him do something for you without looking weak in the eyes of his people," Dee said sagely. "I sho' don't b'lieve Mr. Mark considers that he owns you."

"He does treat me like a sister," Jess remarked.

Dee grinned, "Somehow, I b'lieves he's gonna think of you a whole lot more than a sister."

The day had been a full one. Both of them went to their respective beds with many thoughts running through their heads. It was a long time before Jess fell asleep.

The next morning, when the milking chores were done, Jess made it a point to start gentling the heifer. She could see that the cow had been treated gently and trusted Carson Lambshead. She purposed that gentling the heifer would be a good gift for Mark.

When the eastbound stage rolled in, Jug and Bozy were making the return trip. They both did a double take when they saw Jess dressed in her new clothes with her hair put up. With obvious fake sincerity, Bozy asked, "Dee, aren't you going to introduce me to this young lady?"

"Go on, now, Mr. Bozy! Don't give Miss Jess a hard time. See how pink you made her face. Y'aughta be 'shamed,'" Dee said, as she wagged her finger at the two men.

Jug said, "You are the vision of loveliness, Miss Jess. What a pleasure it is to find you in such a setting."

Katherine Lambshead exclaimed, "Why, Jug, you have revealed that somewhere in your upbringing there was culture and manners!"

It was Jug's turn to turn pink. "With a name like Jug, I try not to let anyone know it."

Everyone laughed and they continued the routine of caring for the passengers and the mules. Bozy gave Jess a report about how things were at Valley Creek and told her that Mark was concerned about how she was enjoying her stay. He told her she could send word with the westbound driver if she had news for Mark.

"I'll send word with Ross Vinson that everything is fine," she said.

Jess did not catch his meaning when Bozy mysteriously smiled and said, "I don't know if that's what he wants to hear."

Edd stayed busy with a batch of whiskey he was running off. As Mark wouldn't get involved in that business, he devoted his time to several projects he wanted to finish.

Pulltight, the paint mule colt, was still too young to pull a load, but Mark began to teach him to drive. Ross Vinson had advised him that the younger you teach a mule, the easier he is to handle. When they threw a fit, they weren't so big as to overpower you.

Mark talked to the colt every time he gave him a behavior cue. He wanted Pulltight to respond to voice commands. He worked earnestly on gee, haw, whoa, and come here. He especially worked on building trust in their relationship.

Edd had sampled an ample amount of his product when he stood at the corral fence. As Mark drove the mule around the lot, Edd said, "See how he backs his ears sometimes when you give him a command. He thinks he should be the boss. It's because he's half mustang and half wild jackass. It sure don't help that he ain't been gelded."

"I don't want to mess up his trust in me by hurting him," blurted Mark.

146

"Well, a horse don't drop his seeds 'til he's about two years old, but a donkey or a mule are born with 'em down. They'll become a nuisance around the females before you know it. Maybe we can get a couple of the boys to help me do it when they stop with the stage, and you can watch from outside the corral," Edd planned.

"I sure would appreciate that," Mark said.

"We need to do it while it's still cool, before the flies get bad," Edd added. "The smaller he is, the easier it will be on man and beast."

"The sooner, the better," Mark agreed.

Edd said, "After supper, we'll gather up what we'll need."

Mark knew what Edd had been up to when he said. "You might want to tell me what we need. You might be too tired after supper."

Edd wasn't so far gone that he didn't catch Mark's meaning. "I see what you mean," he said. "Let's see, now. We'll need a short piece of soft rope to hobble his front feet, two pieces of rope about twenty feet long and a good stout halter with a ten-foot lead rope. We need to mix a double handful of flour mixed with a handful of salt. Finally, we need a jug of my whiskey."

Mark raised both eyebrows and asked, "Who's gonna drink the whiskey, you or the mule?"

The question struck Edd so funny that it was nearly a minute before he stopped laughing. "We're gonna pour it over my knife before I use it and then pour some in the wound to keep it from festering. We'll use that flour and salt to help stop the bleeding and help draw out any corruption."

Mark replied sheepishly, "I didn't mean nothin'. I ain't never seen this done. Ada and Cricket didn't need nothin' like that."

"It's alright, boy. I 'spect me and the boys won't let the rest of the jug go to waste, afterward. I might just send it with 'em to repay their help."

"How is this different from marking pigs?" asked Mark.

"Not a whole lot, except you need to be sure and get everything. A proud cut mule ain't worth the bullet it would take to get shed of him."

"Would you please work him before you start on the other part of that jug?" Mark was trying to be respectful and he added, "I sure would hate to mess him up."

Edd patted him on the back. "Sure will! We need to get the work out of our help before we pay 'em."

The next day, Ross Vinson and Slick Newton were on the box when the coach rolled up in the yard. Mark took the two passengers into the station to make them comfortable and to dish them up the buffalo stew they had for lunch.

Edd made the deal with Ross and Slick.

Ross spat tobacco juice on the ground and said, "Me and Slick ain't much on drinkin', but we'll take it with us to trade for somethin' else. We would do it for Mark for nothin', but we appreciate the gesture."

After everyone had eaten, Edd had Mark haltered the young mule. Edd took him into the yard and hobbled him. He tied a rope around the mule's neck with a knot that would not let the noose tighten around its neck and pulled a hind foot up to the noose with the tail of the rope. He then prepared to do the same thing on the other side and handed the tail of that rope to Ross. He ran the lead rope to the halter under the hobbles and handed the tail to Sick.

When Edd gave the order, the other two men pulled on their ropes.

Both front feet of the mule were pulled up to his chin, and each back foot was pulled up to his neck. Edd half-hitched each rope around the feet and the mule was trussed up like a Christmas turkey.

When Edd finished the operation, he applied the whiskey. He let the wound bleed and drain for a minute and then applied the powder. He took off the half hitches releasing the lower hind foot first. He took off the hobbles and said, "Ross, put your foot on his withers, and pull his nose up to you. He can't get up, if he can't get his nose down. When I get the hind foot untied, let his nose loose. We'll see if he wants to get up from there.

Ross complied with the instructions, but Pulltight just laid there. Ross bumped him with his boot, and the mule just groaned.

Mark's face was a picture of worry. "Is he gonna die, Uncle Edd?"

Edd said, "Naw! He'll get up. He just needs it "'splained to him."

Mark said, "I don't want to beat him!"

Edd comforted, "I ain't gonna beat him, I'm gonna smother him up.

Watch!"

The man picked the mule's nose up off the ground and placed the heel of each of his hands in the mule's nostrils, placing his thumbs on top on the nose. With his remaining fingers, he held the mule's mouth shut. After about twenty seconds, the mule decided he needed some air and began to struggle.

When he came up to his feet, Edd released the nose. He said, "He could get up, he just didn't want to."

Slick Newton, who was a man of few words, said, "I've seen a lot of mules and horses cut, but I learned some things, today."

Ross spat in the dirt and said, "I reckon a man learns something every day he wakes up, but I have to say that was slick."

Edd said, "I just happened to be around some folks a whole lot smarter than me. I'm glad Mark could watch the whole thing without concentratin' on holdin' that mule down. He should have learned some things from all three of us."

"I did, Uncle," came the reply. "How long will I need to leave him alone before I start back working him?"

"You can start tomorrow. He'll be sore and won't want to argue much. I like to start riding a bronc the day after I cut him. He usually ain't interested in doing much bucking."

Before everyone bedded down for the night, Ross mentioned that Jess was thriving with the Lambsheads. He said, "That girl is bright as a penny in more ways than one. She looks like a different person in her new clothes and learns everything so quickly."

Mark had a slight pained expression when he said, "She may not want to come back and live with two bachelors."

Slick said quietly, "She'd come home tonight if she thought she had learned everything. She's just doing this because Edd and the Lambshead think she needs to."

Edd said, "I guess we need to make her a room so she can have some privacy, but we can't just stack rocks like we did for the garden and the jug cellar. I wish we had something to make mortar like they used for the station."

"Well, they've got that quarry and the old lime kiln over at Fort Concho. There ain't no soldiers there now, and I don't see why you can't get some for mortar. That's what they used when they built this station."

"I'll need some way to haul it," Edd noted.

"With the business slowing down at Fort Belknap, you might be able to pick up a rig from somebody moving on. Why don't you go east with us when we come back through," asked Ross.

"I'll give that some thought," Edd said. "If I'm gonna be able to haul my liquor, I need a rig, anyhow."

The next couple of days were spent in preparing for Edd's trip.

"It will be a good opportunity to check on Mattie," he told Mark.

"I'll take ol' Snuffy and the stone boat to gather rocks while you're gone," Mark planned.

"I shouldn't be gone much more than a week, if that long," Edd prompted. "If you stay busy, it won't seem so lonesome around here."

"The coaches will be coming through and I can get word back and forth with Jess," Mark said confidently. "I've stayed by myself before. I'll be just fine."

"I know you will, Mark. Just keep your pistol with you. Remember what happened the last time I left."

"Yes, sir. I'm just glad I don't have to worry about Jess and that baby this time." Mark seemed up to the challenge and added, "Hawk will let me know if there is someone around."

"You know, that dog has become an expert at doing his job and staying out of the way. I don't know what we'd do without him, but I forget he is around," Edd testified.

"Have you noticed him checking out the stage passengers? He don't bother nobody, but he passes judgment on every one of them." Mark's eyes were full of pride.

Edd agreed, "Yep, and he's a real good yardstick. You listen to his instincts, 'specially when you're here by yourself. I'm glad you mentioned him. It will be a comfort to my mind."

When the east bound came through, Edd was ready to go with it. He told Mark, "I'll be back with us a wagon. I hope to get one we can use single or double. I'll probably just buy one animal to pull it home and we can hitch double with ol' Snuffy when we need to. It's been so long since we have sent Snuffy with the stage, he's about to forget the route."

Mark grinned, "Yes, sir. When he rolls his eyes and gets them rollers in his nose, I threaten him with a stage run."

Edd's tone turned serious. "You take care of yourself, and the station. I can't have you hurt. You've really stepped up, and you are my right arm."

Mark blinked, "Thank you, sir. You take care, too. Give my regards to those at Mountain Pass, and say hello to Miss Mattie."

With a shout from its driver, the coach left at a gallop.

Mark stayed busy hauling rocks and piling them outside the station, as well as turning the ground for his spring garden. It wasn't time to plant yet, but he shoveled manure across the corral fence, and worked it into his ground.

When the westbound rolled in, Bozy had Mark a special surprise.

He said, "Mark, I brought you a newspaper. I know you do most of your readin' in the Good Book, but you might need to know what's goin' on in the country."

Mark said excitedly, "Thanks, Mr. Bozy. I may not go to bed quite as early while I'm here by myself."

Bozy said, "When you get through with it, let Edd read it. When y'all get done, I'll take it on a run west and trade it for somethin'."

"I'll take real good care of it, Mr. Bozy," Mark promised.

"I know you will," Bozy said. "There's some more folks down the line that need to know what's rumblin' back east."

"You mean there's more than one purpose for you bringing me the paper," Mark asked?

"I guess it's like killin' two birds with one rock," Bozy replied. "I guess when you've driven a stage as far as I have, you hate unnecessary trips."

Mark said, "Yes, sir. Uncle Edd went for a wagon, but I know he went to see Miss Mattie too. Jess went to learn from Dee and Miss Lambshead how to cook and act, but it wasn't just to learn. It was to keep down trouble. I guess you ain't the only one with more than one purpose."

Bozy grinned as he pointed up toward the graves on the other side of the creek. "I guess if anyone understands two birds with one rock, it's you."

CHAPTER 18

The Winds of Change

W HEN MARK SETTLED IN FOR the night, he called Hawk in to sleep by the fire. He barred the door, fed his dog, and ate a supper of cornbread and gravy. He set the lamp on the table, and opened up the newspaper.

The paper was printed in Anderson, South Carolina. It was called the Anderson Intelligencer and was dated January 3, 1861. The headline read, GLORIOUS INDEPENDENCE! SOUTH CAROLINA FOREVER! THE SECESSION ORDINANCE PASSED DECEMBER 20, 1860.

There were several words in the headline that were not in Mark's vocabulary, but by reading the articles, he got the general idea. When he read the Secession Ordinance, he learned that South Carolina had ratified the US Constitution in April of 1788. The State Assembly voted to repeal that action and dissolve that union.

He didn't know how far it was to South Carolina, or how Bozy got his hands on a newspaper from there. He did know that there seemed to be a lot of people with stirred up emotions. He could not know that these events were going to eventually affect his family.

Over at Mountain Pass, the Lambsheads were letting the news soak in, as well. Katherine Lambshead had been raised in Alabama and she had received news by mail from her family. She knew that her slave-owning relatives were extremely dissatisfied with the election of Abraham Lincoln, and there was serious talk of Alabama following the example of South Carolina.

In spite of the nervous discussions between the Lambsheads, Dee and Jess continued to trade their skills. Because she had used stone knives to skin and cook with, Jess was a whiz with a good metal knife. Dee marveled at her skill and let her cut up most of the meat.

Dee, on the other hand, was an excellent seamstress. She was able to teach Jess about cloth instead of leather, and how to make her stitches tiny and evenly spaced.

One of Dee's favorite times of the day was when they read the Bible ideas. Her questions were humble and sincere.

Dee told her, "Honey, if everybody had a heart like yours, there wouldn't be no troubles back east."

Four days later, Edd rolled in to Mountain Pass in a wagon pulled by a big sorrel mule. The wagon was loaded with planks and had a wagon tongue with a double tree on top of the load.

Carson Lambshead said, "Edd, that's a pretty good load for that mule. What do you need all that lumber for?"

Edd called Carson closer and said in a low voice, "I've decided to add a room on the side of the station, instead of trying to partition off one inside. This is the roofing material."

"I see," Lambshead returned. "You addin' it for the girl?"

"Yeah," Edd confirmed. "It won't be hard to come off the side. We can put in a window, and a small fireplace."

"When are you gonna tell her?"

"I'm just gonna let her see it when she gets there," Edd said. "I see you've got a tongue. Why didn't you get a team?"

"Well, I didn't want the company squawkin' about feedin' my stock, and this mule will match up with ol' Snuffy if we need to. I'll be gone on my business runs with this mule and I won't need a team for those runs."

"I'll quit meddlin'," Carson promised. "I shouldn't have got in your business. Looks like to me that you know what you're doin'."

"Aw, I value your opinion. After all, I made a special trip over here for advice," Edd said sincerely. "How's that girl makin' it?"

"Beats all I ever saw," said Lambshead. "Seems like you just show her somethin' one time and she's got it."

"I'll tell you!" Edd was in full agreement when he said, "You ought to see her and that boy take on a task. They seem to have guaranteed our safety from the Comanches all by themselves."

"I think that besides their brains, what makes 'em such a wonder is that they both are so openly honest," Carson inserted.

"Yeah, there don't seem to be a devious bone in their bodies." Carson asked, "How much longer do you think she'll be over here?"

"I guess we need to let the women folk tell us," replied Edd. "They'll probably know better than we will. That wife of yours is as wise and good as there is in the country. You are a very lucky man."

Lambshead corrected, "I am a very blessed man. The Good Lord deserves all that credit."

That evening at supper, Edd mentioned all that was going on to the east. "The word is that South Carolina pulled out of the Union the day after the soldiers left Fort Belknap. The government must have had a pretty good idea that it was going to happen."

Katherine Lambshead informed, "My people in Alabama wrote that secession is imminent there."

Edd said, "They already pulled out on the eleventh of January, and there is to be a move for Texas to join in later this month."

"I hate to see such rash action," stated Carson. "I know that many did not like the election of Mr. Lincoln, but he is not to even be inaugurated until March. The could at least wait to see what he would do, before they go off halfcocked."

"I don't know what it will do to our business," speculated Edd. "If we are no longer part of the United States, they won't want to run the mail through here."

"It sounds like it's gone so far, that all we can do now is pray," murmured Katherine.

The next morning, Edd pulled out for Valley Creek. With the rolling terrain, he didn't push the single mule and it was mid-afternoon before he rolled up at the station.

Mark was impressed with all his uncle had brought home with him.

He said, "Uncle that is a good-looking rig, and a good stout mule."

"Yeah, ol' Pulltight ain't big enough to use yet and we might need something of our own before long. The folks back east are cuttin' up somethin' fierce."

"Yes, sir. Bozy brought me a newspaper from South Carolina. I don't understand it all, but I can tell there might be a tussle before it's all over," Mark reported.

"Let's hope they come to their senses before that happens," Edd suggested. "If all the slave states pull out of the Union, they will probably move the mail run north.

"Do we need to fix that room, then?"

Edd said, "We ain't doing a whole lot else this time of the year. We might as well since we might not move with the mail run. The stage line won't need this station and we might just stay here."

Mark was convinced. He said, "I'll help unload the wagon. What are we going to do with this lumber?"

Edd answered, "I thought we'd build a room on the outside instead of inside. This is the roofing material."

Mark said, "That's sensible. As we gather more rock, we can stack it where we need it. We won't have to carry each one through the door and across the room."

"I'll make a trip to Fort Chadbourne tomorrow for mortar material and you can look for some good saplings to use for rafters. We'll lay our rock flush to the building to just under the overhang of the roof. We can slope the roof of the room the same drop as the station roof."

"How many rafters will we need?"

"We won't need more than four. We are just talking about a room big enough to keep the fireplace from setting the house on fire," Edd replied. "We can put a window in it for ventilation with a heavy shutter that bars from the inside."

"I saw some good saplings when we hunted the buffalo," remembered Mark. "I'll take ol' Snuffy and skin them home."

"No, I need ol' Snuffy to double up with the new mule to haul the load from Chadbourne. You can wait till you change out the stage team, and take one of the mules that come in."

"If I have to make more than one trip, I'll change out mules."

"That's good thinkin'," replied Edd. "If I get a real early start, maybe I can be home before dark."

It took two weeks of steady labor for the pair to complete the ten by ten room on the north side of the station. They had knocked a hole in the wall of the station and framed in a door. A fireplace had been placed on the east end of the room with a chimney as tall as the peak of the station.

Uncle Edd explained, "We need it as tall as the peak so it will draw well."

On the west wall, there was a window. This would allow for fresh air to come in when the weather was warm. Stone buildings tend to be cooler in hot weather, and warmer in cold weather than wooden structures.

It was the first of March 1861. Much had happened during the fortnight since Bozy had brought the newspaper. Texas had passed a referendum on secession on February 23, and passions were running rampant on both sides of the issue in advance of Lincoln's inauguration March 4.

News was the most important thing traveling the stage line these days. Passengers were anxious to get to their destinations in these uncertain times, and the amount of mail had greatly increased.

Jess had sent word that she was ready to come home, and Edd had sent for her to wait just a few days longer. Mark worked like two men trying to complete their project because he was more ready than Jess was. Edd finally sent word for her to come on the stage.

Ross delivered a message saying, "She wants Mark to come and get her. She has a surprise that she can't carry on the stage."

Mark said, "I can borrow the new wagon and go get her."

Ross said knowingly, "No, just ride a mule and lead her one. That's the way she wants it."

Edd chuckled, "Demandin' little cuss, ain't she?"

Ross said, "It means a lot to her, Edd."

Edd turned to Mark, "Alright, Mark. You can take ol' Snuffy and Brazos when you get ready."

Brazos was the mule that Edd bought with the wagon.

Mark was excited, "If I start pretty quick, I can make it before dark. We can come back first thing in the morning. We've got a little surprise of our own."

Mark started stirring around making preparations. Obviously amused, Slick uncharacteristically spoke up, "Didn't take 'im long to make up his mind."

Sure enough, just as the sun dropped over the western horizon, Mark rode into the yard at Mountain Pass Station. He was greeted by Carson Lambshead who told him, "Tend to your stock and your dog, son. We'll wait supper on you."

Mark said, "Thank you, sir. I'll hurry."

Carson went into the house and announced Mark's arrival.

Jess was busy helping to get the meal on the table when Dee said, "Go on out dar and hep 'im, gal. We wuz gettin' food on the table befo' you came, and we kin handle it, now!"

Jess looked at Mrs. Lambshead and the lady smiled and nod-ded. Jess walked up behind Mark, who was unsaddling Brazos.

She said shyly, "I'm glad to see you."

Mark whipped around to face her and his smile lit up the dusky light. "I'm so glad to see you, too."

There was no embrace because both were afraid of making the other one uncomfortable. They stood silent, looking at each other, for what seemed like a long time.

Mark said, "I'll jerk this saddle, and wash up."

Jess said, "Yes, the food is ready."

After the meal, Jess made sure to carry the scraps to Hawk. Biscuits and gravy had been conveniently thrown in with them.

The Lambsheads and Dee did most of the talking after the supper chores were finished. Jess and Mark didn't say much about their activities because neither wanted to spoil their respective surprises.

Before dawn, Jess was up preparing breakfast. She was eager to show Mark she could make biscuits, and wanted to be ready to leave after first light. Everyone complemented on her meal. Mark especially enjoyed the biscuits. He only ate four! While Dee and Jess cleaned up, Mark went out to saddle the mules.

When Jess came out, he asked, "Where's this big surprise you can't carry on a stagecoach, but you can carry on a mule?"

Jess went into the corral where Carson Lambshead was milking. She put a rope halter on the heifer, and led her out to Mark. She told him, "I had to call her something, and Dee thought Rosebud sounded nice. She's ready to be led home."

Mark was pleased and said, "Rosebud it is. It looks like you've done a good job gentling her."

Carson cautioned, "She might not want to go when she realizes her ma ain't goin'. Be sure and keep her penned up secure for at least a couple of weeks so she won't show up back over here. We ain't the only ones that like milk for breakfast."

Mark said, "I haven't brought you any hog meat, yet. I don't want to be owing you."

Carson reassured him, "The next cold spell, I'll ride over and we'll have a hog killin'."

Mark said, "We'll look forward to it."

The two tied Jess's belongings to her saddle and Mark took the heifer's lead rope. They rode west for the sixteen-mile trip.

After lunch, the pair rode up to the home station from the southeast. Because of the rock corral fence, Mark didn't think Jess would notice the addition of the room on the north side of the building. However, "She who watches" lived up to her name.

"The station has been made bigger," she noticed.

"That's your surprise! Come on in and look at what we've done," he beamed.

They tied the mules to the gateposts and turned the heifer in the corral. Edd met them at the door. He greeted Jess warmly, but he let Mark guide her to the door of the new room.

Mark said, "We made this room for you, Jess. You will have some place to get away from some of the rough characters who come through here. We thought it might make you feel more at home here."

Jess was appreciative, "I thank you for your kindness, but I don't know if there is a way to feel more at home than I already felt."

Edd said quietly, "Jess, we already knew you are a lady, and hopefully, we treated you that way. This tells everybody that comes through here that you are."

Mark interjected, "Yes, and when it's cold, you'll always have a place by the fire. When you want it, you'll always be able to open the window for fresh air."

"It is a large space for me to sleep. It seems empty."

Edd laughed, "You can put anything you want to in here. Men folks don't know how a lady wants her room. We left it for you to fix it like you want it."

She examined the window and how the bar worked. She noticed the latch on the door, which had a latchstring that could be pulled in to keep others from opening it from the big room.

Mark saw her looking at the latch. "You won't have to let anybody in, if you don't want to."

She said, "If the teepee flap is closed in a Comanche camp, no one will try to enter."

"You're talking about neighbors. What about enemies?" Edd asked.

"I hope we don't have enemies in the station," she said.

Mark said, "I hope we don't either, but we've had 'em in here before."

The rest of the day was spent in several different activities. One was getting the heifer settled in, as she was bawling for her momma. They decided to pen her in the garden as she would be weaned before planting time. They dug a hole to set an empty barrel in for water so it would not be too tall for he, and gave her some hay.

One of the roosters was boiled and they had chicken and dumplings for supper. Jess had learned the recipe from Dee.

Mark showed off how Pulltight was responding to voice commands. When placed in the driving lines, he understood gee, haw, step up, and whoa. They built a fire in the new fireplace and Jess moved her bedding in her room. They were about to bed down for the night and Jess said, "I can't remember ever being by myself to sleep. If it won't keep me from being a lady, I would like to leave the door open."

Edd said, "Honey, there ain't never been a question that you are a lady with us. It's your door, you be the judge of when it's proper to close it."

She nodded with a satisfied look and they all went to bed.

The next morning, Edd said, "I'll help with the stage at noon. Today, they'll eat here and go on the twelve miles to Chadbourne. When they leave, I'm gonna get the wagon loaded and head to a place called Waco. It's closer than Austin, and I won't have to cross any big rivers. There's lots of folks headed farther south because of the war talk and I should be able to sell the whole load to the saloons in the settlement.

"Is that through Indian country," Mark asked?

"Son, this is all Indian country. The Comanche's seem to leave us alone because of Screech Owl and I will do my best to avoid trouble. Even when we were back home, there was always risk to haul a load of squeezin'," Edd reasoned.

Mark looked thoughtful, "Don't get mixed up with no trouble in Waco and be careful when and with who you decide to share a jug."

Edd teased, "Dog, if you don't get more like your Granny every day. Try to remember that you ain't my momma."

Mark winced. "I ain't tryin' to boss you. I just worry about you."

Jess said in a low voice, "We won't be around to take care of things while you are 'sleeping from the jug'."

Edd's manner turned serious. "I thank you both for carin' about me. I'll try to keep my mind on business and gettin' on home."

After the stage pulled out just after mid-day, Edd hitched the new mule to the wagon loaded with jugs covered with a tarp. He said, "No need temptin' folks by showing off."

Mark asked, "How long will you be gone, Uncle?"

"Near as I can figure, it'll take about a week to get there, and a week to get back. If I allow a couple or three days to finish my business, I should be back in about seventeen or eighteen days. If I'm a little longer, don't get to frettin'."

"We'll keep the place looked after," Mark promised.

"I know you will. You've done a lot of growin' up in the last six months. I guess you had to," Edd concluded. "You've got some good help in Jess and you can go to the Lambsheads if you need something. Keep your guns loaded and handy."

Jess and Mark watched the wagon 'til it rolled out of sight.

CHAPTER 19

Freedom's Definitions

EDD TRAVELED EAST FOLLOWING THE instructions he had received from Ringo Smith. He kept on a due east trek that led him to a crossing on Pecan Bayou. He then kept his trek east which took him a little north of the headwaters of the Leon River. When he struck the Bosque, he followed it southeast to the Waco settlement where it merged with the Brazos.

He had seen smoke from two different Indian camps, but he had not been accosted. He felt like someone was watching him for part of his trip and he had his rifle and horse pistol ready. He was thankful for no trouble when he rolled into the Waco settlement.

When he rolled down the main street, he was looking for establishments that might be interested in what he had to sell. He rolled to a stop in front of a building with a sign with the crude message "Ax Brady Salune." He mumbled to himself, "Hmm, a country boy. Maybe he's honest."

When he set the brake, he noticed a greasy looking individual with long hair and a long, full beard approaching with purpose in his step. The man growled, "Hey, you. What you got in the wagon?"

The man's manner flew all over Edd's sensibilities.

He growled back, "Well, whatever it is, it belongs to me. If I ever get ready to tell you, I'll let you know."

The man yelled, "Don't give me none of your guff. I want to know what's in that wagon!" As he said this, he started to pull back the wagon sheet.

Edd's move surprised the man as well as all those who had stopped to look. With one motion, he came off the wagon seat with his pistol in his hand and took the man over backwards by his long hair. He placed his right foot on the man's throat and placed the business end of the gun barrel against his forehead. There was total silence in the crowd when he said, "It's loaded with caskets, but you ain't gettin' one. We'll just kick you off in the river, and let the catfish have you."

There was a mixture of fear and pleading in the eyes of the man and Edd was ready to make good his threat. However, he heard a shout as a man wearing a star on his chest came running down the street. "What do you think you are doing to my deputy?"

"I'm about to keep him from having to take any more manners lessons!"

Edd uncocked the pistol and stepped back from the prostrate deputy. "He didn't tell me he was a deputy and what he did say to me started the ball rollin'."

The sheriff was about to take Edd off to jail when two well-dressed men stepped from the crowd. The larger of the two said, "Sheriff, I am Frank Terry, and this is Tom Lubbock. We have just come from Austin as representatives to the Secession Assembly. This deputy was abrupt and abusive, and did not identify himself. This man acted in a manner to defend his freedoms."

The sheriff was obviously impressed with the two men and must have known them by reputation. He said, "Alright, I won't haul you to jail, this time. You just see that you ain't so quick to go on the warpath in my town."

Edd said, "Sir, I just came from two hundred miles to the west to bring that load to Waco. I've not slept real well in about a week, guarding that load. I want to sell what's there, but I ain't gonna have no greasy, lowlife, goat-smelling louse just come up here and take over."

The sheriff had the hint of a grin and asked, "Well, sir, if I asked politely, would you tell me what you are loaded with?"

Edd said, "I'd be happy to, sir. It's loaded down with jugs of good, sour mash whiskey. It's all for sale except two jugs. One is to take with me on the trip home and the other is for these two men."

He indicated Terry and Lubbock.

A man wearing an apron was standing in front of the door to the establishment. He stepped forward and proclaimed, "Sour mash! I would buy the whole load, if it samples out good."

Edd stuck out his hand. "I'm Edd Singletary and I've come a long way to meet you."

The man returned, "I'm Ax Brady and I'm glad you came."

Edd said, "We can haggle on a price, but I want empty jugs to replace the full ones. I might want to bring you some more. Pull back that sheet and pick your poison. That way you won't think I've got a special jug for sampling."

Brady said eagerly, "We can handle all three of those things."

He pulled back the sheet, and picked up one of the jugs.

After Edd and Brady had made their business deal, Edd sat down at a table with Lubbock and Terry. He said, "I want to thank you men for backing me up out there, and the drinks are on me."

Terry said, "We thank you very much, but don't feel obligated."

Edd replied, "You didn't feel obligated when you did me a good turn."

Lubbock said, "No, nothing like that. We just believe in standing up for our rights and appreciate those who do."

Edd asked, "Didn't I hear you say you had been representatives at the Secession Assembly?"

Terry answered, "Yes, sir. Texas is no longer part of the United States.

We won't be told by the government that we must give up our livelihoods; and whether you hold with slavery or not, it's our right to make our own decisions.

Lubbock jumped in, "We like the way you stand up for yourself. We will probably be forming a force from Texas to help defend the states that hold with slavery."

Edd scratched his head, "You just pulled out of the United States. Are you talking about fightin' about it?"

Terry said, "There's seven states who are pullin' out. That new president they are fixin' to inaugurate ain't gonna let us go."

Edd said, "He ain't even President yet. Maybe we ought to give him a chance before we start a tussle."

Lubbock grinned, "You didn't give that deputy a whole lot of time before you were gonna give him a free trip to the Promised Land."

Edd said humbly, "Well, it just struck me the wrong way."

Both were smiling, but serious when Terry said, "Exactly!"

"We've just spent about a month listenin' to those who would have us wait. We had to hold a special convention because Sam Houston didn't want us to join the other states in a Confederacy. The people voted late this month to ratify our secession statement and they'll vote on the Confederacy soon after Lincoln is inaugurated. We've already rolled the dice, man," Lubbock said with passion.

"Well, I guess you boys feel as strongly about this as I did that sorry excuse for a deputy," Edd concluded.

Terry said, "It comes down to this question. Whose freedom is more important, ours or the slaves?"

Lubbock told him, "When we get all these elections over with, we'll be organizing a force from Texas. We are impressed with capable men who fiercely defend what they think is right. If and when you hear the call, look us up. We'll welcome you with open arms.

Terry said, "We are going to meet with the Confederate government in Montgomery first. When we get back, we'll probably organize in Houston. Just take a riverboat from here on the Brazos down to Fort Bend. I have a plantation there. If I'm already gone, my people will get you where you need to be."

Edd said, "I've got a young nephew and another youngster look out for. It will take a lot of thought before I jump off into the fray."

Lubbock said, "We all have obligations, but don't think too long. You'll be left behind and we need men like you. I'll remind you that you didn't think about that deputy. You acted."

Edd said, "I see your point."

They passed a pleasant evening, but Edd limited his drinking. He had a lot to think about.

The next morning, Edd bought supplies to take to Valley Creek. The load was considerably lighter because of the empty jugs.

He said, "Step up, Brazos!" and they started west.

Edd considered the name of the mule and thought of the river of the same name. It was certainly a lifeline to the state with its headwaters considerably north and west of Valley Creek. From Waco south, it even provided decent transportation down to the sea. Once you passed Washington on the Brazos, where it merged with the Navasota, the river passage was even better.

Edd had seen the prices of goods in the settlement of Waco, and decided that he could get a better deal on his needed supplies at a settlement on the Brazos. It was cheaper to ship them up from the coast by riverboat than to have them freighted down the Butterfield Trail. With the soldiers abandoning forts, the pressure from Indian attack would get more frequent.

Edd wondered how things were running back at Valley Creek. He couldn't know that it had been an eventful week and a half there, also.

Two mornings after Edd headed east, Mark stepped out of the door just before the sun peeped over the horizon. He was holding one of the biscuits that Jess had made in one hand and he had a cup of coffee in the other hand. He was thinking how pleasant and still the morning was when he heard the sound of a screech owl.

Jess had noiselessly stepped out the door behind him and he jumped when she spoke. "It is Screech Owl. He wishes to talk."

Mark asked, "How do you know it ain't a real owl?"

"I know his call," she said simply. "We should step out into the yard to let him know he is welcome."

Mark was always impressed with what Jess knew; and when she seemed sure of herself, he complied with her suggestions. He walked out into the middle of the yard with the girl at his side.

Sure enough, the Comanche brave stepped into the open on the other side of the creek. Jess spoke to him in his own language and he started forward across the creek leading a black mare. He was carrying the two saddlebags Mark had traded for Jess. They were empty.

Jess told Mark, "It is customary to offer him food. I'll get a blanket and the biscuits I made for the coach passengers. I can make more before it gets here."

She quickly disappeared into the station.

By the time Screech Owl walked up, she had returned. She spread out the blanket and placed the food in the middle. She told Mark, "Hold up your hand with the flat part forward. Tell him he is welcome and motion for him to sit down and eat."

Mark spoke the words and made the motions. Jess translated and Screech Owl sat on the blanket. He took a biscuit, and tasted it tentatively. He nodded and took a bigger bite.

Jess said, "Ask questions like you are talking with a relative or friend you haven't seen for a while. He will come around to telling you what he wants in his own good time."

With Jess translating, they talked about the weather, the countryside, Little Horse, and anything else Mark could come up with.

Finally, Screech Owl came to the point.

Jess said, "He came to make a trade. He wants to trade you that black mare for those saddlebags full of sugar."

Mark said, "That's not a fair trade. That's a good-looking mare, and she's sure worth a whole lot more than two saddlebags of sugar."

Jess said, "Don't act like you are displeased. He will think you want more and he will be offended. He wants to give you a gift without losing prestige with his people. He knows you saved his son twice and he feels he owes you."

Mark said, "He doesn't owe me. I just treasure his friendship."

Jess said, "I know that mare. She is about three years old, and he was training her for Meadow Lark. She is one of his prize possessions and you need to feel honored."

Mark said, "Tell him I will trade, if he will also take food for his journey."

She said, "No, don't offer more. That would be an insult. Complete the trade, then invite the braves with him to come and eat."

He asked, "What braves?"

She said, "There are three on the other side of the creek."

He said, "Well, talk to him and make me say the right thing."

After a short conversation, she took the saddlebags and handed them to Mark. She said, "They can get salt, but the sugar is something they can only get from white men."

Mark said, "Tell him I will go and get it."

He took the bags and went into the station. When Mark returned, there were three more Comanches there with four horses. Mark motioned for them all to sit.

When the men sat down, Mark handed the bags to Screech Owl. He took them and handed the lead rope to Mark. Mark led the mare out in the middle of the yard and rubbed his hands all over her. She let him pick up each foot without any hesitation. Mark could see she was well trained and completely gentle. He looked at Screech Owl and nodded his appreciation of the fine animal.

He said, "Jess, tell him I've never seen a finer mare. We will take good care of her."

Jess conveyed the message and Screech Owl nodded.

One of the other braves said something to Screech Owl, and the Comanches began to make ready to leave.

Jess said, "Mark, send the other biscuits for the brave who watches on Sentinel Hill. I'll tell them, but you say the words."

Mark did as he was instructed and the men took the food and the sugar. They mounted and crossed the creek, and vanished over the upper bank.

When they had gone, Mark asked, "How did you know there was one on the hill?"

"Prairie Dog told Screech Owl that the flying wagon is coming. I noticed him watching the hill for a signal. I saw a white rag waving at the top," she explained.

"They probably know the stage schedule better than we do," he said. "We'd better make some more of your biscuits."

Jess went into the house to do just that and he took the young mare to the corral. After the stage rolled out, Mark and Jess went out to look at the new mare.

Mark said, "I guess that mare belongs to Uncle Edd. I traded his sugar for her."

Jess said, "I am sure he won't worry about that."

Mark said, "No, I 'spect he wouldn't. She reminds me of his mare that we sold when we left home. He called her Cricket, so I think I'll call this one Katydid. Maybe Katy for short."

Jess asked, "What is a Katydid?"

He said, "That's another kind of hoppin' bug. I sure hope she don't live up to that name."

"Comanches are good with horses, but they don't ride like white men," Jess cautioned. "They direct the horse with their legs and they get on and off the other side than white men do. You'll need to get her used to a bit, because all they have used on her is a war bridle."

"Can you help me rig one up? I'm dyin' to try her out!"

When she had retrieved the rope they would need, Jess walked into the corral. She held out her hand and talked low in Comanche. She made a loop in the middle of the rope, and slipped it over the lower jaw of the mare.

When she had adjusted it behind the bottom teeth, she pulled it up snug where it wouldn't fall from Katy's mouth. She placed the two ends of the remainder of the rope on each side of the horse's neck and told Mark, "Get on this side, she is ready."

He said, "She sure seems to know you."

Jess confirmed, "She was part of the family. Screech Owl spent much time with her. She was to carry his wife and baby."

When he was straddle of the mare, he gathered up the reins. The mare began to stretch out her nose, fretting against the pressure.

Jess said, "Loosen your hold on her. She listens to your feet and legs. Just sit still and lower your hands to her neck. I'll tell you what to do."

Mark lowered his hands to the mare's withers, and relaxed his legs.

When he just sat there, the mare stood like her feet were nailed to the ground. As long as Mark didn't move, the mare didn't move.

Jess said, "Pick up the reins, and point your toe to the right."

When Mark did as she said, the mare turned to the right. When he pointed his left toe, she turned left.

Jess said, "Now turn both toes out and squeeze her with your legs just a little."

When Mark complied, the mare began to back up is a straight line.

When he stopped squeezing, she stopped backing. He said, "She does it so easy."

Jess said, "Comanche horses need to be guided with your legs. You can't shoot a bow with one hand."

"Meadow Lark wouldn't need to shoot from her back," Mark said. "She would probably have belonged to Little Horse when he got old enough," she said.

"Well, why didn't he save her for Little Horse?" he asked.

"I think it was too painful for him to look at her and think of Meadow Lark," she said. "Screech Owl knows that I love the mare, too. He knows she will be treated well."

"We'll be easy with her teaching to take a bridle and saddle," he said. "I 'spect she'll teach me more than I teach her, but I'll try to use it on Gimpy's colt out of Jackrabbit's stallion."

"I was surprised that Gimpy took the stallion, I never saw a fall colt in the Comanche herds," she said.

Mark said, "Say, that's right. Uncle Edd says it takes nearly a year for a mare to carry a colt. A fall colt ain't common, but I guess 01' Gimpy has to do things in her own way. Pulltight was born late in the year."

When the westbound stage rolled through the next day, there was a passenger on board named Dude Heald. He was lean and as tough as a blacksnake whip. He wasted no motion, and he seemed to take in everything at a glance. After the meal of cornbread and stew, he asked, "You kids here by yourselves?"

Mark said, "Yes, sir. We are right now, but Uncle Edd should be back in a day or two."

"Well, y'all seem to have things well in hand. That was a sure enough good stew. Where'd you get that buffalo jerky?"

"We made it ourselves," Mark informed him.

"I'd like to buy a couple of saddlebags full of some like that. I'm headed out west of Van Horn Wells to scout for the army. You got any you might sell?" Heald asked.

"We would sell you some, but I don't know how to price it to you," Mark returned.

"Did you take care of the hide?" Heald queried.

"Yes, sir. Jess cured both of them."

"Can I look at 'em'?" the man asked.

The rolled-up hides were brought out from behind some of the supply barrels in the corner and unrolled for Heald's inspection.

He whistled and said, "Say, that's good work. I don't believe a Comanche could do better. Are they for sale?"

Mark said honestly, "Like the jerky, Mr. Heald, I don't know how to price it."

Heald said, "Young man, I believe you are an honest man. I want you to know that I am, too. The mark of a good horse trade is when both parties are happy. How about I tell you what I'll give and you can decide if you'll take it?"

Mark looked him in the eye and said, "That seems fair to me."

"These are quality items and hard to come by without lots of luck or lots of work. I'll give twenty dollars each for the buffalo robes, and ten dollars for the jerky. Do you know your sums enough to know how much that is?" Heald offered.

"Yes, sir. That would be fifty dollars. That's a lot of money," Mark observed.

"It is, but it's fair. I might want to do business with you again sometimes. If your satisfied, then I am," Heald stated.

The goods and the money changed hands and the stage rolled west in short order.

Jess had remained silent throughout the transaction, but she spoke up when the stage left. "You do not think we need the meat or the robes?"

"I know we put a lot of work into getting those things, but we need to have some money of our own that doesn't come from the whiskey business. The more we read the Good Book at night, the more problems I have with that still," he said.

She relayed her study with Dee and said, "We talked much about the Good Book each night I stayed at Mountain Pass. With the things that are going on in the east, we talked much about slavery."

He nodded, "I guess with her being a slave, it interests her very much."

Jess said, "She is not a slave. She lets people believe that because Texas doesn't allow free black people to come in. The Lambsheads treat her like family, and they keep down trouble with the way things look. I guess it's like me changing my clothes and hair to keep down trouble."

"I wouldn't have thought of it in that way, but her secret is safe with me," he said sincerely.

Jess said, "If we must make money in the right manner, then we need to spend it in the right manner. We need to use it as God would have us to use."

Mark said, "There ain't a church out here to give anything to, but we can use some to help other folks. There ain't no doubt that God had his hand in us getting the buffalo, and then dropping someone in our lap that wanted to buy it."

Jess agreed. She looked Mark and said, "When Uncle Edd gets back, we can hunt some more before the weather gets too hot. Meat will be easier to haul home with the wagon."

Mark chuckled, "Always lookin' and plannin'."

On the eighth day of Edd's absence, the weather turned off cold. The next morning, Carson Lambshead showed up in his wagon with the necessities needed for a hog killing. He said, "I told you I'd come when we got a cold snap. How many do you want to kill?"

Mark said, "We'll get you one and then get us one. We won't need much more than that in the smokehouse, right now."

Carson said, "Good enough. How are we gonna get em?"

Mark scratched his head and then pitched his idea. "Let's tie that heifer to a post and then coax them hogs into the empty garden. I think there is still some soured mash left in one of Uncle Edd's barrels. He likes to keep a little to help start the next batch. I think those hogs will come in for that, and we can shoot the ones we want as we get to 'em."

Carson teased, "We might as well pickle that pork before we butcher it.

We need to save as many steps as possible."

173

Mark and Carson laughed at the joke, but Jess expression never changed. She would wait until Lambshead left before she asked Mark what pickle meant. They loaded a couple of barrels on the slide and brought them full of water from the creek. They built a fire and put the wash pot on to heat water. They also used every container they could think of to put on the fire to heat more water. They dug a hole in such a way that a barrel rested solidly in it at about a forty-five-degree angle. The placed that barrel at the edge of a rock shelf that offered a clean place to scrape hogs. With buckets, they flushed off the slab, and they were nearly ready to scrape a hog.

When they had penned the hogs, Carson picked out a good-sized barrow. He waited until the hog was relaxed and eating. He took aim with his rifle and shot the animal in the ear hole. The hog never knew what hit him. They drug him out of the garden and Lambshead "stuck him" so that he would empty of blood.

They put the hog on the slide and carried him to the rock shelf. After they dipped hot water from the wash pot and the other containers, they put enough cold water with it to make the temperature right. Carson explained, "The water needs to be just hot enough that you can quickly dip your middle three fingers in two times in quick succession and then you just can't stand to do it a third time. When it's just that hot, the hair will slip. If it's too hot, you'll set the hair."

When the water was just right, Carson grabbed the right legs and Mark grabbed the left. They stuck the hog in the barrelhead first and pushed him as far as he would go. They sloshed him around in the barrel to get him scalded good and then pulled him out of the barrel. They reversed the carcass and repeated the process.

With the hog lying flat on the rock, Mark and Carson started scraping the animal with their belt knives. The hair and outer layer of skin slipped off leaving a white, clean carcass. Jess didn't remember ever seeing that event and she stood back to stay out of their way.

Mark said, "Jess, if you'll stoke up the fire and refill the pots, we'll do another one in a little while.

When the hog was scraped clean on both sides form the end of his nose to the tip of his tail, Lambshead asked, "Have you got a loose singletree?"

Mark retrieved on and they cut between the bone and the tendon on the hind legs just above the dewclaws. They hooked the ends of the singletree to the proper legs and put the hog back on the slide. They took him over to the corral gate and pulled him up to hang from the overhead gate brace.

The left the slide up under him covered with clean flour sacks that Lambshead had brought with him. They then retrieved the heart, liver, and the sweet breads from the offal. They didn't keep the rest of the innards since Carson didn't intend to make sausage.

They removed the head and placed it in a flour sack.

"Katherine sure makes a good hog head cheese," Carson said.

Each shoulder, each ham, and each side of ribs were placed in separate sacks and loaded in Lambshead's wagon.

When they had completed the second hog and the meat was hung in the smokehouse, Carson said, "It should stay cold enough for that meat to hang for a few days. Then you may want to pack it in some salt to let it cure before you smoke it."

Mark asked, "Do you think it will be okay 'til Uncle Edd gets home? He should be home within the week."

"I'm sure it will, if it don't turn off too warm. Just keep an eye on the weather." Carson advised.

"I sure thank you for your help, Mr. Lambshead," Mark said.

Lambshead returned, "Thank you for the trade. It's not easy finding ham and bacon in this country. I hope that heifer makes a great milk cow."

Mark was appreciative, "She's already a pet thanks to Jess. Like I heard the other day, I'm happy if you are."

"You know I am. You folks be careful, and don't wait on Edd to try some of that fresh pork back strap."

With that, Lambshead mounted the wagon and headed east.

By the time Edd arrived back at the station, the pork had been packed in salt to cured; Katydid had been gentled to a bridle and saddle; the heifer had quit bawling for her momma; and chores had fallen into a comfortable routine. Mark apologized for trading off the sugar without asking and told Edd about selling the jerky and the buffalo robes.

Edd said, "You ain't got to apologize to me. You used your head and made a couple of good deals. That's a fine-looking mare and we can get plenty of buffalo around here. If they will bring that much, it might be a better business than the still."

Mark said, "Yes, sir. You know I have a problem with money from the still."

"I know you do, but that's what I know," said Edd. "With things heatin' up about war, it might not be a business for long."

"What do you mean, Uncle Edd?" asked Mark.

Edd related his experiences in Waco and added, "I'm worried that it might affect the Stage Line. I met some fellers who are big in the politics of Texas and they say we'll be part of the Confederate States in short order. The United States might not send mail through here, after that."

"How do you feel about that?" questioned Mark.

"I don't particular hold with slavery, but I sort of think those who are agin it are not practicin' what they preach. The way Frank Terry puts it, they are tellin' people what they can and can't do when they say you can't tell people what they can and can't do. They are controllin' somebody's freedom as to whether they can control some-body's freedom. You understand?"

Mark said, "I don't hold with slavery, pure and simple. Dee was a slave and Jess was a slave. Neither one was a slave or servant by choice. Dee serves the Lambsheads now because she wants to and that's alright, but I don't like it because others still treat her like a slave."

"I don't like that, either," said Edd. "In both those times, the family they were slaves to came to recognize who they were. The Lambsheads treat Dee like family and that Comanche family knew what they had in Jess. I don't want nobody to be unjustly ruled by anybody and that includes me. I saddle my own broncs and I don't need no jaybird from Washington off in my business."

"Dee and Jess studied that book in the Bible about Philemon. Jess and I have read it and talked about it. The way I read it, it says it don't matter if you are a slave or a slave owner. It just says be a good one! The Book says it don't matter if you are Jew or Greek, or bond or free, Jesus died for all of us," Mark said.

Edd said, "Sometimes when you are quotin' that book, I could swear that your Granny was standin' behind me promptin' you."

Mark's eyes twinkled, "I'll bet that deputy in Waco wished Granny was there readin' to you from the book."

Edd scoffed, "He came close to hearin' Saint Pete read it to him."

Mark said, "I guess I shouldn't make light of somethin' so serious."

Edd said, "It wasn't funny at the time, but I figure he'll approach his duties with a few more manners. I know there was a few snickers about it before I left town."

"Maybe he thought his job made him free to treat people anyway he wanted," Mark surmised.

Edd said, "There's that word again. People's freedoms seem to overlap each other's. Freedom belongs to you! It's like I told you about using that pistol I gave you, there comes a time when you have to protect you and yours. You have to put a value on it and decide what you are willing to give up."

"That's seems to be what the Good Book talks about," said Mark. "Do you want to do what God says, or be free to do what you want to?"

Edd asked, "Is your Granny standin' behind me, again?"

CHAPTER 20

A Change of Direction

THROUGHOUT THE MONTH OF MARCH 1861, with every west-bound coach, there was news of the turmoil in the east. Seven states had seceded before Lincoln was even inaugurated on March 4; and by March 11, there was a new Confederate States of America.

The imaginations of each one carrying news seemed to fan the fires of passion on each side of the issue until fiction became fact and reason was not possible. Those, on the side of maintaining, the Union learned to keep their opinions to themselves while traveling the stage line in Texas.

When it began to look like war could not be avoided, Edd started to make plans to maintain their ability to survive. He kept his ear to the ground with trusted stage drivers as to what the company was apt to do.

Bozy told him, "There's a rumor that the company will move its line to the north of Texas and stop carrying mail through the slave states. They'll give us the chance to move with it, carry their stock to the new route, and abandon this route altogether."

Edd asked, "When do you think that will happen? I don't know, I think they are waiting to see if there's war," he replied. "Don't seem like they'll have to wait long, from what we hear."

Edd took another load of whiskey to Waco, and this time, had no problems with the local deputy. In fact, it seemed the man took pains to avoid Edd.

On the way back, Edd stopped at a little settlement on the Leon River called Stephenville. The population of the town was shrinking because of attacks by the Comanches, and he bought a turning plow from a family who was going back to Louisiana.

When he got back to Valley Creek, it was the first of April. He and Mark took 0l' Snuffy with the plow and made short work of breaking ground in the garden.

When they had their vegetables planted, Mark said, "We'll trust in the Good Lord to bless us with a planting rain."

Edd said, "You bet! I'm ready for some fresh vegetables, but I'm sure counting on those seed we got from the Fort Chadbourne station. I've got my mouth fixed for one of them watermelons."

"Jess is sure gettin' good at cookin' since she stayed with Dee. She might get us fat if we give her something to work with," Mark purposed.

"If we can catch a cool day, we need to butcher those other two hogs and get 'em cured. You need hog meat to season fresh vegetables," Edd said. "We need to scope out some of these meadows to cut fodder, too."

"How much will we need if the stage line moves?" Mark inquired.

"We'll cut like they ain't movin'," Edd stated.

"If the stage line don't need it, we'll have it ourselves. If they do decide to move, we'll need it for ourselves. I intend to stay right here and you've gathered up a bunch of mouths to feed. You've got two mares and one of them is expectin'. You've got a mule and I've got one. I'd like to trade the company out of 0l' Snuffy if they move. You've got goats, hogs, chickens, and a heifer that all have to eat, so I guess we'd better put up all we can."

"I see what you mean," Mark said. "I count my blessings that Ned Brackin did such a good job last year."

"Ned was a man well prepared. He had these critters you traded for and he seemed to be prepared to stay. If he had had a little company here, he probably would have," Edd said.

"I hope he made out well, wherever he wound up," wished Mark.

"I'm sure he did," Edd contended. "Your little meeting up with Screech Owl has taken some worry off of us about the Comanches. Ned had to watch himself all the time without any help. That can wear on a man."

Edd had been learning to handle Katydid by using his legs. He was impressed by the training she had received from Screech Owl and told Mark, "I can see why the Comanches are so feared. With their horses trained like they are, they can do a lot of fighting from the back of a horse. We both need to learn to handle our weapons horseback and we need to work on the mare so she won't be gun shy."

"Yes, sir, and we need to train Gimpy's baby to handle like that," the boy replied.

"I don't imagine it would hurt to train Pulltight, either. That's handy whether it's horse or mule."

"I've got him pullin' light loads, and responding to commands, now. When he gets another year on him, I'll break him to ride."

By the third week of April, the garden was growing well. There was a new litter of pigs, baby chicks were following several hens, and the nanny goat had twin nanny kids. Spring was in full swing, and nature was renewing itself with green grass and baby critters.

The westbound stage clattered into the yard and Ross Vinson stepped down. He handed Mark a newspaper and said, "It's war, son. The Confederates fired on Fort Sumter in Charleston harbor."

"Mr. Ross, I've been dreading it. I may have to kill somebody else sometime, but I don't want it to be in anger. I sure don't want to kill somebody because somebody else is angry at 'em," Mark confided.

Ross Vinson was a man of common sense and he knew it when he heard it. He said, "You said a mouthful. I hope you don't ever have to."

Edd was unhitching the team, but he heard the conversation. He said, "I've always said you kill only in defense of you and yours, but that would include your rights. I won't be run over."

"There's lots of folks that feel like that," Ross reasoned. "I just hope both sides don't get more than they bargained for."

The door to the station was open and good smells were coming from inside. Slick Newton asked, "What is that powerful good smell?"

Mark grinned, "We got fresh eggs, cornmeal mush, and cured ham. One of the pigs I traded Ned out of, and hot coffee."

Ross rubbed his belly and said, "Well, let's not let it sit there and ruin. Let's eat."

Jess had done a good job with the meal, and the stage employees and passengers ate like they had not eaten in a week. There were no leftovers when the meal was finished, and everyone complemented Jess.

Before the coach departed, Edd took Ross to the corral under to pretense of looking at the black mare. When they were alone, he said, "Ross, I guess we need to be checking back up the line with Gilder to see how we stand. I'm thinking about making the trip, and I would like to take somebody with me that I trust. You're the one."

Ross said, "I wouldn't have a problem going with you, but I would need to send word up the line to switch out with drivers going and coming. That would cover the company and not leave us short for a run. It would take a week or so to send word, but we can probably swing it."

"That's fine, and I thank you. I'll wait on word from you," Edd affirmed.

"I figure there are some more folks that would like to have word, like the Lambsheads. They are set up well enough that it would take some time for them to get ready for a change," noted Ross.

By the time all plans have been made, it was the first week of May when they made the trip. They traveled straight through with Ross acting as driver on one leg of the trip while Edd slept. Then Edd would ride shotgun the next leg to let Ross rest. Ross had made all the arrangements and Edd knew he had the right companion for the important meeting with Gilder.

Passions were running high in all the towns over the war, but the two men didn't have the time or inclination to do any debating of the issues. They just stayed focused on their mission. Ross had been able to make the trip arrangements by promising to bring back word and there were lots of people counting on them.

When they met with Gilder, they explained that they needed to know how to prepare for what the company had in mind. "We ain't plannin' to leave you in the lurch, we just need to prepare a little. The other folks you got working for you want us to bring them word, too," Edd informed him.

"I'll tell you boys, it looks like we're already be out of the running to keep operatin' your part of the route. About the time the Confederacy organized in March, the legislature in Washington revoked our contract. We'll stop service through your area the last of June. We're gonna change the route west to a track further north of Texas. We'll make arrangements to move operations at that time. Any of you that want to be part of the new route can sure move with us. We ain't disappointed in none of you, we've just got it to do."

"What are you going to do about the station buildings you are leaving down there?" asked Edd.

"We may come back someday, who knows. In the meantime, you can stay as long as you want. It would be better for them to be kept up than to be abandoned to the Comanches and the elements," Gilder said.

"How do we need to let you know if we'll stay on and make the move?" Ross asked.

"I'm gonna make a trip and talk to each station. I'll start in about a week and a half," answered Gilder.

"I can give you my answer now," said Edd. "We won't make the move from Valley Creek. We'll just look after it 'til y'all get back."

"That's fine, Edd. You and that boy have been an asset and we hate to lose you. I also understand that the stage line is just one of the endeavors at Valley Creek," Gilder replied with a knowing look.

"You know about the girl," Edd asked.

Gilder nodded, "Word travels fast on a stagecoach."

"I've got to figure out how this will affect those young folks. It's sort of like your route move. I didn't exactly put in for it, but I've got it to do," Edd said.

Ross put in his two cents. "If he wasn't gonna do it, I would. That's two-top notch young folks, and we've all claimed 'em."

Gilder agreed, "I think the world of that boy, myself. If I had to choose, I'd run Edd off and keep the kid."

Edd said, "And I'd have to agree with that choice!"

Gilder said, "Edd, you know you get paid after the job is completed. How do you want to arrange to pick up you last pay?"

Edd said, "When you come out, we'll talk trade. I want to keep a certain one of the mules and I probably will want some of the harness and supplies."

Gilder said, "That would keep us from having to move them. I'm sure that will be satisfactory."

On the return trip, Hugh Peoples had a deep conversation about what the war might mean to all of them. He said, "It's already gonna root up you folks from your jobs in Texas. Just don't let Mark get involved, if you can help it. We don't need him shot down over other folks business. We'll need men like him to help us all rebuild."

Edd said, "He won't be, if I can help it. I appreciate your interest and advise."

Peoples told them, "You tell that young man that I'm willing to help with anything he ever needs. I mean that from the bottom of my heart, he's got a friend if he ever needs one."

"Thanks, Hugh. You know, that boy seems to make friends wherever he goes. Something in his nature makes folks naturally like and trust him," Edd commented.

Peoples said, "You know I do."

The return trip let them pass on the news to the drivers, shotgun riders and station agents along the way. Some of them took the news hard, and some took it in stride. Whatever their reaction, they were thankful to know in time to prepare for the change.

Their timing was such that Ross stayed at Fort Belknap to begin his regular run schedule, and Edd traveled on toward Valley Creek. He had an interesting meeting with the Lambsheads at Mountain Pass, and they told him they would have to think about their situation because of Dee. They thought it might be better if they moved with the company to a state that was not still a slave state.

Edd said, "I'm getting pretty set up with those two at Valley Creek. The stage won't travel the run anymore, but I feel like we will still have some folks pass through. I may set it up as a place folks can pick up supplies."

Katherine Lambshead said, "Yes, and you might be far enough from the action that the war won't touch you, much."

Edd raised his eyebrow, "Yes, ma'am. It's that 'much' part that worries me."

When Edd returned to the home station, Jess and Mark took the news without much emotion. Mark said, "We'll make out alright, Uncle Edd. We always have."

Edd asked, "What do you think, Jess?"

She said, "I have no other place to go. I'll do my part in whatever you decide."

"I'm open to suggestions," said Edd. "You two always seem to think things through. If you have an idea, I want to hear it."

"What kind of preparing should we do?" Mark inquired

"I think we need to just keep on with what we've been doing," the man suggested, "we've got a good bit of paper money, I think I'll try to change as much as I can into coin. I'll also try to set in a store of supplies we can sell to those who head this way to get away from the war."

"Where will you set in your supplies?" Mark asked

Edd laughed, "Looks like I need to make another run to see my favorite deputy."

"What do we need to do while you are gone, Uncle Edd?"

Edd scratched his head and said, "We are gonna need a place to put the money I bring back. It needs to be a place nobody will look and one that we won't leave a trail to. Y'all think about it and see what you come up with."

"You need to be careful on your trip, Uncle Edd. If somebody figures out how much money you are carrying, they might try to take it away from you," Mark remarked. "Why don't you take my pistol with you?"

"If they see me loaded for bear, they might know something's up. You need to have it here for just in case," Edd stated.

"Keep it hid with the money," Mark insisted. "We can make out with Grandpa's shotgun. We won't need to hunt and the stagecoach will be through regular."

"I hate to leave you without enough artillery, but that might just make the difference in a pinch," Edd said. "That might be something we need to take in trade instead of money is some more firearms. Folks headed west will have things they will trade for supplies."

"Yes, sir, and they will probably need to buy ammunition," added Mark.

"That's a good idea, Mark. We can keep a big supply to trade, but we'll have it, if we ever need it," Edd agreed. "I'll be loaded heavy coming home, so don't get worried if I am gone more than two weeks."

"We'll do fine," Mark said. "If we have trouble, we'll go to Mountain Pass. There's plenty to do in the garden, and Hawk keeps an eye out."

"I forget about that dog," Edd said. "I'm glad you brought him with us."

Edd left headed east the next morning. He wanted to return before Gilder made his trip through on the stage route. He and Mark made a false bottom for the wooden box that held the food supplies. Edd planned to carry the coin money in that box on the way home. He wore his money belt to carry the nearly eight thousand dollars in paper he wanted to exchange.

Mark had saved his money that he had earned, and he sent all but a hundred dollars with Edd to be exchanged as well. He had secretly kept the money because he had a purpose for it.

When Ross Vinson came through headed east, he pulled him aside and asked, "Mr. Ross, could I ask a favor of you?"

Ross said, "You know I'll help you if I can."

"I want you to take this money and see if you can locate another pistol like Uncle Edd gave me," he said.

"You mean that big ol' thang that shoots for a week?"

Mark confirmed, "That's the one."

"You can't hardly carry one of those. Why do you want two?"

"Mr. Ross, times are gettin' desperate. I want Uncle Edd to have one when he travels by himself and I want one here to protect Jess," he answered.

"Do you think it will cost a hundred dollars?" Ross asked astonished.

185

"I hope not, but I know Uncle Edd paid forty dollars for mine. They might be a little more scarce since the troubles have started," Mark told him.

"Well, I can't promise I can find one, but I'll be glad to try," said Ross.

"I thank you so much. There's not many folks I would give a hundred dollars to," Mark said gratefully.

The next day, a column of soldiers under the command of a Captain Lee came through headed back to reassignment. They had abandoned Camp Stockton and were eager to get out of Texas.

Mark and Jess were polite and accommodating and Captain Lee said, "I thank you for your hospitality and for your attitudes. We haven't been as well received at some of the places we've traveled through."

Mark said, "Sir, the Bible tells us to treat others like we want to be treated."

The Captain said, "If everyone adhered to that one instruction, we wouldn't have this fight we are facing. Then we would only have to worry about the Indians."

Mark paused and then said, "Captain, that instruction seems to have worked for me with the Comanches. We have no trouble with the Antelope band of the Comanches since I helped Screech Owl."

"You know Screech Owl?!"

"Yes, sir," Mark said in a low voice. "The young lady over there was his wife's slave. She and I together helped save the life of his baby son."

"You two must be the only white people to see him and live to tell about it," the Captain surmised.

"No, sir. My Uncle Edd has seen him. He hasn't bothered the folks here on the stage line since we saved the baby last fall," Mark informed him.

"I'll remember that if and when we come back to Texas," said the Captain. "It might come in handy if we try to work out a peace."

"We would be happy to help," Mark told him. "I wish you good luck as you try to get out of Texas."

"We are going to strike southeast from here and try to make it to the coast," Lee told him. "I trust you will hold that in confidence. I am going to gamble that secessionists won't expect us to go that way."

"I will not betray you," Mark promised, "I don't want blood to be spilled by either side, sir. May the Good Lord keep you safe."

"And you also. It has been my pleasure to meet you."

The Captain ordered assembly, and his column moved out down the creek toward the Colorado River.

The pair kept busy weeding the garden and taking care of chores with the livestock. They lured the hogs into the rock corral and Mark used his dog to catch the young pigs to mark. They would lift the pigs over the fence to keep the rock wall between themselves and the nervous sow.

Jess had learned well from Dee and with plenty of eggs and milk along with fresh garden vegetables they ate well. Mark was at the age where he was growing like a bad weed and his clothes were beginning to get tight.

Jess said, "If you will let me measure you, I will take some of the deer hides we have saved and make you a shirt."

"You know how to make a shirt?" Mark asked.

"Comanches wear clothes, too," she answered.

"Not many, as far as I can see," he replied.

"You remember that Screech Owl had a shirt when it was cold weather?" she reminded him.

"That's right. As I recall, it was a pretty fancy shirt," he said.

"Thank you. I made it," she said.

"You don't need to go to that much trouble for me," he said. "I just need one larger than this one. Is there anything I can do for you to make it easier?"

She said, "I would like to use the things that you and Uncle Edd use to sew the harness when it needs it."

"I wouldn't have thought of that. Granny always used a needle and thread, but she was sewing cloth and not buckskin," he said. "I'll fetch it from the harness shed."

By the time Edd returned from Waco, Mark was proudly wearing his new shirt.

Edd said, "We just got Jess to start dressing like a white woman, and now you are dressing like a Comanche. Where did you get that shirt?"

"Jess made it for me," Mark answered. "I was about to bust out of my other one."

"If you like it after you wear it awhile, I may need one," Edd said. "Looks like she did a first-rate job."

Mark smiled, "First rate is the only kind of job she does."

Jess asked, "How was your trip?"

"I had my work cut out for me changing out all that paper money," he returned. "I had to take about eighty cents on the dollar to get it done, but I have it in the false bottom of that box."

"We made a wash stand for Jess's room with a way to remove the back. There is no opening at the front and we don't think anyone would ever notice it. We can put the money in there," Mark said.

"Who came up with that?" Edd inquired.

"Jess had seen one at the Lambsheads and she thought it might work," Mark said.

"What did we ever do without her?"

"Speaking of that, we thought about one of her talents while you were gone," Mark mentioned. "It might be a good thing to lay in a big supply of buffalo jerky. It'll keep well, and might be a good trade item. I don't look for us to be able to do a lot of cash business, but we might even do some trading with Screech Owl. He seems to like salt and sugar."

"I wouldn't refuse to trade with him," Edd mused. "But we had better keep our ammunition supplies out of sight. We don't want to furnish the supplies for an attack on folks. For that matter, we need to be careful and feel out folks character before we sell any ammunition."

"Maybe, we could just keep a reasonable amount out where it could be seen and keep the rest hidden. When someone traded for that, we could act that's all we have available." Mark thought a moment and added, "We wouldn't be deceiving them, because that would be all we had available for them."

"That's what I admire about you, Mark. You solve problems before they come up. You must have got that trait from your Granny," Edd smiled.

"I don't reckon I did," Mark grinned. "She still had that trait when she passed on."

"If we trade with the Comanches, we can trade on a blanket in the front of the station. It is not their custom to trade inside," Jess spoke up. "We don't have to show them what is inside."

"Now, that's a right good custom," Edd observed. "Granny ain't the only problem solvin' woman in the world."

They had all their trade goods situated and the garden was beginning to come into full production by the time Mr. Gilder showed up the second week of May. Word had come down the line that he was coming, and Jess and Mark had tried to make a feast for his arrival.

After buffalo steaks, fresh squash, butter beans, and cornbread, Gilder pushed back from the table and said, "If I had known we had this kind of eatin' on the stage line, I'd have made more trips to check on things. You young people spread a fine table."

Mark and Jess beamed their appreciation and began to clean up the dishes.

Edd offered, "I'd be glad for you to sample my handiwork."

Gilder said, "Edd, you know I don't use that scamper juice. I know you've made some good money on it, and I've heard folks brag on its quality, but if you keep that around, it'll bring nothin' but trouble.

Edd was solemn and nodded, "I've been thinkin' on that. These youngsters can't have no trouble with drunks when there ain't nothin' to make 'em drunk.

Gilder went on, "Out here, as isolated as you are, it might be a good thing to keep your wits about you. You ought to get off that stuff."

Edd confessed, "Momma always said it would be my downfall. With times like they are, I need to do some serious thinkin' without my mind clouded."

Gilder replied, "I'd sure feel much better about these kids' chances."

Edd and Mr. Gilder came to an agreement about settling up in June.

The last run would be in about a month, and a crew would come through to pick up the mules and equipment. Snuffy would stay along with two sets of harness.

Gilder said, "I notice one thing you need, and I'll send it with the crew that picks up the stock. I see you have three people and only two saddles.

I'll send a saddle to fit Jess, if you'll fix the crew up with enough jerky, corn meal, and what ammunition they need."

"Well, we ain't got but two mounts to ride. The young mare and 01' Snuffy are the only ones broke to ride."

"Now, Edd," Gilder scolded, "I can see that paint mule will be ready to break in before long, and I know what a trader Mark is. Don't try to tell me that you won't have another one in short order."

"Alright," Edd grinned. "I just didn't want you to feel like you didn't have to put on your tradin' britches."

Gilder snuffed, "You know I'm givin' more than I'm getting!"

Edd conceded, "I know what you're doin' and don't think I don't appreciate it. You've been good to me and the boy."

"I got you out to this lonesome place, and I feel responsible."

Mark said quietly, "Don't worry about us, Mr. Gilder. The Lord's finger is in everything."

Gilder raised his left eyebrow a little bit and asked, "Mark, what makes you so calm and sure about the Lord taking care of you?"

Mark thought a minute and said, "Granny always finished her bible reading to me by quoting a line from Proverbs 3, 'Trust in the Lord with all your heart, and lean not on your own under-standing. In all your ways acknowledge Him, and He will direct your paths.'"

The thick silence in the room was broken by Jess. She said, "That's how you got the trust of Screech Owl. You gave credit for your kindness to your God, and let him know that it was also his God."

Mark grinned, "I still give God the credit. When that happened, I can't say that I was real calm and sure."

Mr. Gilder laughed and said, "Being with you kids is like going to school. I learn something every time we talk."

Ross Vinson called Mark aside after the meal. "I've got something for you, but I didn't know if you wanted anyone else to know. I found you one of them hip cannons you were looking for. I haggled 'em down to seventy dollars, but that was the best that I could do."

"Oh, thank you, Mr. Ross. That's wonderful, and I know you did your best for me," Mark beamed. "I'd be happy for you to keep the other thirty for your time and trouble."

"No, sir. Friends help friends and it was my pleasure," Ross returned. "I know you would do the same for me, if the shoe was on the other foot."

"I'll put it away and give it to Uncle Edd at the right time. He might want you to take it to try to get my money back, if he sees it before you leave." Mark grinned, "What he don't know won't hurt him."

"That's about the way I see it," chuckled Ross.

The next morning, Mr. Gilder explained that he was traveling to the end of the southern route and would come back along the route they were setting up.

He said, "I won't see you folks again, unless you come north to visit. I'll get a couple of guides and some good horses, and scout the new route. I'm honored to know you, and may the Good Lord bless and keep you."

Edd extended his hand and said, "The same goes for us, sir. It's been an honor, and a pleasure."

When the dust settled from the coach rolling out of the yard, Edd turned to the youngsters and spoke, "Well, there ain't nothing like a new-found freedom to make you realize your new found responsibilities."

CHAPTER 21

Life is about Choices

A WEEK PASSED AND IT seemed to be business as usual, with the exception of war news coming in with every stagecoach. Edd tried to edit what Jess and Mark heard, but it was hard to stop them from talking to passengers who were headed west to stay out of the conflict.

Edd received word that some of the men he had met in Waco were going to muster troops at Galveston. Their intentions were to travel north to Waco to muster more troops there. They wanted to march northeasterly through Arkansas on their way to join Robert E. Lee.

After an exceptionally good meal of vegetables and fresh venison, Edd asked Mark to sit down with a cup of coffee and make some important plans.

Jess said, "I will leave you alone."

Edd came back, "No, you need to hear this."

Jess got some cups and put the coffee pot on the table. This sounded like it might take more than one cup.

Edd began, "Mark, you know how I feel about folks getting in other folks business. Well, the reason for this war has to do with the North telling the South what they can and can't do. I don't hold with slavery, but I won't stand by and let my neighbors be bullied. I want to get you and Jess settled, and I am going to help them. I wish it could be different, but I've got it to do."

Mark was silent for a little while, then he spoke in a solemn and measured tone. "Uncle Edd, I could never raise my hand against our neighbors. At the same time, I could never support slavery. Dee and Jess have both been slaves, and I would not wish that on anyone."

Edd replied, "I don't want you to raise your hand against anyone. I want you and Jess to stay on right here so I'll have somewhere and someone to come back to. I understand your feelings about Jess and Dee, but their masters treated them well."

"Yes, sir, if you can call losing your family being treated well. I believe the reason they were treated well is that they acted the way the Good Lord would have had them act. God spoke to slaves and masters as well when Paul wrote that letter to Philemon."

"I see you have been studying up on the subject, boy."

"Jess is reading so much faster, and we are able to cover more territory when we read the Bible at night."

Edd scratched his head, "Well, who did Paul say was wrong, the master or the slave?"

Mark said, "The way I read it, he admitted the slave was wrong for running off, but Paul offered to make that right. He told both of them to act like brothers in Christ, and to love one another. He hinted that the right thing to do would be to let the slave stay and help Paul, but he didn't command it. It was like he was trying to give the slave's master the opportunity to get his heart right without being ordered to."

"I see you have some strong opinions about this slavery issue. Why do you think you see it so differently than a lot of our neighbors?"

"Because of Jess, I realize that skin color doesn't save you from slavery.

According to the Good Book, we can even be slaves of sin."

"Are you referring to my drinking, boy?"

Mark looked at his uncle respectfully, "No, sir, but since you brought it up."

Edd said, "I promised Gilder I would give up that business. I don't want you and Jess to have to sell it, and then deal with drunks. Tomorrow, I'll get rid of the still. You need to keep a few jugs hidden well for medicine purposes, but I'll empty the cellar so y'all can use it for a root cellar."

"Uncle Edd, I'm not trying to force you into anything. You were the one who wanted to talk."

"I know it and we ain't through talkin' yet. I want to go over some things that you need to be prepared to do, if you need to. The first thing is that I don't want you serving in the army on either side. You need to be here for Jess. If they come to force you to serve, get away and go to Screech Owl. He thinks enough of you, he would make a Comanche out of you. He knows that you and Jess are why Little Horse is alive."

"I hope it doesn't come to that, but we will if we have to."

"Good! The next thing is, when somebody shows up, if at all possible, one of you stay out of sight to keep them covered until you know they are all right. War turns desperate people into something ugly. Don't trust folks until they earn your trust."

"We will do our best, Uncle Edd."

"Thank you. The next thing is, trade for as much as you can with folks passing through. That will keep you from having to go to towns much, and it will be hard for both of you to go at once because of all your stock. If you do have to go, you might work out something with our Mexican friends over at Fort Chadbourne station. Y'all could trade out looking after each other's stock while the other goes to Fort Concho for supplies.

"You've been doing a lot of thinking."

"It pains me to go off and leave you two, but I've got faith in you."

Mark looked up, "I'm glad you mentioned faith. I've been trying to find a way to tell you that I need you to help me figure out how to get baptized. Mark 16:16 in the Bible says it pretty plain."

Edd said, "I don't study your Granny's book like you two. What does that say?"

"He that believeth and is baptized shall be saved. He that believeth not shall be condemned."

"Well, you believe don't you. Ain't that enough?"

"Granny always said those little words like 'and' are some of the most important. I don't want to be guilty of a half way job, I want to do everything the Book says."

Jess had not said a word since the conversation began, but she shyly said, "I would be baptized also."

"I should have known! Well, I guess y'all have been readin' it together.

I don't know who the closest preacher is, or where we might find one."

Jess said, "When I stayed with the Lambsheads, I was told that before they came west Mr. Lambshead preached at a church."

"Is that right? I'll ride over and see if he would come baptize you in Valley Creek. We probably need him for another little chore, as well."

"What might that be, Uncle Edd?" asked Mark.

"We need him to preach your wedding."

"What are you talking about?"

"Listen, boy! I'm not going off and leaving you two not properly married. I know you two love each other, but you just haven't really given it any thought. Since you want to make things officially right with God, let's make everything right with God."

"But Jess might not want me," Mark offered.

"What about that, Jess? Would you like him to be your husband?"

Jesse's eyes shone like diamonds when she said quietly, "I have belonged to him since he bought me from Screech Owl."

Mark looked pained with guilt when he said, "I don't want to be the kind of husband that my father was. I would never wish that on Jess."

Edd stood up and grabbed Mark by both shoulders. "Listen to me. You were never influenced by that no account. He loved only himself and it's obvious that you love Jess. If you didn't love her like you do, you wouldn't worry about it. Don't you want her with you always?"

"More than anything!"

"It's settled then. When I leave here, you will be Mr. and Mrs. Mark Singletary."

"But, Uncle Edd! I don't know nothin' about being a husband, and Jess don't know nothin' about being a wife."

"Don't bet on it," Edd retorted. "You've witnessed Ma and Pa. You've seen how the Lambsheads are. You've witnessed how not to act by seeing what happened with your Pa. Jess has been taught by Mrs. Lambshead and Dee, and there ain't a more loyal wife than a Comanche squaw. Y'all will figure it out in short order."

Jess blushed as she said softly, "I could be a good wife."

Edd nodded, "I 'spect as good as they come. Don't mistake being stupid for being modest, boy."

Mark looked earnestly at Jess and said, "I guess Jess and I need to talk this thing through. This decision is for a lifetime."

Edd agreed, "That's shore right. I figure there's a few matters that need to be decided before I ride over to talk to the Lambsheads. We know we are going to need him for the baptizin'. If he has to do the other chore, the women folk will want to help. They'll want to come for one or both."

"We probably need to go over and help them to prepare for their move north. It's gonna be different with them gone and the stages not rolling through." Mark's face lit up and he added, "Uncle Edd, we might need to buy some of the things they can't take with them. They might need some cash money to get settled up there."

Edd approved, "You're right. It would probably help both parties and it would be the neighborly thing to do. Good neighbors are priceless, no matter how far away they live."

"This is a lot to chew on. I need a little time and room to chew."

Edd chuckled, and then looked thoughtful. "Well, they tell me that the way you have to eat a buffalo is one bite at a time."

After what seemed like a long moment of silence, Jesse said, "Meadow Lark used to say that the morning will bring new light."

"The more I find out about Comanches, the more I respect 'em. A good night's sleep would help us all."

Mark remarked, "Who's gonna sleep?"

They all laughed, and retired for the night.

After breakfast, Mark explained that he was going up on Sentinel Hill to look over the countryside and to think awhile. He rode off on Katydid and left the other two to their own devises.

When midday approached and Mark had not returned, Edd called Jess out to the corral. "Girl, why don't you rustle up something you can take up the hill for you and Mark to eat. The top of that hill will be a good place for y'all to talk things out. I'll saddle Snuffy for you."

"I would not intrude on him while he seeks wisdom."

"There's those Comanche customs coming out again. Don't you understand that if he is seeking wisdom, you need to go up there and give him some?"

"What wisdom could I give him?"

"You need to let him know what you think and how you feel. Shucks, you two have been teaching each other ever since you showed up. It seems to me that when one of you comes up short in a situation, the other one takes up the slack. When you were staying with the Lambsheads, Mark was like a duck out of water."

"It was not the same to be without him, either."

"Well, hustle that mule up the hill and tell him, and you don't have to hurry back. I'll look after things around here. When she reached the top of Sentinel Hill, Jess found Mark sitting on a rock looking off to the west. He came over and helped her down from the mule, even though she was quite capable. He said, "I'm glad you came up here, Jess. We need to talk."

"I brought some jerky and some water. Uncle Edd thought you might need to eat."

"Thanks, but I haven't been thinkin' about food. When I get one thing kind of settled in my mind, another thing comes to mind and stirs up the first worry."

"Uncle Edd said you need to eat this one bite at a time."

"Did you ever take a bite of meat, and the more you chewed it, the bigger it got?"

"You told me that your Granny always said that whatever came up in life, the Good Book had the answer. It might not be what we want to hear, but it's the answer just the same."

"Yes, and that if we were called to God's purpose, everything would work together for good."

Jess waited for a long half-minute. "What is the first bite you are trying to chew?"

"This war! It makes no sense to me. Why would men kill each other over something they could settle by talking it out? It is the root of all the problems we are looking at. The stagecoach line moving, Uncle Edd leaving, our being by ourselves are all because of this war."

"I know how much sorrow comes from war. The Comanches have been at war with the whites for a long time. I lost my family to that war, but later came to respect the Comanches. I even grew to love some of them. That war was the reason I later came to be here. I can see how bad things can work together for good. It even brought me to be called to God's purpose, as you are."

Mark brightened a little as he understood her thinking. "Granny also used to say that, when you have troubles, you do your best and give God the rest."

"The stage line depends on us, much more than we count on them. It is nice to be able to get things brought to us, but we have a good shelter with plenty to eat. We don't have to move our camp like the Comanches. They know we are here, and whites passing this way will stop. We can trade with both, and live at peace with both."

"I don't have a problem with being without the stage line, but I hate to see Uncle Edd going to kill or be killed over other people's thoughts."

"When those men who are buried across the creek were killed, it was because you stood up against what they were thinking."

"I had not thought of that. Uncle Edd said that the Bible even teaches that you have to stand up for you and yours. He feels strongly about being his own man who is free to make his own decisions. He thinks he's standing up for freedom."

"Isn't that what both sides are fighting for? One side is fighting for the freedom of slaves, and the other is fighting for the freedom to have them? The men we know who don't own slaves, but fight for slavery, also fight fiercely to free white folks from being slaves to the

Comanches. If they could come to really know Dee, it would change their mind about a lot of things."

"You've said more in the last few minutes than you have since I've known you and you've hit the nail on the head with all of it. I don't know what's got into you, but I like it."

"I'm at a place where I need to stand up for me and mine. What does that mean 'hit the nail on the head?'"

"It means that everything you have said has been right."

She nodded that she understood and then said, "We do not have a choice about the stage line moving, and its Uncle Edd's choice to go to war. We need to make the choices that we can make."

"I can see that you are right again. We'll just do our best and give the rest to God."

"Uncle Edd would tell us that we've got it to do, we'd better get at it."

Mark looked at her with a combination of pain and tenderness.

"Well, then, what do we do about this wedding idea of Uncle Edd's? I don't want to force you into something that you are not ready for."

She looked into his eyes and asked, "Is it something that you are not ready for? Do you not want a wife? Do you not want me for a wife?

"It ain't none of that, Jess. I can't stand to be without you. It's just that I don't want to rush you into something because of other folks going off halfcocked. You need to be the one making plans for your future, not other folks trying to settle their own minds."

"I have belonged to you ever since you bought me from Screech Owl, and you have been responsible for me ever since you saved me and Little Horse. I am not worried about other people's minds being settled. My mind has been settled for a long time."

"I didn't know you felt that way!"

"How could you? You said that I don't talk much."

"I don't know much about love and being a husband."

"You have a warm lodge and are a good provider. You are known as a great warrior who will fight to protect his tribe. You are patient and kind like we read about love in the Bible. You know things that you didn't know that you knew."

"There are still a lot of things we don't know about being a husband and wife," he said seriously.

"We could learn them together."

"Does that mean that you would marry me?"

"If you would have me, I would."

He took her in his arms and hugged her. After a long moment, they mounted and rode down the hill to tell Edd. You see, there were still some things they hadn't learned yet.

CHAPTER 22

Giving the Rest to God

EDD WAS EXTREMELY PLEASED WITH the decision of Mark and Jess. He set about doing his part to make everything come together. The first thing was to get rid of the still. He poured out all but six jugs and placed the empty jugs back in the dugout. He took the full ones up to the house after he kicked the copper pot into the creek and watched it float downstream.

He told Mark, "I want you to put one of these jugs in your hiding place for your money. You may never need to use it, but I want you to have it for wounds and sickness. God won't care if you use it for sickness."

"Alright, Uncle Edd. I saw how Granny used it for medicine when I had the croup. I would use it to ease suffering."

"I'm gonna take a jug to the Lambsheads for the same reasons. I'll give a jug each to Bozy, Jug, Ross, and Slick when they come through. One or two of them might immediately get sick so they can use it."

Mark smiled a knowing smile and said, "I could probably tell you which ones before it happens. What should I do with all those empty jugs?"

"Just leave them alone. There may come a time that you need to carry water with you, and you'll have something to carry it in."

Edd spent the morning getting the wagon ready to go over to the Lambsheads. He hitched up Snuffy and Brazos and told Mark he would spend the night at Lambsheads.

Mark asked, "Are you carrying so much over there that you need a team and wagon?"

"I might be bringing that much back. Get me two hundred dollars in coin to take with me Remember your idea about them needing money for their trip?"

Mark fetched the money and Edd mounted the wagon. He waved his hat and started east. In a few moments he was over the rise.

When he was out of sight, Mark called Jess outside. "I'm glad Uncle Edd left his saddle here. Let's use his holster for his horse pistol, and make another one to fit his new gun. We can give it and Katydid to him when he gets back.

"Do you want to use deer hide or buffalo?"

"Let's use buffalo. Where he's going he'll need something tough that's built to last."

Jess brought a piece of buffalo hide and went to retrieve the tools they used to sew harness.

Mark brought out the gun to help make the holster a custom fit. By looking at the other holster, they were able to make a comparable model for the new pistol. As the first holster was mounted by the right side of the pommel, they attached the other a little behind the right cantle. In this manner, Edd could draw either pistol with his right hand.

They busied themselves with the garden and fed all the stock. They fixed and ate a meal together, then cleaned up the dishes. Mark lit the lantern, and they barred the door for the night.

Carson and Katherine Lambshead were working around the barn when Edd rode into the yard. Carson raised a hand in greeting and said, "Step down, Edd. It's good to see you."

"Thanks, Carson. I guess we need to see how we can help each other before the stages stop running. I 'spect we both have a list."

Katherine said, "I need to do some trading with the kids for some jerky and such. I hope they might have a ham or two we could trade for."

"I know that won't be a problem. They have a couple of things they would like Carson to do for them, and would probably consider it payment for his services."

"Whatever could that be?"

"If Dee has some of her good coffee on the stove, let's sit down and discuss it. I know it ain't proper to invite myself in, but we've got a mouthful to chew."

Ever the southern lady, Katherine Lambshead smiled and said, "Of course, Edd. I apologize for not beating you to the punch."

Edd blushed a little, "I won't ever be caught in a punching match with you."

Carson grinned at Edd's discomfort, "Well, come on in and let's start chewin'."

When the three were seated at the table, Dee placed a cup of hot coffee in front of each one. She started to leave the room, but Edd stopped her.

"Dee, some of what we are going to talk about may need to have your thinkin'. I would appreciate it if you would get you some coffee and help us work these things out."

Carson saw Dee's pained loo, and offered, "He's known you are not a slave for some time. You don't have to worry about what your place is. He respects your ability and your opinion."

Relief seemed to creep into her features. She humbly nodded and sat down.

"Since we are sort of on the subject of a slave's place, I need to do some explainin'. I have told Mark and Jess that when the stage line closes, I am going to Waco to join the Confederate Army. I don't hold with slavery, but I won't fight against my friends and Texas. I reserve the right to my own opinion without some Yankee know-it-all telling me what it will be. I think it is a matter of state's rights."

Carson said, "I understand your thinking and I have some what of the same opinion. I am torn about fighting for the right of slavery. Yes, I was raised around it, but my study of the scriptures has convinced me that I cannot own them myself. We will move to the northern stage route, especially because we love Dee."

"We love her, too. I hope she won't hold my actions as a personal insult to her."

Dee looked at Edd and said, "No, suh. The Book say we is to lub one another. I hold freedom to be precious, and I can see that you believe you is fightin' for freedom. I know you ain't tryin' to take mine."

Katherine said, "We will pray for your deliverance, Edd. What are Mark and Jess going to do?"

"That's what's next on my list. Carson, you know that Mark has taught Jess to read by using his Granny's bible. Well, they have read enough that they both want to be baptized. I know that you preached at a church before you came west. Would you consider baptizin' those two?"

"It would be a pleasure and an honor. We could do it right there in Valley Creek. When would they like me to come?"

"Well, that ain't all they want. You see, I don't want to leave them here without them being married proper. Could you marry them the same day?"

Katherine smiled, and her eyes sparkled. She said, "We'll all have to be involved in that blessed event. This will take some planning."

Edd said, "Now, wait a minute. Carson hasn't said that he would do it."

Carson laughed out loud. "Do you possibly think Kathy and Dee would let me say no?"

Dee asked, "How much time do we got to prepare?"

"I plan to ride out right after the stage line closes and the last run will come west on the twenty-eighth. It will return east on the twenty-ninth."

Katherine went to the desk in the corner and retrieved a small book.

She looked at a homemade calendar and said, "We had planned to leave headed north on the first of July. The thirtieth of June is on a Sunday. How fitting."

"We could have a baptizin', a wedding, and a going away party all at one time."

Carson said, "The driver's tell me that they will be gathering the extra stock to drive north. We are taking three wagons to move and we'll use some of the stage line's mules to pull them. That will get our wagons and their mules to the place they need to be. If we gather the extra stock ahead of time into your big corrals, maybe the drivers that matter could make the wedding."

"That's a good idea. I'll send word back with Ross Vinson and make the arrangements."

Dee asked, "What that child gonna do about a weddin' dress?"

Edd said, "I know she's been workin' on something she don't want us to see, but you may need to ask her."

Dee said, "If the missus don't care, I could ride the stage over to check things out. I'd find out what she need, and ride the next stage back."

Katherine said, "That would be wonderful."

Edd replied, "That would be good, but you all might want to come trading. I know there are some things you can't carry with you and you could trade them for some things more practical to take."

Edd and Carson set about to finish up what the Lambsheads were doing at the barn while the ladies were fixing supper. Edd gave Carson the jug of liquor with the explanation that it was for medicine purposes. "You never know about sickness or wounds on a journey. You can't find a doctor behind every tree."

"Thanks, Edd. I know your intentions are honorable. We'll be glad to have it in an emergency."

"Thanks for what you are doing for those two at Valley Creek. This is quite a step for a seventeen-year-old kid, but those two will make it when anybody else might not."

"Edd, is it love or lust?"

"Carson, I can tell you it sure ain't lust. That boy bends over backwards to be proper and I don't know if he knows what lust is. As for the girl, I suspect she knows more than he does about that, having lived with the Comanches without much privacy. From everything I've seen though, she don't know what forward is. I don't know that it's as much love as it is devotion."

"If that's the case, all the other will come. What made them decide to get married?"

"They have read so much in his Granny's bible, they both want to keep things right in the sight of the Lord. They know I'm leaving and Mark won't have anyone think or say anything bad about Jess. He's already killed two men defending her."

"That comes awful close to 'loving your wife as Christ loved the church.'"

"Yeah, I have no doubt that he would lay down his life for her."

"Do you think they will be alright out here without us?"

"Well, you can't get two better allies than the Good Lord and Screech Owl in this country."

"Isn't it funny how understanding makes allies out of enemies?"

"I've thought about that, and Mark's knowledge that there is just one God is what brought about the understanding."

"That's a lot of wisdom for seventeen years."

Edd laughed, "Well, he sure didn't get it from me!"

At sundown, they went into the station to a fine supper. The ladies buzzed about planning the wedding while the men discussed plans for shutting down the stage line. Edd rolled out his bedroll by the door and they retired for the night.

The next morning, Edd told the Lambsheads that he had come prepared to buy things that they couldn't take with them. He said, "I've got money in coin. I know that you may need some to get set up when you get to where you are going."

"I don't think our milch cow would make the trip. I would like to see the kids have her. I thought she might make a good wedding present."

"That's mighty nice of you, but I want to buy some things. I have the money and I want to see that you have what you need. You have sure been there in my hour of need!"

"I have a couple of barrels of oat seed, a good harrow, and a doctor's buggy that I would get rid of. I didn't know how I was going to take them with me."

"What will you take for the whole lot?"

"I'll let it all go for one hundred and ten dollars."

"Let's load the oats and the harrow, and I'll ride a mule back over and pick up the buggy. That can be my wedding present."

Edd arrived back at Valley Creek just as the westbound stagecoach rolled into the yard. He and Mark changed out the teams while the passengers and stage employees went in to eat buffalo steak and fresh vegetables.

When Ross Vinson came out, Edd cornered him to tell him about the upcoming events. He didn't say anything to the youngsters, but he couldn't stop grinning at them. They thought he was acting a little daffy.

Mark called him aside and asked, "Did Uncle Edd tell you about us?"

"Yes, and I think it's about the best news I've heard this year!"

"Thanks, Ross. I just hope I can make her a good husband."

"Don't you worry. You two are just about the best match I ever saw."

"Mr. Ross, I need to ask you another favor."

"I'll help you if I can."

"Uncle Edd is going off to war, and I want a Bible to send with him. I know he won't take Granny's because she left it to me. I'll send whatever money you think it will take and some for your troubles."

"Don't send no money. I'll check with the Sheriff at San Angelo. Sometimes, some of those unfortunates that get killed in a bar fight have personals that nobody knows who to send them to. I'll see if maybe there is a Bible. I'll let you know on my way back through."

"Thank you, sir. You are a true friend."

"Shucks, boy. You would do the same for me."

The days began to fly by. Lots of activity associated with the stage line took up lots of time. Passengers were taking the opportunity to use the route before it closed down. Most were heading west to escape the threat of war, while a few were going east to take care of business while they still could.

Armed men were riding east headed to join in the fighting and would trade for jerky and provisions.

Katherine Lambshead, and Dee came riding into the yard in the doctor's buggy pulled by one of the stage line mules.

Katherine said, "Carson said to leave the buggy and the mule here, and we'll ride the stage back home. The mule can go in with all the stock to be gathered here to drive north."

"When are you going to pick up the buggy?" Mark asked.

Edd slapped him on the back and said, "That's my wedding present to you two. Won't ol' Pulltight look good pullin' that fancy buggy. You'll be the envy of all the neighbors."

"What neighbors?" Everyone laughed.

Dee said, "They sho won't be no question who be the high roller around here."

As they were unloading the buggy, Mark unloaded a big piece of mattress ticking.

He asked, "What's this for?"

Dee laughed out loud and said, "You'll be findin' out by and by."

Mark looked at it questioningly for a minute and then both his ears turned bright red. He put the bundle down like it was hot and found something that needed to be done at the barn.

The three women went into Jess's room and put down the bundles.

Katherine said, "We came over to see what we needed to do to help you get ready for the wedding. What do we need to do about your dress?"

Jess went behind the small bed and reached for something under the bed. She placed a bundle wrapped in cloth on the bed and untied it. When she unfolded it, there was a dress made of soft doeskin. It was decorated with patterns made of porcupine quills and tiny mussel shells. It was a beautiful thing.

Katherine exclaimed, "It's beautiful. I have to see it on you. We'll step outside and you put it on. When you are ready, call us back."

When they returned, the teenage girl was transformed into a beautiful young woman. The dress fit perfectly and accentuated every curve. Dee said, "That dress will make his ears turn red."

Katherine's eyes twinkled. "Did you do all that work yourself?"

"I had three good teachers."

"Who besides us?"

"Meadow Lark taught me how to measure and decorate the skins. She made beautiful garments."

"She must have been good to you."

"Yes, she treated me like family instead of like a slave."

Dee spoke in a husky voice with a knot in her throat, "I know sumpn' 'bout that."

Katherine said, "Let's change the subject before we all start bawlin'."

Jess asked, "What is bawlin'?"

The two older women laughed. After they explained the meaning, they continued with the planning.

"We don't want to get your wedding dress wet, so you will need another dress to be baptized in."

"Can I not use my work clothes?"

The black woman said patiently, "No, Honey. You are going to become one of God's chilluns. You need to look nice for the 'casion."

"I took the liberty of bringing one of dresses from my younger years with us. If you will let us measure where it needs altered, we will bring it with us for the baptism."

"I could not. It is too much!"

"Nonsense. You are as close as a daughter and I would be so honored if you would wear it."

The girl beamed and the woman understood her acceptance. The women continued to flit around from one plan to another like a bunch of candle flies. Before they knew it, the eastbound stagecoach came through to take them home.

Katherine told Edd and the youngsters that they would come back on the day before the wedding to help get everything ready. "We will come in one of the wagons we are traveling north in, so don't worry about sleeping arrangements for us. The way I hear it, there will be enough help around you won't be able to stir 'em with a stick."

When the stage rolled over the rise, Mark asked Edd to wait inside the station for a few minutes so he and Jess could get something ready to show Edd. When the older man was called out into the yard, Katydid was saddled with his saddle. Both holsters held revolvers.

Mark said, "Uncle Edd, you gave us our wedding present and we thank you very much. We feel like you have done so much for us already. We want you to have this for your going away present."

Edd shook his head and said, "I ain't takin' that cannon I bought for you, and I ain't takin' that girl's little mare."

"Uncle Edd, I knew that's what you would think. My gun is in there where it belongs under the bar. We bought this for you before we knew you were going off to war. We thought you might need more than the jawbone of a donkey."

"That was sure thoughtful of you and I thank you. I still ain't takin' the girl's mare."

Jess said softly, "Uncle Edd, we want you to go on her because she knows the way to bring you home. She is controlled with your legs, so you can use a jawbone in each hand. We won't make you keep her, we just hope that you will use her."

Tears rolled down his face and he simply said, "I'd be honored."

Mark said, "If you will check the left saddlebag, you'll find something else we knew you needed for your time away from us. Come on Jess, let's start on supper."

When the two went inside, Edd opened the saddlebag to discover a Bible. When he opened the cover, he discovered a man's name had been marked through. There was a fresh inscription inside, which read: This Bible is lovingly presented to Edd Singletary by Mark and Jess. Granny said that all the answers are in this book and that all we can do is our best then give the rest to God.

On June 28, the last stage rolled eastbound out of Valley Creek Station. Bozy Combs, Jug Myers, Ross Vinson, and Slick Newton had brought their saddles and stayed behind. They busied themselves packing provisions for the trip driving the stock north. They knew the mules from all the times they had handled them and had already picked out their mounts. There were a dozen mules from each of the four closest stations, so besides their mounts they would be driving over forty mules north.

Early the next morning, Jug and Bozy each mounted a mule and took an extra one with them.

Jug said, "We are gonna climb that hill, and see if we can see something to cook. A weddings got to have a real feast."

Then they rode off toward Sentinel Hill.

The Lambsheads and Dee arrived about mid-morning. They took lots of good things to cook off the wagon and took them inside.

Dee said, "We ain't got room to cook all o' dis in one little bitty ol' fireplace. We are gonna need a cook fire outside, and plenty of wood."

Ross piped up, "Me and Slick will handle gathering some wood. Come on Slick, saddle up and we'll drag some up."

About noon, Jug and Bozy came back with a fat buffalo calf pulled on a travois by the extra mule. Bozy said, "I made a running shot on this one. I figured we'd cook what we want to for the wedding, and everybody can take some with them for their journeys. I'm sure Jess and Mark will know what to do with the rest."

It was a long day of preparations and everyone was ready to go to bed after a wonderful supper of stew and cornbread. Everyone was tired but happy and Hawk kept watch while they all slept.

After breakfast the next morning, Carson Lambshead told them all to get cleaned up for a worship service and a baptizin'.

Bozy and Jug had each brought Mark a new shirt so he would have a new one for each service. Ross and Slick had each brought him a string tie. Ross kidded him, "Now don't forget to comb your hair."

When they all gathered on the banks of Valley Creek, Carson led them all in the singing of "Rock of Ages." He then talked about the fact that God gives us the freedom to choose. Choices are made many times in a day.

Sometimes choices have grave outcomes. He said, "Mark tells us about the only two choices we have concerning eternity. In Mark 16:16, we read that he that believeth and is baptized shall be saved and he that disbelieved shall be condemned."

Carson asked Jess to step forward. When she had, he took her by the hand and asked, "Jess have you made your choice. Do you believe that Jesus is the Son of God?"

"Yes."

"Bless you girl for that confession. Mark, what about you? Do you believe that Jesus is the Son of God?"

"Yes, sir. I do."

Before Carson could speak, Edd said, "Me, too!"

There was stunned silence for a moment. Carson broke the silence, "Does that mean you want to be baptized, too."

Edd nodded, "I sure do."

Carson said, "Praise God, and bless you all for your confessions."

Carson waded into the creek and asked each of the three to come to him in their turn. With each one he said, "Upon your confession of faith, I now baptize you for the forgiveness of your sins in the name of the Father, the Son, and the Holy Ghost."

After the service, Mark said, "Uncle Edd, I am so proud and thankful. I didn't know you were even thinkin' about it."

"Well, the thought of going off to fight makes a man do some soul searching. I have learned from you that fightin' ain't always the answer, but when you have to fight make sure the Lord is on your side."

Katherine said, "Dee, Jess, and I are going up on Sentinel Hill to get ready for the wedding. Y'all come on up in about an hour."

After they rode off on their mounts, Mark asked, "What in the world will they do up there for an hour."

Carson giggled, "I 'spect you'd be surprised. I 'spect you will be surprised."

"Come on, sprout. Let's get out of these wet duds and get ready for your weddin'."

When the men folk rode up Sentinel Hill, they found a rope stretched between two small trees to hitch the mounts to. They walked up the rest of the way to the top. When they reached the top, only Katherine and Dee could be seen.

Katherine told Carson where to stand and for Mark to stand beside him.

When Katherine called out to her, Jess appeared from the west side of the hill.

Because of the baptism, Jess had wet hair when they started getting ready. They braided her hair in two braids, Comanche style. They had braided red and white ribbons in with the hair. She had a flower over each ear that had come from Katherine's flower garden. The doeskin dress must have been stunning, for every man on the hill stood there with his mouth wide open.

Carson waited for Jess to come and stand by Mark.

"It's customary to ask who gives this woman to this man."

There was a moment of silence, then Slick Newton (who seldom said anything) said, "Screech Owl ain't here, so God does."

Jug said, "Amen."

Carson continued, "We are gathered here to unite this man and this woman in Holy Matrimony. That is the only kind authorized by God and that is why these folks want it. I would like to mention that they were baptized this morning because they read the instructions in God's Word. I hope they will read His Word together all of their lives. Proverbs 31 is known for telling a woman how to be virtuous. That's not all it is about. It's about telling a man how he is supposed to act, and how to pick a good wife. I believe Mark has picked one."

"Solomon said, 'unless the Lord build the house, they who build it labor in vain.' I am under the firm belief that it was God that brought these two together. You see, it was Mark's belief in the one God that allowed him to rescue Jess."

Carson turned to Jess, "Jesse Louisiana Behannon, do you take this man to be your lawful wedded husband? Do you promise to be the helper that God made to be suitable for him? Do you promise to be his alone as long as you both are alive?

Jess beamed, "Yes, sir."

He then turned to Mark, "Mark, do you take this woman to be your lawful wedded wife? Do you promise to be God's man that will love her as Christ loved the Church as long as you both are alive?

Mark's eyes were as big as saucers, "Yes, sir."

Carson grinned a knowing grin and said, "Then before God and this company, I pronounce you man and wife. Mr. Singletary, you may kiss Mrs. Singletary."

Marks ears turned bright red, but when their lips touched, he got over it.

There was a lot of hand shaking and kissing the bride on the cheek, then they hurried down the hill.

The wedding feast was just that. There was enough for two or three times the number of people there. They topped it off with a cake that Dee had baked.

The drivers started to hustle around to get started with the stock. It was the last day of June in west Texas and there was a lot of daylight left. Bozy kidded, "Since the married couple ain't leavin', I guess they'll have to throw rice at us."

Ross admonished, "If we don't get a move on, they'll probably throw rocks."

Each of the drivers separately told the couple if they needed help to send for them. They all shook Mark's hand, hugged Jess, mounted and started northeast.

The Lambsheads weren't far behind. All the women had to shed a few tears and Carson graciously wouldn't let Mark pay for his services. Mark and Jess loaded them up with jerky and sent cornmeal with eggs stored in it.

Before they left, Dee said, "You two men come in here and help me.

We got one more thing to do."

They went inside and she directed Carson and Edd to move Mark's bed frame in and put it next to Jesse's. She looked at the couple, "Y'all can get on out to the straw stack and fill up that mattress tick now." She cackled and went to get on the wagon.

When the Lambsheads rolled out, Edd went to saddle Katydid. Mark said, "Uncle Edd, you don't have to be in that big of a hurry."

"There's no need of dragging it out. Son, this is your wedding night.

I'll ride over and spend the night at the Lambsheads. I'll be there to help them get hitched up and loaded in the morning. They helped us so much, I feel the need to neighbor up."

"I understand, but we sure hate to see you go. We are afraid we might never see you again."

"Whatever God wills. I'll just do the best I can and I'll give the rest to God."

"I love you, Uncle Edd."

Edd hugged him up, "I love you, too. Y'all be here when I get back, or leave me a note in the money hiding place."

Jess hugged Edd long and hard, and then spoke Comanche to Katydid.

Edd asked, "What did you say?"

"I told her to bring you home safe."

Edd rode over the rise with the young couple, watching arm in arm. Valley Creek continued to bubble and flow heading south to the Colorado. It brought life to parched country, life to thirsty animals, and for at least three people, the hope of eternal life.

About the Author

CARL MCDONALD WAS A WORLD War II hero, a beloved educator, an elder in the church, and a child of the depression. He was the youngest of fourteen children and was raised by his mother after the death of his father when he was four years old. He lived many of the survival skills described in the book.

Herschel McDonald, his son, found the manuscript of the first six chapters of the book twelve years after his father's death. He had spent much of his life and career horseback in the areas surrounding the story. He has also served as an elder in the church, and the Christian principles exhibited in the book were learned from his faithful parents.

CPSIA information can be obtained
at www.ICGtesting.com
Printed in the USA
LVHW040311311222
736049LV00001B/253